BROTHER'S KEEPER

Born and raised in Atlanta, Georgia, C.E. Smith studied English at Stanford and medicine at Vanderbilt. In 2013, he won Shakespeare & Company's international Paris Literary Prize. He lives with his wife and children in Nashville, Tennessee. *Brother's Keeper* is his first novel.

Brother's Keeper

C. E. SMITH

Atlantic Books
LONDON

First published in trade paperback in Great Britain in 2015
by Atlantic Books, an imprint of Atlantic Books Ltd.

This paperback edition published in Great Britain
in 2016 by Atlantic Books.

10 9 8 7 6 5 4 3 2 1

A CIP catalogue record for this book is available
from the British Library.

Paperback ISBN: 978 1 78239 427 3
E-book ISBN: 978 1 78239 426 6

Printed in Great Britain by Clays Ltd, St Ives plc

Atlantic Books
An imprint of Atlantic Books Ltd
Ormond House
26–27 Boswell Street
London WC1N 3JZ

For Brooke

1

The squawking radio, some kind of prayer, is torture to Burkett's headache. The driver speaks no English, or so it seems when Burkett asks him to lower the volume. He'd lower it himself, sacrilege or no, but a wire partition confines him to the back of the cab.

They're next in line at a military checkpoint, where a one-armed man with the dark skin of a native Khandari endures a painstaking search despite his advanced age. The old man watches impassively as the soldiers, in flagrant disregard for the standstill traffic, mount his wooden flatbed and jostle the sisal bales and overcrowded birdcages. It could be the missing arm that aroused their suspicion: he could have blown it off making bombs.

Whatever the case, their scrutiny doesn't bode well for Burkett, even if he just cleared customs without a problem, and even if most of the drugs he's carrying are perfectly legal. Of the hundred or so packages of antibiotics, he'll simply repeat what he said less than an hour ago at the airport: these medicines have been donated to the people of Khandaros, to a clinic that treats the poor free of charge.

But his personal stash of Xanax and Valium, a week's worth, could earn him up to ten years in prison. A week for ten years: it seems on the surface like the risk of a madman, but only a pharmacist or a certain type of addict

1

would notice the discrepancies of pills and labels. At least that's what he's been telling himself in the days since his summons to this impoverished island.

The drug laws here are rather harsh for a new democracy boasting social reform: life in prison for a kilogram of marijuana, death for five grams of heroin. In some ways, nothing has changed since the draconian years of Quadri the Behemoth. It is well and good to disband the secret police, to hold fair trials and rock concerts, but to Burkett's way of thinking, the concept of westernization isn't complete without some degree of permissiveness in the area of pharmacology.

But he isn't worried. The customs inspector at the airport hardly bothered with his shaving kit, much less any pills inside. Why should he expect any different from troops at a checkpoint? They have more important things to consider, like their fledgling government's war with Islamic militants. They wouldn't waste their time on minimally addictive drugs when a suicide bomber could be sitting in the very next car.

The driver shuts off the radio as he pulls up to the checkpoint. Burkett welcomes the silence, though in a way it grants the soldiers a measure of respect he isn't sure they deserve. There are signs of poor discipline: an unsnapped holster, a missed belt loop, even food stains on the taller one's shirt. Burkett doubts he'd concern himself with such superficial details if the two men weren't armed with assault rifles.

'Salam,' the taller one says, studying Burkett. 'Passport, please.'

Burkett hands his passport through the window. He waits while the soldier confers with someone in a parked SUV. He hears the word 'American' and the SUV's door opens. This one is older, more professional in his bearing. A member of the old guard, Burkett guesses, maybe a player in the coup nearly twenty years ago that brought an end to the ancient line of kings and paved the way for Quadri.

The older officer flicks through Burkett's passport. He reads the name aloud – Ryan as 'Ron', Burkett as 'Buckett' – and lifts his sunglasses for a closer look at the picture, which shows Burkett in the goatee he wore during medical school.

'What is your profession, sir?'

'I'm a surgeon,' Burkett says, which draws a look of confusion. 'A doctor,' he says. 'But I'm here for personal reasons.'

In the heat Burkett wants to follow the driver's lead and get out of the cab, but the soldier blocks the door while trying to compare the passport photograph to the real thing. He takes much longer than necessary, perhaps because of the goatee, and eventually shakes his head as though resigned to the impossibility of verification.

'Why empty?' he asks, thumbing through the pages.

Perhaps he thinks the new passport is fake. The single stamp represents his first international trip in years.

'I haven't had much time for travel,' Burkett says. How could he explain more than a decade of surgical training at less than minimum wage?

The soldier slides the passport into his shirt pocket. He yawns and mutters something to the cab driver, who reaches through the window and pops the trunk.

Burkett gets out to watch while his luggage is searched for the second time today. The soldier lifts the shaving kit by its strap, the pills inside faintly rattling, but sets it aside in favor of a stethoscope. Holding it up he grins and says, 'Doctor surgeon', as if only now comprehending Burkett's profession.

He opens the duffel of antibiotics and begins shuffling through the boxes as if looking for a particular label. If he had such difficulty with the word 'doctor', what could he possibly learn from a pharmaceutical box? He opens a package and draws out a plastic card with rows of tablets in transparent domes. He squints at the words on the peel-away back.

'Ciprofloxacin,' Burkett says.

Apparently satisfied that Burkett isn't smuggling narcotics, the soldier moves on to the other duffel, which produces a froth of mosquito netting as he pulls back the zipper.

'What is this?' the man asks.

Mosquito netting works just as well, if not better, than the expensive mesh surgeons typically use for repairing hernias. Burkett makes cutting gestures and points to his groin, but the soldier has lost interest. He's found something else buried in the duffel. His hands emerge from the white folds with a bottle of bourbon.

'This for surgery too?' the officer asks. Is he making a joke?

'Duty free,' Burkett says. 'Do you understand duty free?'

The officer rotates the bottle, appraising the label.

'Do you understand the prison?' he asks.

Burkett remains silent. He'd gathered online that the ban on alcohol applied only in name, and almost never to foreigners or non-Muslims. The customs agent at the airport was so preoccupied with the antibiotics and their expiration dates that he hardly seemed to notice the bourbon. Or rather he noticed but chose to avoid the paperwork of reporting it.

'Pardon me,' the officer says, and carries the duffel to the SUV. When he returns with the bag, Burkett can tell from the lighter weight that his duty free bourbon has been confiscated.

'Can I have my passport?' Burkett asks.

'There is a fine for liquor,' he replies, fanning himself with Burkett's passport. 'The fine is one hundred dollars American.'

The cab deposits him at a crowded intersection supposedly in the vicinity of the medical complex. He unfolds a map but without knowing the street names he can't even be sure of his own location. In the niche of a doorway, he sets down his luggage and sorts through his backpack. Both of his flasks are empty and yet he finds himself unscrewing the caps and hoping a drop might fall on his parched tongue. From his shaving kit he takes two pills, swallowing them dry.

A boy sits in the shade with a pair of wooden crutches that look like Victorian relics except for the armpit cushions of duct tape and foam. At the sight of Burkett the boy, whose left leg is encased in plaster, extends his open hand. Burkett offers a five-dollar bill, which the boy receives in silence.

In the cab he had only limited success with his Arabic–English diction-ary, but again he opens it and speaks the words for 'hospital' and 'morgue'. The boy says something and points in the direction of a cylindrical tower that stands out for its height as well as its covering of elaborate fretwork.

To reach it Burkett has to navigate a warren of crowded alleys and side streets congested with stalled traffic. A welter of humanity fills the court-yard outside the building, no doubt the encamped families and friends of patients. Women in burqas sell food and bottled drinks from an old refrigerator turned on its back. A group of elder Khandaris with seashells in their beards stand around a brazier and glare at the passing white man. Children gather around him, a swarm of brushing hands.

He crosses an ambulance bay and enters the hospital through sliding glass doors. He pauses at a security desk, expecting to be questioned, but the uniformed guard merely smiles and nods. In the crowded waiting area he checks his pockets and realizes his smartphone has been stolen, probably by the urchins in the courtyard. There is no way of knowing. He glances toward the security desk but there's no point. At least his phone was password protected. At least he still has the disposable he purchased at the airport.

Patients lie on beds parked in the hallway, leaving little room to pass. He tries to keep his luggage from bumping the bedrails and IV catheters. A frail jaundiced woman reaches for him, and he feels a chill at the touch of her fingers. He searches her face for some hint as to the meaning of her feverish muttering, but her eyes suggest delirium.

'I'm sorry,' he says. 'I don't understand.'

Many of the signs have English translations, so he's able to find an information desk manned by another security guard. On the wall hangs a photograph of President Djohar, the self-proclaimed reformer who came to power in this island nation's first free and fair election. One of his earliest duties as president was to supervise the hanging of his predecessor, but the televised event became an embarrassment when the gallows fractured under the Behemoth's weight. Burkett wonders if this was the hospital where the former dictator languished for months in a coma before his eventual death obviated the need for a second hanging.

The security guard's irritated look softens when Burkett asks for the morgue. Mumbling into his shoulder radio, the guard escorts him to the elevator. They descend two floors and pass through an abandoned ward where empty patient rooms form a circumference around the nursing station. They take a staircase down yet another level, and in a subterranean corridor Burkett has to stoop to keep from bumping the rusted, antiquated pipes, which in some cases are suspended by frayed rope.

They come to a metal door with an intercom. The guard holds down the button, producing a buzz so muffled as to seem buried. From down the hall comes an elderly physician in a white coat stained with what looks like blood. His expression of surprise makes Burkett wonder if he heard the buzzer at all. The guard speaks into his walkie-talkie and turns down the dim passage, ignoring Burkett's thanks.

The physician puts on his glasses for a better look at the American. Recognition passes over his face: he knows why Burkett is here.

'I am Dr Abdullah, chief of pathology,' he says.

The doctor waves his name-badge over a sensor, the metal door unlatches, and Burkett follows him into an anteroom where shelves are stacked with protective gowns, gloves, and masks. At the doctor's urging, Burkett leaves his bags, but he's reluctant to set them on the floor, this being a morgue, so he hangs his backpack from one of the hooks and props his two duffels in a chair.

They put on rubber gloves and surgical caps and walk through an autopsy suite, where three cadavers lie covered on stainless steel tables. One of the heads is exposed, a man in his forties or fifties with a full beard and ligature marks on the neck.

The next chamber is lined with freezer doors. After checking a handwritten chart on the wall, the doctor pulls open one of the freezers. He slides out a body bag on a tray. He unzips the bag, exposing a face identical to Burkett's except for the pallor and bruising. The doctor brings over a metal folding chair but Burkett refuses to sit down.

'Show me,' he says, waving a hand over the body.

'Are you sure?' the doctor asks.

Burkett doesn't need to reply. The doctor pulls down the zipper. There are incisions from shoulders to pubis, stitched with twine. Two gunshot wounds to the chest, no visible powder burns. Burkett turns the body on its side looking for the exit wounds, but there are none.

The doctor holds up a finger and mumbles, 'Pardon,' and disappears through a door.

Burkett can make out the knot in the left clavicle – an old wrestling injury from their time at Penn State. His brother became something of a legend for winning the national championship despite having sustained that fracture during the second period of the final match. Of the twins Owen was always the better wrestler. He was a better surgeon, too.

There are contusions on the right hand, and when Burkett lifts it he feels the shifting fragments of bone: a boxer's fracture, which means Owen must have hit someone very hard.

The pathologist returns with the bullets, amorphous lumps of metal in separate plastic bags.

'Kalashnikov,' the doctor says.

He conducts Burkett into a small windowless office cluttered with textbooks and journals, the walls adorned with diplomas. On the desk Burkett recognizes a recent issue of *The Lancet*. It is an office no different from those he might have found in the department of surgery back at Emory.

Burkett signs a series of documents, most of them in English. He's given copies of the autopsy report, death certificate, and – the doctor nearly forgot – a large manila envelope containing the items found on the body: wallet, keys, belt, a pocket notepad, and a cross on a lanyard. Right away he sees that something is missing.

'He wore a silver ring,' Burkett says.

Dr Abdullah gives an apologetic shrug and says, 'There was nothing else.' He absently pats his pockets, which seems for a moment like grounds for suspicion, but it turns out he's only looking for another pen.

'I understand from the embassy that you would prefer cremation,' the doctor says.

'That's right,' Burkett replies. 'It's what he wanted.'

'I see.'

'Is there a problem?'

'No,' he says, smiling. 'We have a – what is the word? Oven?'

8

'Crematorium?'

He nods. 'Crematorium. Yes, this is forbidden by Islam, but the natives do request it.' He shrugs. 'The graveyards are filling up, so to speak, and very expensive.'

2

On the ground floor of Burkett's hotel is a bistro frequented by journalists and aid workers. Sandbags and poured concrete shut out the midday sun. He doesn't mind: when drinking he prefers an atmosphere of perpetual twilight. No alcohol on the menu, but the waiter, who seems hardly surprised by Burkett's order, serves him bourbon in a porcelain teacup.

His brother's notepad bears signs of long hours in a back pocket – sweat stains, crushed rings, the pages molded in a vaguely gluteal curve. Burkett pages through the lists of drugs and medical supplies, trying to see something of his brother in the handwriting, the minuscule letters that look like claw prints. He reads the list of items necessary for a lumbar puncture, the differential diagnosis for optic neuritis. There are occasional verses and snippets of prayer.

Grant me the words to pray as You'd have me pray.

When Nick Lorie arrives, half an hour late, Burkett's on his third bourbon but not as drunk as he'd like.

'Welcome to the Rock,' Nick says as they shake hands.

A former Navy Seal, Nick bears little resemblance to the soldier Burkett envisioned from their correspondence. He has a beard and mussed hair, and he's shorter than Burkett. Tattoos cover his forearms – geometric patterns, cross thatch grids or jagged lines in parallel – but none of it, as far as Burkett can tell, suggests any kind of military affiliation.

'I brought some of Owen's things,' Lorie says, placing a wrinkled paper bag on the table.

Burkett glances inside: a stethoscope, sunglasses, a pharmacopeia, two novels, a deck of cards, and a photo album. A picture in a frame: the two of them in the days of college wrestling. It's getting to the point that he might need another suitcase for his brother's effects.

'Did he not have a phone?' Burkett asks. 'Or a laptop?'

'Taken,' Nick says. 'Along with the car he was driving.'

'He used to wear a Celtic-style ring on his index finger. It had an inscription inside.'

'I remember it. It must have been stolen as well.'

'I never thought of Islamic militants as thieves.'

Nick's gaze lingers on Burkett's teacup. Perhaps he's a teetotaler like Owen. Bourbon could easily pass for tea, especially in this dim light, but the cup seems to make Nick uncomfortable. Perhaps he fears someone might see it and mistake him for a drinker. Burkett pulls it closer to himself.

'How was your flight?' Nick says. 'You came through Frankfurt, right?'

'And New York before that,' Burkett says. 'I got in yesterday.'

Nick speaks to the waiter in Arabic. Burkett finds this impressive, but Nick insists that anyone would know a language after ten years. Besides, the dialect isn't much use anywhere else.

'Ten years is a long time,' Burkett says.

'We love it here,' he replies with a shrug. 'This is our home now.'

He and his wife Beth hadn't planned on staying this long. It was meant to be a one-month trip, a temporary medical clinic, but they decided to stay.

'The Lord wanted us here.'

These words are jarring to Burkett. It's the kind of language he might expect from his brother's journal, but not in conversation with a stranger. Could this be the way he spoke with Owen? They were close friends, after all. Perhaps Nick has to remind himself, moment to moment, that this man with Owen's face is in fact someone else.

Nick looks at the duffels as if noticing them for the first time.

'Supplies for the clinic,' Burkett says. 'Antibiotics, mosquito netting – some of the things Owen said you needed.'

He'd carried the drugs for months in the trunk of his car, planning to send them to his brother by mail. They were given to him by a sales representative from the pharmaceutical company, a woman he used to sleep with. The mosquito netting he bought the day before his flight at an army surplus store.

'We're always in need,' Nick says. 'I can't thank you enough.'

'I'm happy to send more,' he says.

'Why don't you stay on and work with us?' Nick says, and off Burkett's smile adds, 'I'm serious. We pay for a mobile operating room twice a week, but without Owen it's sitting empty. If you had the slightest inclination...'

'I don't share my brother's religious convictions,' Burkett says.

'You'd be working as a surgeon, not a missionary. International Medical Outreach would pay you a stipend, along with your travel expenses. You'd have free room and board.'

'After what happened to Owen...'

'Look, it's obviously dangerous, but Owen – that was a fluke.'

'Aren't you worried about the political situation?'

'If things get hairy, my friend Mark Rich, an American army officer, has guaranteed seats for us on the first helicopter out.'

'I didn't think there were American troops here.'

'He's an advisor for Djohar's drone program,' Nick says.

Burkett shakes his head, smiling to soften what he says next: 'I could never live in this place.'

'I can't begin to describe the difference you'd make.'

'I'm sorry,' he says.

But there's a certain appeal in the idea of walking away from his life in the States: his medical school debt, the latest drunk-driving conviction, and his embarrassing dismissal from the fellowship program at Emory. Would it even be possible? He can't help but wonder if the clinic stocks benzodiazepines. He could stretch the supply in his shaving kit two weeks. He has an arrangement with another physician in Atlanta, a kind of prescription exchange, but that wouldn't do him much good overseas. How long would he stay? A month, a year? But the question is moot: he's already signed a contract with a surgical practice in Atlanta.

'Let me show you the clinic,' Nick says, opening his laptop. He uses Burkett's room number to access the hotel's wireless service. He pulls up the IMO website and clicks past the memorial to Owen – the short biography that neither confirms nor denies the real nature of his work here – to a map that fills his screen: an island shaped like a dagger, with its blade-like flatlands to the north, and the southern half whose mountainous topography suggests the nubs of a grip. He zooms in on the north, prompting an overlay of colored roads and labeled towns.

'Here's Mejidi-al-Alam,' he says, pointing and then expanding the image till the scant buildings and roads are visible as tiny squares and lines. Colored graphics highlight a cluster of buildings, the medical clinic.

'How far are you from the coast?' Burkett asks.

'About an hour's drive.'

He shakes his head. It seems fitting that his brother would travel halfway around the world only to deny himself an ocean view.

A couple sits down at the next table – an Arab in western garb, and a white woman who speaks English with a French accent. He gathers from their tone that they're colleagues. A purely professional relationship, he thinks, as he steals another glance at the woman. From the Arab's camera bag, Burkett decides they must be journalists.

Nick magnifies the vicinity of the clinic. He points out the nearby military outpost, separated from the clinic by a tributary of some kind.

'Show me where they found him,' Burkett says.

The cartoon hand follows an unnamed road till there is nothing on the map except for the road. And when Nick switches to the satellite view, the background wrinkles into a brownish landscape of rock and shadow. The last thing Owen saw must have been stone and sand. Some desert hell.

'He was on his way home,' Nick says.

'Was he set up?' Burkett says. 'Was it the patient he visited?'

Nick doesn't know much more than Burkett – only what he's gleaned from the newspaper accounts. The national police have repeatedly emphasized their commitment to the case by specifying the number of officers involved at each stage: three interviewed Owen's last patient, ten scoured the scene for clues.

What kind of clues? What would a clue possibly signify? He pictures some functionary crawling around with a magnifying glass. What are the odds of an arrest or punishment? The culprits are known already – they've taken credit, claimed responsibility. Heroes of Jihad, they call themselves. Does it even matter which of them pulled the trigger? Of course Burkett would like to find him. He's probably young, educated in some madrassa, if at all.

When he gets back to his room, he empties the brown paper bag on the bed. The deck of cards, creased and dogeared, is held together by a rubber band. He should have recognized it sooner, what with the swimsuit models on the backs of the cards. He flips to the ten of hearts, the one they liked best, the one they called Lydia – a beautiful brunette with her back to the camera, her face in profile. The inflated 1980s hairstyle dates the picture as much as the sepia tint. At Penn State, Burkett and his brother used these cards to guide their push-ups. They would shuffle the deck and work their way through, counting the face cards and aces as twenty each.

The framed photograph shows the two of them at the NCAA wrestling tournament – Owen's arm in a sling, the first-place medal dangling from his neck. Burkett's expression in the picture conceals his own anger at not placing. How he'd hated his brother that night – not just for winning, but for the injury, which only enhanced his glory. Why would Owen have kept this particular photograph? Perhaps it summarizes their relationship: Owen with the championship medal, Burkett with nothing but bitterness. He rubs his thumb against the glass, as if to palpate a barrier he imagines between the two wrestlers.

Still annoyed by the confiscation of his bourbon, Burkett negotiates with the concierge for another bottle from the hotel's stock. The concierge demands fifty dollars – added expense to cover the risk of losing his job or running afoul of the Ministry of Vice. Burkett takes out his wallet. At this rate, his supply of cash won't last the weekend.

'If you like,' says the concierge, 'I can give you something stronger.'

He conducts Burkett through a large kitchen, down a back stairwell and into the basement. The man looks both ways before unlocking a closet and pulling the cord inside to light a bare bulb. He kneels and slides out a cooler and opens the lid to reveal stacks of clear plastic bottles. He glances up at Burkett.

'*Siddique*, my friend.'

'How do I know this won't make me blind?'

'Please,' he says, 'this is the highest quality.'

To prove it he unscrews one of the caps and sips. He winces at the taste.

'See, no problem.'

'How much?'

'For you, ten dollars per bottle.'

'I'll take five,' he says. 'And the bottle of bourbon, too.'

Back in his room he tastes the *siddique* – a burning pleasure, but without the sweetness of bourbon. A useful substitute, he thinks, for drinking when already drunk, when his taste buds are numb. He unscrews the new bottle of bourbon and fills his two flasks, catching the run-off in a plastic cup. He takes two Xanax and lies down with the cup and bottle.

He wonders if he has grieved enough for his brother. Does he owe it to him to shed tears? If there were some kind of duty to grieve, surely Burkett would fall short of the obligation. What he feels more than grief is guilt for his grief's inadequacy.

Another pill to help him sleep, to help him stop thinking like this. Perhaps this is the very character of grief, that it can't be separated from its shadow, that the aggrieved must also ponder the idea of grief. How much simpler grief would be if left alone – if he could experience it without thinking about it. Are other emotions like this? Does happiness demand an account of itself?

He calls it grief, but grief was what he felt as a boy of ten when his mother died. His brother has left him with an emptiness – a piece of himself gone. No, not a piece. This is not the same as an amputated limb. The loss is more diffuse, more complete, but at the same time more subtle. As if the absence represented a tiny portion not of himself but of every cell, every atom in his body.

'Owen.' He mumbles the name as if speaking directly to his brother

– as if his brother were a casual presence here in the room. But the name seems out of place – like a familiar word in the wrong context. Names are words whose meanings can suddenly change. It was rare that he and his brother actually called each other by name.

He turns on the bedside lamp and opens his brother's notepad to a random page. The jagged, minuscule handwriting is so similar to his own – perhaps indistinguishable. The medical notes could easily have been written by either of them, but then there are the strange religious jottings:

> For what is your life? It is even a vapor that appears
> for a short time and then vanishes away.

Probably a Bible verse, it brings to mind yet again the question of an afterlife. Beliefs that came so easily as a child now seem absurd.

He thinks of that quirk of physics, where particles once linked but now separated continue acting as though linked no matter the distance between them. *Strange interaction at a distance.* What is the distance between him and his brother? If one particle is annihilated, shouldn't the other one be annihilated as well?

There is no afterlife, he tells himself, as much as he might wish otherwise. But if a single particle can exist in two places at once, or if two can be linked across any distance, then perhaps life and death represent flickering states in a more permanent scheme. Perhaps somewhere else, in some kind of parallel universe, it is Burkett rather than his brother who is dead.

The body lies in a cardboard box and wears a white gown provided by the morgue. A Catholic priest lends an element of religious formality, but it's Nick Lorie who prays and utters words of remembrance. Burkett and his brother were brought up Catholic – non-practicing, as they liked to say. The family's religious affiliation only seemed to have relevance on holidays.

The way Burkett remembers it, he and his brother were alike in every way till Owen's religious conversion. They were fifteen, at a Christian sports camp. Burkett was amazed when his brother responded to the altar call. Had they not heard the exact same sermon? Did they not have the same DNA, almost identical brains? God, if he existed, seemed to have chosen one brother over the other. How could his brother believe in a God who would make such a distinction?

He sees the conversion as the beginning of their separation – and also when Owen first chose the path that would culminate in his own death. If Owen had ignored that altar call perhaps the two of them would have ended up doing residency together and joining the same practice.

Burkett's anger is large enough for Muslims and Christians alike. The pastor at the sports camp, Nick Lorie, and any other Christian who inspired Owen to risk his life. He could write a treatise on the evils of religion.

'We thank you,' Lorie says, 'for the promise of eternal peace. Amen.'

The priest makes the sign of the cross. The orderly covers the box and pushes it on rollers into a stone furnace and bolts the cast iron door.

Burkett waits while the body burns. There is no smoke from the grate, no odor of burning flesh. The only evidence of fire is the heat radiating from the furnace. A barrier seems to surround him, a barrier composed of nothing but heat. He is cut off from the others, sealed in a thermal pocket all his own. They are separated from him by only a few feet, but it could be miles.

For the remains he's given a cylindrical plastic container with a screw-on cap. Like Tupperware, he thinks, as he scoops ashes and bits of bone from the furnace. He wishes he'd thought to bring some kind of urn.

The wood-handled garden shovel seems clean enough, but he can't help wondering how often it has been used for this very purpose. Are his brother's ashes mingling with those of others? Does it even matter? He can taste the floating dust as he fills the container. The orderly is no doubt breathing it as well. To collect the last of it, the orderly produces a small broom and dustpan.

3

Burkett takes a shower and puts on fresh clothes and goes down to the bistro for another drink. He has no good reason for bringing his brother's ashes with him. It just seems like a bad idea to leave them unattended. What if a housekeeper poured them down the drain? He sets the canister on the table and lifts his teacup. *My brother the martyr.*

He listens to the only other customers, a group of older men, Germans and Italians as far as he can tell, but speaking English. They are probably journalists. He counts six empty wine bottles, one for each man. He is sitting on the opposite side of the room, but they speak loud enough for him to hear.

'Djohar is right,' an Italian says, jabbing his smokeless pipe in the imagined direction of the Khandarian president. 'Why should terrorists be appeased with a country of their own?'

The man beside him nods. 'My question is this: if you give it to them, who can guarantee that the bombings would even stop?'

'You rebuild the Khandarian Wall,' says one of the Germans, his sarcasm clear despite the thick accent. 'Simple, no problem.'

'I agree, this is ridiculous,' says the man with the pipe. 'The separatists in parliament are always talking about the wall but none of them have any idea how to pay for it.'

The French woman he saw before enters the bistro and removes her coat. She wears a headscarf, but her sleeveless blouse and knee-length skirt are wildly audacious by local standards. The journalists, suddenly silent, acknowledge her with glances or outright stares. She takes a seat at a table near Burkett. She meets his eyes, quickly looks away, and after a moment looks again. It is the second glance that justifies his approach.

He senses malevolence in the journalists' refusal to look at him. He resists gloating. After all, he's the youngest man here by at least twenty years. He might look old for his age, now thirty-four, but he's a picture of youth next to them.

The circumstances aren't well suited to his usual strategy of sitting next to a woman without speaking.

'Mind if I sit here?'

With her foot she slides out the closest chair. He sits down and places the canister of ashes in the chair beside him.

She asks, 'Do you always bring Tupperware when you drink?'

'Only on special occasions.'

'Is this a special occasion?'

'Maybe,' he says. 'Ask me again in ten minutes.'

It is the sort of idiotic banter he only uses with women in bars. Tonight he is more conscious of it, almost wincingly so, perhaps because of the presence of Owen. He can see his brother shaking his head and rolling his eyes – his brother who as far as he knows never drank a sip of alcohol, much less seduced a woman in a bar.

Does this actually work for you? Owen is asking. *How can anyone take you seriously?*

Véronique is her name. A journalist in her mid-thirties, she's covered militant Islamic groups for more than a decade. It turns out she's heard about what happened to Owen. She has a particular interest in the Heroes of Jihad, whom she sees as much more of a threat than the typical fanatics. It is because of the Heroes and their organized campaign of bombings that the public and many in parliament are seriously considering a referendum on the secession of South Khandaros.

'Two years ago,' she says, 'there were literally hundreds of groups claiming responsibility for attacks in the capital. Now it is just the Heroes.'

'How did that happen?'

'You could say the jihadists had to pool their resources to fight their assorted enemies – warlords, the national army, you name it. Secularists, unionists, foreigners.'

'Why did the Heroes rise to the top?'

'Their leader, Mullah Bashir.'

'Didn't someone kill that guy?'

She nods. 'Six months ago, probably a drone attack. It was a political victory for President Djohar, a strike against terrorism, but Bashir was loved by many, so his death served to inspire even greater hatred, especially against the west.'

'Isn't it amazing how drones always inspire hatred for Americans, even when those very drones are owned and operated by someone else?'

'Americans are hated not just for selling drones to the regime, but also for sending missionaries to convert Muslims, for exporting pornography and fast food. For being the great Satan.'

He stares at the ashes in the chair beside him. 'The group that funded my brother's clinic, International Medical Outreach, claims he wasn't here as a missionary but as a health worker.'

'To say otherwise would endanger those working at his clinic. It is illegal here to preach Christianity. What your brother was doing was akin to espionage. A foreigner doing illegal work under a pretext. Medicine was his cover, so to speak.'

'What a waste,' he says.

She shrugs. 'Do you disapprove of your brother's proselytism?'

'You can't expect to come to a place like this and impose your beliefs on others. It's certainly not worth dying for.'

'By law, if a Muslim converts to Christianity, he forfeits all of his property. Missionaries should consider this when they come here with their religion.'

'I thought there was a new constitution,' he says. 'I thought it was approved by western monitors.'

'Have you read the new constitution?' She pauses, but he doesn't think she's waiting for a reply. 'The law against apostasy was one of many concessions to conservatives in parliament.'

'What about the tribal religion?' he asks. 'Do the Islamists hate it as much as Christianity?'

'Samakism,' she says. 'There are not many actual practitioners, not enough to have any real influence.'

'What exactly do they believe?'

'There was a powerful being,' she says, 'a *Jinn*, who created this island, El-Khandar, by dropping a great jewel into the sea. To protect the islanders, the *Jinn* sent a demigod, a one-eyed shark named Samakersh. You occasionally see his symbol on doors and buildings.'

She uncaps a pen and on her napkin sketches an eye, a simple oval with a dot near the center, and beneath the eye a jagged line like the edge of a saw. An eye floating over mountains? Not mountains, he realizes, but teeth – the teeth of a shark.

Though she hasn't yet finished her wine, he gestures for the waiter to bring another round. She has a kind of dark-eyed beauty, but what he finds most alluring is her voice – not just her raspy eloquence or French accent, but the odd formality of her language, her reluctance to use contractions.

'How do you feel about Djohar's use of drones?' she asks.

If Burkett were honest he'd place his opinion on drones somewhere between apathy and disapproval. But what does he really know about it? He imagines soldiers with joysticks, a disturbing overlap of gaming and killing.

'He has no choice,' Burkett says. 'He lacks the manpower to keep his country from falling apart.'

'There has been an outcry over civilian casualties, particularly from America, where private companies are selling him the drones in the first place. But you are right, what choice does he have? How else can he deal with the unofficial mini-state in the south, people paying tax to a separate Islamic regime?'

'Unofficial?' he asks. 'If I'm not mistaken, the caliphate of South Khandaros has already been recognized by Hamas and the Taliban.'

'With endorsements like that who can argue!'

'A far cry from the United Nations,' he says with an easy laugh.

After a period of silence he says, 'I think I'm too drunk to talk politics.'

'And I,' she says, 'am perhaps not drunk enough.'

When the bistro closes, they walk through the lobby toward the elevator. He isn't sure what will happen, how he should go about suggesting she come up to his room. But when the elevator doors close she turns to him and they kiss. He presses her against the wall and runs his hands up and down the sides of her body. They hardly disengage when the elevator arrives at his floor. She clings to him as they approach his room. Though still in public, technically, they seem to have dispensed with whatever decorum they might have observed downstairs.

Now they're in bed. She lies beneath him and her lips move against his ear, muttering in French what could be either obscenities or endearments, possibly both. When drunk he has a tendency to feel abstracted, distant from himself, which adds to the strangeness of this foreign woman and this foreign place. He feels like he's in a kind of free fall, the darkness beneath him opening wider and wider as he braces for impact. Afterward he rolls off her and waits for her to speak, but she says nothing, and in only a matter of minutes he hears the nasal rasps of her drunken sleep.

Just past four a.m. he wakes in a panic. He left his brother's ashes in the bistro. At his table or Véronique's, he can't remember which. He races down to the empty lobby, and bangs his fist against the door of the bistro until a uniformed bellhop walks up behind him. The bellhop doesn't have a key to the bistro. Only after Burkett hands him a twenty-dollar bill does the man call security. It takes half an hour for the guard to arrive and open the door. To his relief, the ashes wait undisturbed in the same chair where he left them.

The clock reads five a.m. when he returns to his room. He goes to the bathroom and undresses and drinks a glass of bourbon in the shower. Afterward he stands in the carpeted room with a towel around his waist. The rising sun casts a bar of light across his bed and the bare legs of the woman lying there.

While she sleeps, he unpacks his computer and checks his email. Two days' worth of unread messages, at least fifty, wait in his inbox. There is a message from the Georgia Medical Board with his license number in the subject line. He holds his breath, feels his heart accelerate. It's been less than a week since the hearing. Could the board have already decided his case?

He skims through the letter, pausing on the phrase 'temporary suspension of your medical license'. After his third drunk-driving charge, the state of Georgia has deemed him unfit for surgical practice. If he undergoes treatment for substance abuse, the status of his license will be reconsidered in six months. The board has been kind enough to provide links to two treatment facilities.

His initial response, after shutting his laptop, is to go to the bathroom for a Xanax and a shot of *siddique*. He stares at his reflection as if waiting for it to give him some word of encouragement or condemnation. He climbs back into bed and drapes one arm across his eyes, but there is little hope of sleep. With the sun coming up he would need a higher dose to escape consciousness.

So he is now an unlicensed physician. He wonders if this is a decision he can appeal. Should he contact a lawyer? Baptist Hospital has hired him as general surgeon, to begin practice a week from today. His future partners gave him a generous signing bonus, which he now might be obligated to pay back. Perhaps even more generous was their offer to postpone his start date when his brother died.

Will they revoke the job offer? The status of his license should be a private matter. If no one asked, he could theoretically begin operating next week as scheduled. Perhaps he could find a local treatment program in the evenings. On the other hand, he would face criminal prosecution if it ever came to light that he was operating without a license.

Substance abuse. The words would have shocked his teetotal brother. Burkett, for his part, had always enjoyed the occasional binge, even when they were college wrestlers, but he wasn't getting drunk on a regular basis till late in his first year of medical school at Emory. By fourth year, he and his classmates were out in the bars every night. During his internship and residency, it wasn't uncommon for him to show up for rounds still drunk and reeking of smoke.

Owen, whose social life revolved around Bible studies and fellowship meetings, finished at the top of his class at Johns Hopkins and became a chief resident in surgery at Harvard. What a surprise it must have been to his attendings when he turned down a fellowship in pediatric surgery and entered the mission field.

Véronique rises and hurries to the bathroom, surprisingly modest of her nudity. With the shower running she reappears in a terry cloth robe to gather last night's clothes. He gets up and makes two cups of drip coffee using bottled water from the non-alcoholic minibar. He pulls back the curtains for a view not of the ocean (his room faces in the wrong direction) but of moldering rooftops interspersed with minarets and columns of greasy smoke where people are burning their trash.

Light glints from a metallic disk hovering among the chimneys and antennae as if suspended by a string. Too small for a helicopter and too still for a plane – it could only be a drone. He notes the blur of propellers, a camera like some kind of proboscis. By reflex he shuts the blinds even though the camera points elsewhere.

She emerges fully clothed and turns on the overhead light, and he's gripped by a sudden awareness of his pasty skin, the hirsute paunch over the waistband of his boxer briefs. It is unclear whether he refrained from dressing out of laziness or a hope of further sex, perhaps some combination. That picture of him and his brother sits on the bedside table, and his younger, stronger self seems to glare in disapproval at what he's become.

Véronique picks up his wadded pants and flings them across the bed. While he dresses she sits with the bowl of complimentary walnuts left in his room last night.

'So how long have you been married?' she asks, no doubt taking his sullen mood for guilt.

'Sorry,' he says. 'I'm just hung over.'

How many times has he used that excuse in the morning? How many times has she heard it? It would be more truthful, perhaps, to tell her he's grieving for his brother, but on this subject he remains silent.

She has a flight home in two days. He'd like to see her again, but she has appointments all day and a party tonight at the French embassy. She programs her number into his phone, but doesn't invite him to the party. Why should she? Perhaps she'll fit him into her schedule, a tryst between appointments.

'So when are we getting together?' he asks when she opens the door.

She glances back at him, a quick smile as she leaves, and asks, 'How about the next time we're both in El-Khandar?'

He stares at the door with a lingering smile, half expecting her to return – or hoping she will. Of course she was joking about their next meeting. She'd have no reason to expect him to visit Khandaros, or El-Khandar, ever again. And no doubt the idea would have seemed absurd to him yesterday, even an hour ago, when he still had a medical license and a career waiting for him back in the States. But what's waiting for him now? His father, his only living family, no longer recognizes him. He still owes fifty thousand dollars for medical school, twenty thousand in back taxes. His debts wouldn't have been a problem on his salary in private practice, but now he wonders how he'll make the payments.

He can't bear to think about money. Debts, investments, salaries, and taxes: such words have little more than a tenuous connection to reality. His inability to grasp financial concepts might be a consequence of growing up in relative wealth. The economics of health care are such that his father, at his prime as a surgeon, earned far more than Burkett ever will.

A message from Nick Lorie appears in his inbox.

We'd love to have you on board. I spoke with IMO about making it worth your while to join us.

International Medical Outreach paid off Owen's debt from medical school. If they would do the same for Burkett, if they would help with his student loans and back taxes, he could stay and continue his brother's work. Here he could practice the kind of medicine he envisioned as an undergraduate: helping those in need without worrying about reimbursement rates and lawsuits. And if he found it unsuitable, he could simply leave. He'd be free to come and go at will.

Of course, he can't ignore the political situation: a tense equilibrium of warlords, jihadists, and government forces. A military comprised of American drones and soldiers ill-equipped to fight the ever more likely civil war against the Islamists in the south. The Republic of Khandaros, 'the Rock', has cracked down the middle: 'A knife broken at the hilt,' as the saying goes. If the situation takes a turn for the worse, Nick and Beth have their plan of evacuation, the promised helicopter.

For Burkett the threat of violence is nothing new, not after almost seven years at Grady Hospital in Atlanta. During his time there, two physicians on separate occasions were assaulted in the very same parking deck, one killed and the other permanently disabled. He's sure he could find statistics to prove Grady at least as dangerous as his brother's clinic.

As he responds to Nick's email he thinks of another reason to stay, one he's surprised not to have considered sooner: he wants to see where his brother died. Not that seeing the place would change anything, or even make him feel better – but what if he uncovered some bit of evidence missed by the police? Something perhaps only a brother would notice. After all, he knew the victim better than anyone else. If the roles were reversed, if Burkett were the one who had died, he has no doubt Owen would insist on visiting the scene of the crime.

4

Three days later Burkett and Nick leave the capital at first light, traveling south on a coastal road. Burkett's passport is stowed in a hidden compartment with a stack of Bibles. When the car takes a hard turn, he feels a slide and a knock under his seat as if the Bibles were crying out to be found. Even if IMO have agreed to the monthly payments on his debt – confirmed in writing just last night – the contraband under his seat makes him question the bargain. After what happened to his brother, why would he consent to ride with translated Bibles? What sort of madness is this?

He and Nick have taken the precaution of wearing turbans and covering their faces with scarves. There is no weapon in the vehicle – Burkett asked – but Nick has military experience, and their driver, Abu, is a hulking presence, well over six feet.

He remembers the official announcement put out by the so-called Heroes. *We arrested a Christian missionary with translated Bibles, so we killed him.* He'd be interested in knowing the original language of the statement, whether it was composed in English, or later translated by the media. He can't help but admire the perversity of *arrest*, the way it casts the murder as an act of law enforcement.

Adding to the risk, yet unknown to Nick, are the ten bottles of *siddique* he bought from the concierge yesterday, bringing the total in his suitcase to thirteen. With the benzos, he could probably maintain an optimal condition of low-grade drunkenness for about twenty days. If he decides to extend his stay in Mejidi-al-Alam, he doubts he'll have a problem replenishing his supply. On the other hand, since sobriety must come to him eventually, it might as well happen here.

They pass a crumbling set of buildings, the burnt-out shell of what looks to have been a grand seaside hotel.

'The Aljannah,' Nick says. 'Raided by militants. Hundreds of guests were taken hostage and ultimately killed.'

It is evidence of the event's magnitude that Burkett remembers it at all. He was in his residency at the time, so completely immersed in work that outside news had to be particularly grim or sensational to penetrate the walls of his narrow existence. One of the televised moments he recalls with disturbing clarity: a masked gunman and kneeling hostage, a single shot to the back of the head. That image haunted him when he learned of his brother's decision to move here. And rightfully so, for now when he closes his eyes it is his brother who kneels and waits for the bullet.

Nick asks the driver to slow down. 'Check it out,' he says, pointing. 'The national army's sorry excuse for special forces crashed a helicopter in the hotel pool.'

Sure enough, the charred tail of a helicopter juts from the rubble like an obscene gesture aimed at a ship in the distance, what looks like an aircraft carrier.

'Quadri, the Behemoth, wanted to make Khandaros a tourist destination,' Nick says. 'He legalized alcohol and gambling in the coastal provinces, so it wasn't long before the resort became a symbol of decadence and moral corruption. Some say it was the photographs of Quadri's poolside antics that led to his ousting.'

'I can't imagine that guy in a bathing suit.'

Nick smiles. 'He wasn't known as "the Behemoth" for his svelte physique.'

They skirt a small bay, where fishermen toss nets from boats. A brightly colored village sits in a depression formed by rocky hills.

'My home,' says their driver in heavily accented English. 'The village where I grew up. Those fishermen could be cousins.'

'Was your father a fisherman?' Burkett asks him.

'All the men of my family have been fishermen,' Abu says, with a sweep of the hand that implies endless generations. 'It was a great surprise to everyone when I chose to go to university in the capital.'

'What did you study?' asks Burkett.

'Economics,' he says. 'But not for long, unfortunately.'

'This was in the final years of the king,' Nick says, 'when the secret police were cracking down on radical student groups.'

'You were arrested?' Burkett asks.

'I went to a meeting,' Abu says, holding up his index finger. 'For one meeting I spent ten months in prison.'

'But it turned out to be a blessing,' Nick says.

Abu nods, but offers no explanation, so Burkett asks, 'How was it a blessing?'

'It was in prison that I met Isa,' Abu says.

'Jesus,' Nick interprets. He glances back as if to check Burkett's face for skepticism.

'It sounds like you made the best of the situation,' Burkett says in a neutral voice.

Abu explains that he had a recurring dream while in prison – a clear vision of a bearded man all in white, standing in a meadow beside a running stream. Abu never heard the man speak, but somehow he understood that it was Jesus, and somehow he knew, simply from the man's gaze, that he was being invited to drink from the stream. He stopped having the dream after his release, but for years afterward he envisioned this man during his prayers. Now he supports his wife and two small granddaughters on a salary of about thirty dollars a month. Not even the other employees of the clinic know of his conversion and baptism. He and the twenty or so other Christians in Mejidi-al-Alam gather in secret for fellowship and worship.

'Like the earliest apostles,' Nick says.

It seems unwise for Abu to discuss matters of faith with a man he has only just met. Or maybe it's that same fallacy encountered all too often by identical twins – the assumption of identical beliefs. When Burkett agreed to work at the clinic, he failed to consider the mild irritation of being mistaken for his brother. Perhaps he should ask Nick to spread word of his religious apathy.

'My wife is an enemy of the faith,' Abu is saying. 'She calls me a great sinner, but she would never betray me. If I die, all my property goes to the nearest male relation. A cousin she hates, a terrible man. She and our granddaughters would have nothing.'

To Burkett he looks far too young for grandchildren, no older than forty. But he suspects this is what happens in a poor, overly religious culture. People marry too early, have too many children. Perhaps Burkett should serve as a different sort of missionary – an evangelist not of faith but of progress.

They pull off the road at a roofless, one-room hut of mud brick and go inside to urinate. They face the wall and keep their distance from a corner used by some previous traveler for defecation.

Burkett lingers inside while Abu and Nick return to the car. He opens his flask and takes a drink only to be startled by a sound in the window. An elderly farmer with shells in his beard stares at Burkett. A pair of oxen wait behind him. Burkett stuffs the flask in his pocket and looks away.

*

The SUV pulls through an open gate into a small, otherwise empty lot. The cluster of buildings is surrounded on three sides by a twenty-foot wall of unpainted cinderblock. Plastic tarps divide the courtyard into separate waiting areas for men and women. Among the men, Burkett spots a goiter, a case of jaundice, and a swollen toe – probably gout.

In Nick's absence, a nurse named Hassad has managed the male side of the clinic. He wears a prayer cap, bright red vest, and baggy pants a few inches above the ankles. They follow him into the anteroom used for triage – a new addition of plywood and corrugated steel that, like the cinderblock wall and portable modules, seems incongruous next to the stone and crumbling brick of the original house at the center of the complex.

It is perhaps another byproduct of Nick's absence that the task of running triage has fallen to a teenager. The boy, about fourteen, sits at a desk and types on a laptop while listening to an elderly tribesman. Posters tacked to the walls feature instructive cartoons on clean water and vaccination. A white woman emerges from a door behind the desk. She's attractive, around forty, with a scarf draped over a blonde pony-tail.

'My wife Beth,' says Nick, as she and Burkett shake hands. 'She's in charge of our women's health and vaccination programs.'

'Welcome,' she says with a smile. 'Now that you're here, we have one doctor for every fifty thousand people in the province.'

'What was it yesterday?'

'One in a hundred thousand,' she says.

Out the window, Burkett can see the section of the courtyard designated for women. The burqas make it impossible to guess their ailments. Fully covered even when sick, he thinks. Nick explains that Burkett won't see any female patients except in cases of surgical emergency. Beth, who has training as both a midwife and a family nurse practitioner, can handle most of the issues in the women's clinic.

'What's to keep the separatists from attacking this place?' Burkett asks.

'We pay a tribal leader for protection,' Nick says. 'A shady character named Walari.'

'He's something of a warlord,' Beth says without sarcasm.

'Ex-warlord,' Nick corrects her. 'He's more of a businessman.'

She begins to speak but catches herself. Perhaps she fears reopening an ongoing dispute, or drawing attention to her husband's recalcitrance, that quality of certainty bordering on arrogance. Burkett could tell her not to worry. He's spent enough time in operating rooms not to be bothered by a personality like her husband's. Among health workers it's typically the surgeon who plays the part of dominant asshole, but this soldier turned nurse resides far from the hierarchy of any hospital.

'A piece of advice,' she says, opening the door to a simple examining room. 'With the people here, we have different views of God, but our word for him is the same. *God* in English is *Allah* in Arabic. Don't be afraid to use those terms interchangeably.'

He stares, trying to imagine a context in which this would have relevance. Perhaps it is evidence of Owen's religious fervor that no one can imagine his twin would not have an identical vocation.

'Something to remember,' she goes on, 'is that Muslims do believe in the virgin birth. Most are interested in discussing the person Jesus, but it's counterproductive to try to persuade anyone through apologetics.'

'I don't expect to do much persuading,' he says.

'Beth,' says her husband, 'he's not a believer.'

A look of vexation crosses her face. Burkett sees that she's well aware of his unbelief. No doubt she and Nick have discussed at length the question of whether a non-believer should be allowed to work in the clinic

– whether his surgical skills outweigh his spiritual shortcomings. So why would she speak to him in such a way? Was her 'advice' on evangelism itself a form of evangelism? A paradoxical strategy of coaxing the agnostic twin? Her husband either missed the point altogether or simply recognized the futility of it.

Burkett places the pocket notepad and canister of ashes on the small wooden desk. His brother inhabited this same room, approximately ten feet by five, equipped with a small sink of stainless steel and a narrow bed that doubles as a desk chair. He opens the single drawer in the desk – a blank legal pad, some loose paper clips, a toothpick, and one of those microfiber rags used for cleaning glasses.

How did Owen live here more than a year without leaving the slightest mark? Burkett scans the walls, but he doesn't know what he's looking for. His brother wasn't the sort to carve some prosaic memorial to his own presence. *Owen was here.*

Burkett might have thought by coming here he'd better understand why his brother gave up his career. Why he turned his back on whatever prestige he might have enjoyed as a surgeon in the States. In any American city, he could have found ample poverty and secular misery on which to train his evangelical sights.

It seems unthinkable that a surgeon of Owen's caliber would have chosen to live like this. How could a man so driven in the pursuit of success end up in such bleak obscurity?

As a wrestler, Owen was known for his relentless desire to win. Of course Burkett too wanted to win, but he lacked his brother's obsession. Mad obsession – the only way to explain the undefeated final season, the NCAA championship, when Burkett, despite identical genes and an identical training regimen, managed to win just a few more matches than he lost. Owen always gave the credit to God, spouting clichés on faith and hard work that annoyed Burkett but inspired church groups and teenage members of the Fellowship of Christian Athletes.

But did Jesus not exhort his followers against vanity and worldly ambition? Owen must have seen the obvious contradiction in the idea of a Christian seeking worldly glory. How would an NCAA champion and Harvard-trained surgeon reconcile his success with his faith? Or was it that very success which drove him to this island, this Spartan cell?

In a cardboard box under the bed he finds wadded surgical scrubs and an old Penn State tee shirt. He puts on the tee shirt and lies on the bed with his arms at his sides. His brother's bed, his brother's clothes: surely this is an exact repetition of some past moment. He lifts the collar of the tee shirt over his nose and breathes in the faint odor of dried sweat. Perhaps something of his brother, his spirit, resides in the odor. If only he could believe in such things. The odor takes him back to the Penn State wrestling room: he and Owen, grasping each other by the neck. He imagines the smell of the tee shirt entering his body and being transformed, and when he exhales, his breath takes the form of his brother's name. Not even a whisper, little more than a modulation of air: *Owen.*

Owen was here. Where is he now? Is he some kind of spirit or ghost? Does his soul or some version of his consciousness exist at this particular moment, here or elsewhere? Even if Burkett became a so-called believer, he wouldn't buy into the sort of afterlife preached to children – not some sunlit family reunion. How much joy could such a place offer, anyway? How could the dead bring themselves to celebrate while the living still grieve?

In reality, what is Owen now but tiny bursts of electricity in the brains of those who knew him? Like an afterimage that follows a flash of light.

That night sleep comes to him only in fits, despite the additional

Valium, which on top of the Xanax and alcohol could be dangerous for even the most desensitized patient. Maybe he's testing his limits, exploring the boundaries of death. Maybe he wants to die. He doubts he would even be missed, except perhaps by his father, in a rare moment of lucidity.

He lies in the dark waiting for a bright light with floating angels – or endless writhing bodies in a barren desert, the armies of the dead. What he sees instead is the face of his brother underwater – his eyes replaced by black ovals, hair wafting in the current. The strength of the current leads Burkett to think they're in the ocean or a strong river. They wrestle as they sink deeper, but shouldn't they be helping each other swim back to the surface? Burkett realizes the effort of their wrestling is entirely his own, the stiffness in his brother's limbs an effect of rigor mortis. So how is it that he can't seem to gain an advantage? They come to a gentle landing, and silt rises in an enveloping cloud of black. He's held his breath till now, but this ash-tasting blackness turns out to be something he can breathe.

The taste of it lingers when he wakes. The clock reads 3:32 a.m. It is the sound of his own name that woke him, his brother calling, *Ryan.* He gets up and opens the squeaking door of his module. The night breeze carries a hint of ocean salt. From beyond the wall of the compound comes his name: *Ryan.* Now it sounds less like the voice of his brother than that of a woman or child. He pads barefoot to the gate and stares out at the street and when the voice comes again he realizes it's not a human voice at all, but merely the wail of some animal in pain. He goes back to his room, but the shrieks rise in volume and frequency. The animal, perhaps a dog, must be closer now, just outside the wall of the compound. No sooner has he put on his jeans and shoes and gone back outside than the noise stops altogether. The animal must have died.

He stands listening, waiting, but for what he has no idea – some agonal whimper from the dying animal, or some chirp or distant howl to bring an end to the silence. All of a sudden he has the sense that he isn't alone, as if the silence itself were imbued with consciousness and waiting for some sound from him.

'Owen,' he whispers.

As though in response, a muffled thud comes from the module Nick and Beth share – something dropped, perhaps, or one of them stumbling in the darkness. Or perhaps a stray sound in the throes of passion. He's had only a glimpse of their chamber through the open door, the layout no different from his, so small as to seem crammed despite the modesty of furnishing. In his mind's eye he sees Beth lying beneath her husband, her eyes closed and lips parted in pleasure, but the image doesn't hold: it is more caricature than reality. He listens further, but there is only silence. Did his brother ever have such thoughts of Beth? No, even in the deepest recesses of his mind, surely Owen, so honorable and gallant, would have respected the privacy of his friends' marriage. How unfortunate, then, if he were forced in death, through some binding of spirits, to endure the lusts of his brother, the very thoughts he shunned in life.

5

Until the arrival of the portable operating room, Burkett and Nick divide the work of seeing patients on the male side of the clinic. Burkett functions as what amounts to a family practitioner, though not a very good one. After five years of general surgery, and almost two more in plastics, he's hardly qualified in the art of physical diagnosis.

He's most at ease treating the minor burns and chronic wounds that happen to pass through his examining room. To a man complaining of urinary frequency, he offers a week's worth of ciprofloxacin. He prescribes the exact same dose to a teenager with what seems to be a middle ear infection, though he can't be sure with the earwax blocking his view of the tympanic membrane. At this rate he's going to deplete the clinic's limited supply of antibiotics.

Several patients with abdominal pain leave him wondering if he missed a case of ruptured diverticulitis or cholecystitis. In his surgical residency, every patient with abdominal pain had a CT scan, but the clinic's capabilities are limited – totally inadequate by the standards of the level one trauma center where he has spent the last ten years. It forces him to hone his skills in physical diagnosis – to try to practice medicine in the old way. For years he's wielded a stethoscope, but he doesn't remember the last time he truly listened to the sounds of the heart and lungs. It was always

41

an ECG that informed him of an arrhythmia, an x-ray of pneumonia.

If all had gone as planned, he would have been content to spend the rest of his career at Emory. He'd been on probation after his second drunk-driving offense, but what ended his tenure as a fellow in plastic surgery was his refusal one night at two a.m. to drive to the hospital. Emergencies in plastic surgery being relatively uncommon, extremely rare in fact, he'd decided not to let the possibility of one ruin every third evening.

That night he happened to be extremely drunk. He was asked to evaluate an obese female trauma victim whose antecubital vein had ruptured during a CT scan. The injected contrast material, rather than entering her bloodstream, had infiltrated the soft tissues of her hand. Normally this requires nothing more than ice and elevation – Burkett had never heard of a severe complication – but in this particular case, the swelling and inflammation cut off the blood supply. A smarter intern would have consulted vascular surgery straight away rather than wasting time on plastics. Whatever the case, he had no excuse, he refused to see the patient, and within days, a portion of the woman's little finger had to be amputated. Burkett, for his part, has no recollection of receiving any call that night, but two nurses backed up the intern's account of slurred speech, his insistent repetition of that phrase *ice and elevation*.

All along his brother questioned his decision to specialize in plastic surgery. Burkett remembers an argument over Thanksgiving dinner in their third or fourth year of residency. His brother refused to see beyond the breast implants and face lifts. There was a kind of irony in Owen's view of plastic surgery, the fixation on its surface flaws. What about repairing a child's cleft palate, or reconstructing the face of a trauma victim? But for Owen, a single cosmetic operation on a healthy patient would negate a thousand acts of medical necessity.

Near the end of his first week at the clinic, he wakes one night to the sound of gunshots. His first thought is that the separatists are attacking the clinic, but the shots are too far away. Perhaps it is the nearby military base that is under attack. He wonders if the clinic has weapons. He reminds himself of Nick's military experience but takes little comfort in it.

He dresses and walks into the courtyard and checks the lock on the front gate. He stands listening. The gunshots seem to have died, but then comes another series of bursts. Are they closer now than before?

The modules are small enough that Nick can open the door without getting out of bed. He is shirtless, and the tattoos covering his torso resemble a map of some non-existent geography. Behind him Beth rises on an elbow, looks at Burkett, and sinks back into the heap of blankets and pillows.

'I hear gunshots,' Burkett says.

'It's just the soldiers at the base.'

'Are they fighting someone?'

'No,' he says, laughing. 'When there's a full moon they like to shoot stray dogs in the air field.'

The door closes and Burkett stands in the dark of the courtyard. He senses movement and turns just as a shadow drifts over the wall of the compound. He realizes he's just seen a surveillance drone – probably the same type he saw from the window of his hotel in the capital. The other day he read online that for surveillance the Khandarian military favors a model called the Phantom. In the photographs it has a distinctly piscine shape, with a snub nose, tapering empennage, and propeller mounts that resemble fins.

It reminds him of a story he heard in the capital: a teenage girl from the provinces was bragging about late night visits from the shark god himself. The girl's father, a Khandari tribesman, was uneducated but by no means stupid, so when he heard this he grew suspicious and started keeping watch. One night around midnight he saw an object hovering at her window. It turned out there was some pervert in military intelligence.

This is the stuff of sexual farce, but Nick finds no cause for laughter when Burkett shares the story the next morning in the kitchen. The problem is either Nick's sense of humor or Burkett's storytelling – or perhaps something of both.

'Anyway,' Burkett says, 'I guess the guy had recorded all kinds of footage of women inside their homes. There's supposedly a black market for it.'

'So what happened next?' Nick wants to know.

'What do you mean?'

'Did the girl's father take a shot at the drone?' he asks as he pours coffee into a foam cup. 'There are people serving time for just that, you know.'

Burkett strains to remember. How did the father react to the voyeuristic drone? Perhaps Burkett missed that part of the story, which he heard by eavesdropping on a drunk journalist in the bistro of his hotel. Burkett was sitting a few tables away but could hear every word – at least he thought he could. Perhaps the journalist attenuated his voice when he realized Burkett was listening. It was only a week ago, but Burkett's memory of it is vague – probably because he was drunk at the time too.

'What about the daughter?' Nick asks. 'How old was she?'

'A teenager – how should I know?'

'Beyond a certain age, she would have been viewed as a disgrace to her family. Something like that could ruin her prospects for marriage.'

'If that's the case why would she brag about it?'

'Maybe she was sent to another town to live with some relative,' he says, as if Burkett needed consolation. 'On the other hand, she could have been beaten or even killed.'

Nick's disapproving gaze seems to implicate Burkett in whatever injustice befell the girl. And even as Burkett shrugs off a twinge of guilt, he

finds reason to accept some small portion of blame. Is he not perpetu-
ating that family's shame by spreading the rumor? He sips his coffee and
looks away. The conversation is beginning to feel like a recapitulation of
some old disagreement between him and his brother.

The site of Owen's death is a twenty-minute drive from the clinic. After
seeing his brother's body, he has no need to protect himself. His eyes have
already been seared by the autopsy wounds and bullet holes. No other
vision can hurt him. And yet as the car stops a voice in his mind tells him,
You don't need this. You've seen enough.

It is late afternoon. The other car eases to the verge behind them. The
pair of armed bodyguards – employees of the strongman Walari – remain
inside with their engine running.

'He was visiting a patient's house?' Burkett asks.

'He'd done an appendectomy on the girl a week earlier,' Nick says. 'He
was worried about a wound infection.'

Burkett is almost relieved to see nothing at the roadside but sand
and gravel. But what did he expect – a chalk outline with overlapping
bloodstains?

'Do you think he was betrayed by someone in that family?'

Nick shakes his head. 'The police say it was random.'

'He was on his way back to the clinic when it happened?'

'That's right – he'd already seen the patient.'

Burkett remembers the absurd 'press release': *We arrested a Christian
missionary with translated Bibles.*

'How does a person get 'arrested' by jihadists? Did they drive up behind
him and force him to pull over? How could they do that? Were they dis-
guised as police?'

Nick shakes his head. 'There were so many insider attacks we had to work out an agreement with the local police. They would never under any circumstances try to stop us on the road.'

Burkett has heard about the controversial program of recruiting separatist militants into the national police force. At some point it must have seemed like a good idea – bolstering security while at the same time depleting the ranks of jihadists – but the only proven outcome has been a rise in the number of suicide bombers dressed as police.

'Owen would be more likely to stop if somebody needed his help,' Nick says. 'Maybe they pretended to have a flat tire, or engine trouble.'

'Trap, disguise, or whatever, they must have known he was coming,' Burkett says. 'My guess is the *Heroes*' – he can't speak the word without a sneer – 'were watching the clinic. They followed him out and set him up on his way back.'

'That seems unlikely to me,' Nick says. 'We'd have known if we were under surveillance.'

Burkett glances back at Walari's thugs and wonders how reliable they'd be in a standoff. The escort wouldn't even be here if Burkett hadn't insisted. Nick seems oblivious to the risks. Does he truly believe that God will protect him, even after God failed to protect Owen?

'You came out here that day and saw the body?' Burkett asks, and Nick nods. 'Where exactly was he lying?'

The patch of sand lies partly shaded by a boulder, without even a hint of discoloration. It seems as though the earth drank his blood and then forgot him entirely. How long has it been, fifteen days? What disturbs Burkett most about the place is its ordinariness, how easily one could pass it without knowing. Perhaps every bit of land in the world has its own forgotten history of violence, and it isn't possible to take even a single step without dishonoring the site of some person's death.

He lies on the ground. Nick watches as if this were perfectly normal and to be expected.

'Which way was he looking?' he asks.

'Your right,' Nick says.

It is the direction of the mountains. Grit abrades his scalp as he turns his head. The last thing registered by his brother's eyes could have been one of those distant peaks, or perhaps something closer, some bit of gravel or clump of weeds.

What happens in the brain at the moment of death? Is there an unprecedented surge of neurotransmitters and electrical impulses? Adrenalin to heighten acuity, endorphins to numb the pain. He has the notion that his brother experienced a dilation of time, the world in slow motion, such that his final second stretched into an entire year. The smoke from the gun barrels stood perfectly still. A year-long respite from time, an interval of pure contemplation: it is an afterlife as believable as any.

That night he calls his father at the home. *The home*: as if the place of senility and bedpans represented some ultimate gathering of family.

'Elysian Fields,' answers a woman in a monotone.

After introducing himself – there is the usual international delay of one or two seconds – he is connected to his father's room, where a nurse says, 'I'm placing the phone to Dr Burkett's ear.'

'Dad? It's me, Ryan. I'm with Owen – at the clinic where he works.'

His father grunts.

'What was that? How are you feeling? Are you seeing your friends in the dining room?'

Burkett talks about the clinic and the patients. He doubts his father understands any of it, but still he feels the need to say something of substance. These unilateral conversations drain him. Add to that the stress of lying – or rather avoiding the truth, speaking of Owen in the present tense. Dementia doesn't necessarily imply psychic fragility, but in his father he's begun to see a kind of child-like innocence. It is a quality Burkett has a strange impulse to protect, even if there is no clear evidence that his father ever did anything of the kind for him or his brother.

After their mother died, they were left in the sole care of their father, which meant a series of relatives, nannies, and housekeepers. What little attention they received from the man himself, the almighty surgeon, it always seemed to Burkett that he favored Owen. This was confirmed when they graduated from medical school. Both Emory and Hopkins allowed parents who were also physicians to award their children's diplomas. The parent needed only to provide credentials to qualify for a temporary professorship. A straightforward matter, the same at both schools – but their father couldn't manage it twice in the same week: he took the stage for Owen's graduation but not Ryan's. Later Owen would cite the apparent bias as an early sign of Alzheimer's – one of the many lapses they'd recall when the diagnosis prompted them to come up with a narrative of cognitive decline. But Burkett had a slightly different explanation: the disease worked on one's personality from the outside in, attacking the shallowest parts first. His affection for Owen must have occupied the deepest place. Burkett he might neglect and even forget, but as long he loves Owen, then something essential remains.

'Dad,' he says. 'Can you talk to me? Do you want to put the nurse back on?'

Perhaps he should pretend to be his brother. Perhaps that would draw out some hint of the former self. But that former self, no matter how weakened, would probably recognize the imposture.

Why this impulse to lie? Why does he want to protect this man like a child? The man who said to his own ten-year-old sons: *Your mother killed herself. She did it by breathing the exhaust from her car.* Always the scientist, he took the opportunity to teach them about carbon monoxide and hemoglobin in the blood. The darkening of blood without oxygen. Burkett remembers it as one of their longest conversations. For a time he was convinced that his mother had died because of a change in the color of her blood, and in a manner of speaking that was accurate.

'Sorry I can't put Owen on the line.'

Faint static comes through his phone. It could be the sound of electrical activity in a feeble brain, the remnant of a brain. When did he cease being our father? He was still our father at graduation. He was our father when he lost the ability to perform those simple tasks put forth by the neurologist: spelling 'world' backward, drawing a clock face.

'Dad,' he says. 'There's something I need to tell you. The reason I'm here is that Owen was killed. He was shot to death by religious fanatics.'

'Ah,' his father says.

An expression of pain or surprise, or perhaps nothing more than a verbal tic, a random flexion of the vocal cords during respiration.

'Did you hear me?' Burkett asks. 'Do you understand?'

6

Burkett's first surgical case is a man in his late thirties whose left foot is swollen to the size of a melon. He walks with a crutch, his massive foot wrapped in a grimy bandage.

'He was your brother's patient,' Abu says.

'Does he know I'm not my brother?' He has to ask now that several patients have made the mistake.

'Yes,' Abu says. 'He knows what happened and offers his sympathy.'

Burkett looks at the man's bloodshot eyes, the skin prematurely wrinkled, and opens the manila folder that serves as a patient record. He recognizes his brother's barely legible handwriting. A single line, dated two weeks ago: *OR 5/4 for L BKA*. Below-the-knee amputation, scheduled for two days after Owen's murder.

The patient unclasps a clothes pin so that Burkett, wearing rubber gloves, can remove the encrusted swaddle. He holds his breath – for the cloud of skin flakes more than the foul odor. He stands and changes gloves, if only as a pretext to let the scurf settle to the floor. He tries in vain to feel a pulse through the shell of warts and scabs. The nub-like toes twitch in response to his prodding, but there is no evidence of pain or active inflammation. No doubt the underlying bones are involved, perhaps destroyed.

This is mycetoma pedis – or Madura foot. Burkett has never seen a case, but it couldn't be anything else.

'How long has it been like this?' he asks.

The man listens to Abu's interpretation and then thinks for a moment before speaking.

'Too long,' Abu interprets. 'The foot has enlarged over so many years that he hardly remembers a time when it was normal.'

'Did it start with an injury?' Burkett asks. 'Did he hurt his foot while working outside?'

'He doesn't recall an injury,' Abu says over the man's voice, 'but many years ago, before the – it got bigger?'

'The swelling.'

'Before the swelling, there were painful sores with blood and pus.'

While the patient waits, Burkett attempts an online search, but the internet service is too slow for anything more than email. In the clinic's small library, he manages to find an entry for Madura foot in a book called *Tropical Medicine for Nurses*. It occurs to him that his brother likely read the same entry in the same book.

Back in the examining room, Burkett makes a chopping motion with his hand. 'We'll have to cut it off.'

The patient was told the very same thing by an identical surgeon three weeks ago, but still he places a hand to his chest and dips his head in gratitude and relief. Burkett can see the emotion in the man's face – his yearning to be rid of the foot.

'Tell him we're sorry for the delay in surgery. We appreciate his patience.' Burkett understands how a man will build up hope, even if three weeks seem short for a problem lasting decades.

It is an operation better suited to an orthopedic surgeon. Burkett was a medical student the last time he scrubbed in for an amputation. There was no shortage of diabetic toes at Emory, but those cases fell under the purview of orthopedic surgery. He reminds himself that Owen wasn't trained in orthopedics either.

'He just wants it gone,' Abu says, while the patient wraps his foot back up.

'Tell him to come in on Tuesday,' Burkett says. 'We'll do it then.'

The patient rises and shakes Abu's hand, then Burkett's, all the while bowing and mumbling his thanks with tears in his eyes.

'See you Tuesday,' Burkett says.

When Nick travels to the capital for supplies, Burkett walks with Abu and Beth to a crowded market in the center of town. Beth wears a headscarf but even still she draws malevolent stares. A gruff bodyguard, who follows in a tireless suit, is presumably returning some of that malevolence. The children begging for money (Abu and Beth have brought coins for this very purpose) instinctively know not to bother with the bodyguard.

A black flag hangs from one of the stalls, signifying that vendor's refusal to sell to westerners, or perhaps just Americans, although in Burkett's judgment few Americans would even know what to do with the variety of bark and roots on display. According to Beth, this discriminatory vendor – an old man in a turban and mirror sunglasses – went blind decades ago when a member of a rival family threw acid on his face. It was one of many reprisals in a feud that lasted until the majority of both families had been killed.

As it happens, the old man became something of a milestone in Nick's endeavor to learn Arabic. When he felt he'd reached a certain level of fluency, he tried to pass for native by purchasing a vial of ylang ylang oil at the forbidden booth. Afterward Nick was so pleased by the old man's friendliness that Beth almost refrained from telling him when she uncorked the vial to the stench of urine.

Burkett waits while Beth haggles with a teenager over the price of apples. A younger boy in the adjacent stall swats a dog when it veers too close to a bucket of crabs. A large tuna hangs from a hook, slabs of its flesh cut away, its fins removed. The boy, when he sees Burkett watching, smiles and gestures toward the fish.

'No thanks,' Burkett says.

Nearby a young man in a white tunic seems to be staring at him, perhaps mistaking him for Owen, but as Burkett passes, the man's eyes remain fixed on some distant point. Burkett experiences a twitch of recognition, but surely he would remember if he'd seen this man as a patient in the clinic.

He risks another glance: the man is walking now, his arms rigid and upper body stiff, like a wooden effigy attached to mechanical legs. There is a sheen of sweat on his face. All at once Burkett understands: it is the look of intoxication – probably opiates. Perhaps he should ask him where a foreigner might buy scheduled pharmaceuticals in this town. But when he looks again the man has disappeared among the stalls.

With her bag of fresh apples, Beth conducts him to the edge of a crowd bidding on livestock. They watch as an American in military fatigues outbids a Khandari tribesman for a horse. This is Mark Rich, Beth explains, an air force captain embedded at the local base. After the final round of bids, they find Captain Rich at the stables waiting for his new horse.

'I'm sorry about your brother,' Rich says as they shake hands. 'We were trying to start a wrestling school.'

'You were a wrestler?'

'Four years at the Academy,' he says.

The captain's interpreter, a white-haired Arab in camouflage fatigues, stares at the bodyguard, whose gray suit and bulging sidearm mark him as one of Walari's men. The aide's fleeting scowl is a reminder of the tense equilibrium between the national army and provincial warlords, former enemies who have found common cause against the Islamic separatists.

'What weight did you wrestle?' Burkett asks.

'One-fifty-eight.'

'Same,' Burkett says.

'Wow,' says the captain, more polite than amazed: it's not as much of a coincidence as it might seem. Of the ten weight classes, those around one-fifty tend to be the most highly populated. The two men stare at each other. For former wrestlers in the same weight class, it's only natural to wonder who was better then and who is better now. Burkett can't remember a single All-American from the Air Force Academy.

'How about helping me get this school off the ground?' the captain asks. 'It gives the boys a sense of purpose. There's a long tradition of wrestling in Khandaros, especially among the natives.'

'No thanks,' Burkett says. 'I'm done with all that.'

Burkett envisions them wrestling, his brother and the captain. He resists asking if such a bout occurred. He prefers to think of himself as his brother's final opponent, even if he hasn't wrestled in years – not since medical school, when he tried to get back in shape by working out with the team at Georgia State. The coach there was glad to have him – at the time the Burkett twins had a reputation in wrestling circles – but in a single practice he sprained his knee and vomited from sheer exertion.

The captain excuses himself when his new horse emerges from the stables. The handler accepts an envelope from the captain's aide before handing over the reins. The piebald horse whickers and tugs against the hackamore while the captain whispers in its ear and pats its neck.

'The wrestling clinic was your brother's idea,' says Beth. 'But Captain Rich wanted to use it for tactical purposes.'

'Tactical purposes?'

'He saw the wrestling clinic as a means of recruiting young men as informants.'

'I thought the American troops were here only as advisors.' He watches as Rich and his aide guide the horse through the crowd.

'Officially,' she says, 'they're here to teach people the art of using drones.'

'I see,' Burkett says. 'And drones aren't much use if you don't know where to send them.'

Burkett notices the man he saw earlier, the drug addict, striding past the stalls. The man's eyes, no longer dazed, are locked on the captain. His hands fumble in the baggy sleeves of his tunic. A feeling of dread comes over Burkett as the young man cries, '*Allahu Akbar!*' and drops to his knees. Burkett shouts but his voice seems to reverse course, as if shoved back into his mouth by a wave of heat.

When he looks again, his ears ringing, a cloud of smoke has replaced the bomber. The captain's horse staggers on three legs – the fourth reduced to shredded pulp and shards of bone – before collapsing amid the flaming debris. Blood from the horse spreads toward a smoking shoe which – it takes him a moment to realize – contains an amputated foot, presumably the bomber's.

He sees Captain Rich hurrying toward an SUV, his aide trailing close behind. Beth, apparently stunned, kneels amid bits of puckering flame to pick up her apples.

Even though it is a Saturday, they leave open the clinic's gates, expecting injuries from the blast, but it seems the only casualties were the horse and the bomber himself. The military closes all roads in and out of town, forcing Nick to spend the night in the capital. Burkett had planned on grilling strips of lamb for dinner, but now feels nauseated by the idea of meat. Instead they eat rice, flatbread, and apples. If Abu and his nephew Karim are disappointed by the meal, they are too polite to say so.

'It must have been a front-loaded vest,' Abu says. 'He was facing the horse when he blew up.'

'Who has to clean up the horse?' Burkett asks.

'People will collect the meat and eat it.'

Burkett can tell from Abu's face that this isn't a joke. 'Wouldn't it be contaminated,' he asks, 'with pieces – of, I don't know, the bomber?'

'Once you cook it and pick out the – the metal balls?' Abu says.

'Ball bearings,' says Beth.

'Once you pick out the ball bearings,' he says, 'you can't tell the difference.'

Abu interprets for his nephew Karim, who expresses revulsion at the notion of eating the horse. He likes horsemeat well enough, but he happens to have known the suicide bomber from childhood.

'They were schoolmates,' Abu says. 'How is it that my nephew could become a successful driver and find a good wife, while his friend would come to this? Isn't it strange how God works?'

When Karim and Abu have gone home for the night, and Burkett is finishing the dishes, Beth emerges from the storage closet with a bottle of wine.

'There's a surprise,' he says.

'An IMO rep left it as a gift. We thought it might come in handy some day as a payoff.'

'I can't speak for your local warlords, but that happens to be my currency of choice.'

Since the explosion he has felt an almost celebratory impulse. Perhaps it is nothing more than the relief of survival. He thought he was alone in this, but the wine would suggest she feels the same. Or else her sudden urge to drink stems merely from the absence of her teetotaler husband. Whatever the case, he decides not to risk changing her mind by asking for an explanation.

The wine alone isn't enough to affect him, not till a couple of pills have melted into his nervous system. He can see the pinpoint pupils of the suicide bomber. Burkett's idiotic notion to ask the man about drugs might well have gotten him killed. After such a close brush with death he should probably be trying to catch the next flight home, and maybe tomorrow he'll wake up and start making calls, but for now he's overcome by a kind of tranquil satisfaction, a feeling of near invincibility, as if he's survived an ordeal through strength and wits rather than sheer luck.

He and Beth sit on the concrete steps behind the clinic, drinking from coffee mugs. His brother seems to occupy the silence between them. Burkett all but holds his breath, listening for some hint of another presence. A distant gunshot breaks his reverie – the soldiers shooting at dogs.

'Did my brother have any kind of – romance?'

She shrugs. 'He didn't have many options here.'

He almost asks: What about you? It would be too direct, too forward, but it's likely his brother, with so few options, would have felt drawn to her. Perhaps she felt something for him as well.

'Did he ever talk about old girlfriends?' Burkett asks.

She purses her lips, gazes upward – almost like an actor's representation of the act of trying to remember – and says, 'I don't think so.'

'So no old flames?' he asks. 'No past regrets?'

She shakes her head. He isn't sure he believes her. The name he's circling is Amanda Grey, a name like an iron splinter in his gut. But why would Owen still pine for a woman he'd loved more than fifteen years ago? He should have forgotten her after so long, or at least forgiven his brother for stealing her. Burkett always meant to bring it up – to end their years of silence on that particular subject. Owen probably would have laughed: you're still hung up on *that*? But now it's a conversation they can never have, another layer of regret.

Beth's phone jingles – Nick checking in, telling her he's safely ensconced in some hotel. His voice is audible from where Burkett sits. He wants to make sure she locked the gate and the side door, that she double-checked the gas level in the generator. Of course she did: she seems increasingly annoyed with the interrogation. She interrupts him with a peremptory 'Love you' and hangs up.

'Does he always give you the third degree?'

'We complement each other,' she says. 'He's the idealist and I'm the pragmatist.'

'He's just so – dogmatic.'

After a pause, she says, 'They say true saints are hard to live with.'

In this she seems to be siding against her husband, so he pushes further: 'Is he a true saint?'

'As close as any I've ever met. He devotes himself completely to easing the suffering of others.'

'Not everyone,' he says.

'What do you mean?'

'Those who live with him – you said saints are hard to live with.'

She shrugs.

He's pleased by this trap of logic, but if he were sober, would he still feel like he'd scored a point? Would he still be pursuing this course? A voice tells him: *Leave it at that, change the subject.*

But he goes on: 'I'm sure my brother was the same way. So rigid. Always spouting aphorisms. God has a plan, whatever.'

He reaches for her hand, but she pulls it away.

'I'm sorry,' she says.

The last of the wine he drinks alone. A scenario forms in his mind: Owen slept with Beth, so Nick killed him, or paid someone to kill him. He almost wishes for it to be true, an easy fiction. As grounds for murder, sexual jealousy is more plausible than religion. At least then he'd understand the reasons behind his brother's death.

He takes another pill to help him sleep, not bothering to check if it's Xanax or Valium. Lying in the dark he tries to summon his brother, but no image comes.

Xanax and Valium, his drugs of choice. Xanax has a stronger, more immediate effect, while Valium works as a kind of baseline stabilizer. Classed as benzodiazepines, or anxiolytics, these drugs are designed for the treatment of anxiety. Shortness of breath, rapid heart rate, dry mouth, and insomnia. The tremulous flutter in his belly. Given such similar symptoms, one would expect the benzos to work just as well for shame and grief, but that doesn't seem to be the case.

The pharmacy here has a small stock of alprazolam, generic Xanax, locked in a glass case, along with several narcotics. The key lies in the top drawer of the desk, in a built-in pencil trough. The drugs are easily accessible. There's no record of access, no need for a forged prescription.

It is so dark that he sees no difference between opening and closing his eyes. Has he in fact succeeded in conjuring his brother? Is this the very darkness in which his brother now finds himself?

Perhaps he should light a candle. A vision comes to him – flickering lights across a dark landscape, beacons for all the dead. But almost immediately he realizes it isn't a landscape. What he sees is a much smaller space: the market in the town square. These lights aren't candles either, but the sputtering flames of exploded bits of flesh.

In the morning he and Beth work together in the clinic. Perhaps too casually he says, 'Sorry about last night, I drank too much.'

She gives him a curious look before turning back to her patient. Is she feigning confusion, or could she be so naïve that she didn't notice his desire for her? He doubts it. She wasn't a married missionary all her life. Whatever the case, he understands all too well. They'll act as if nothing passed between them. It is a role he's played before.

7

The family Owen visited that day lives less than a mile from where he was shot. It is a compound of stone and crumbling mortar, with rows of sisal plants in the yard. A boy of around ten emerges with a partially deflated soccer ball. Behind him stands a little girl who smiles when Burkett gets out of the car. They have the dark skin and high cheekbones of Khandari natives.

'*Salam*,' Nick says.

The boy scurries back inside, but the girl remains. Probably five or six, she wears a dirty shawl, a shirt down to her knees, and baggy pants. Nick kneels before her and places a hand to his abdomen as he speaks. Burkett thinks he recognizes the phrase *Kaifa haloki?* How are you? The girl lifts her shirt to reveal a fresh bandage, and Nick peels away the tape and gauze, which is stained with antibiotic ointment. Burkett bends down for a closer look at what could have been his brother's final incision, almost completely healed. The girl offers him a rubber dinosaur missing one of its legs.

'Thank you,' he says.

'She thinks you're Owen,' Nick says.

Burkett smiles and pats her head the way he thinks his brother would have done. It feels awkward but she doesn't seem to notice. He's almost disappointed when Nick explains to her that this is a different doctor.

Nick laughs at her response.

'What did she say?' Burkett asks.

'That all white people look the same.'

They follow her into the dusty courtyard, where the boy dribbles his ball past a tethered cow. An old man appears in a doorway – probably the grandfather, or great-grandfather, of the children. He shakes hands with Burkett and Nick.

'*Marhaban,*' he says. Welcome.

He conducts them into a large room, where rugs and pillows surround a smoldering fire. A pot hangs from a gambrel. An old woman, apparently his wife, ignores them as she flicks an orange powder into the pot. With a wooden spoon she stirs and tastes. The man utters something, a command of some sort. She ignores him, so he repeats himself, only louder. Without looking at him she disappears through another doorway and moments later returns with a bowl of dates and sets it on the floor with a clatter.

A pleasant aroma spreads in the dry air – some kind of spice, whatever the woman sprinkled into the pot – as Burkett listens to Nick and the old man. He's heard enough Arabic now that he can detect the difference in Nick's accent – the fricatives softer, the vowels rounder. Perhaps the natives find him hard to follow, the accent too thick.

'He and his family offer their condolences,' Nick says. 'Your brother was a friend, an honorable man.'

'Tell him thank you,' Burkett says. 'We need to find out how many men live in this house.'

'It's rude to ask a man directly about his family.' Nick pauses and adds, 'He's the only man here at the moment.'

'Why do you think that?'

'When a guest arrives, the men of the house typically present themselves.'

'What about the father of those kids?'

64

Nick eats one of the dates. 'Maybe he's out working?'

Burkett looks at the fruit but only takes one after the old man nudges the bowl.

'Ask him what happened the day Owen came here.'

Nick returns to Arabic, gesturing toward Burkett. The woman reappears to stir the pot and sprinkle in more of the orange powder. The children's voices and the sporadic thump of the deflated ball echo from the courtyard.

'He says that after Owen examined his granddaughter, and gave her medicine, the two of them, he and Owen, had coffee. He thinks the killers were waiting for him while he was here.'

'Why does he think that?'

'He heard another engine start when Owen got into his car.'

'He didn't see the other car?'

'No,' he says, but inquires again, just to make sure, and the old man shakes his head.

'An engine is a common sound,' Burkett says. 'It could have been a coincidence, a neighbor.'

'None of his neighbors have cars.'

'Did he tell the police about it?'

Nick relays the question, and the old man nods.

'What did it sound like? Could he tell what kind of car?'

'It was an old car,' he says.

'All the cars here are old.'

Another woman emerges, this one wearing a burqa, but he can tell she is young from her hands, from the lie of fabric over her breasts and shoulders. He feels a twinge of desire as she bends down and places a tea kettle directly into the fire. He catches himself staring and looks away. Normally he is not one to stare – he can assess a woman in just a glance. He blames the burqa, its dual effect of blocking his view while also creating a false sense of privacy, a freedom to stare without being seen – as though it concealed him just as well as her.

'Ask him if there's a phone in the house,' he says after the woman disappears.

Nick speaks for longer than necessary, no doubt to avoid the impertinence of direct interrogation. The old man draws a flip-phone from his pocket.

'This is the only phone,' Nick interprets. 'His son had one, but now his son is dead.'

'I guess that answers our question about the father of the children,' Burkett says. 'Do any of the women have phones?'

'No.' Nick doesn't bother conveying the question. 'Unmarried women don't have phones.'

'What about the old woman, his wife?'

He can tell he's testing Nick's patience, and yet Nick complies, or seems to comply, by turning to the old man and asking a question. But it's obvious from the somberness in the old man's voice that the conversation has moved beyond cell phones. The silence that follows lasts till the water on the fire reaches a whistling boil.

'His son died in a suicide bomb attack last year,' Nick says as the young woman emerges with three cups on a tray. 'An attack the Heroes of Jihad claimed responsibility for.'

Burkett meets the old man's stare. He wonders if he should feel some spiritual connection since they have this terrible thing in common. Does a similar rage lie behind the old man's placid eyes? Burkett looks down at the bits of leafy debris floating in his cup. When the old man speaks again he gazes over the fire as if searching out his words in the smoke.

'He says the night after his son's death, the shark god Samakersh came to him in this very room and swore that his son would be avenged. This is how he knows that the Heroes of Jihad will be annihilated.'

Nick doesn't interpret the exchange that follows, but Burkett catches *Isa al-Mesih*, Jesus the Messiah. Burkett excuses himself and ducks into the courtyard. The boy and his sister are nowhere in sight. He notices figures carved in the lintel: the eyeball and shark teeth.

On the way home, Nick says, 'In some ways these pagan shark-worshippers are harder to convince than Muslims, but Owen was on the verge of a breakthrough. He might have given him a Bible. But of course, the old man sees Owen's death as divine punishment, evidence against Christianity.'

It is nightfall when they return to the clinic. Seven men, including the supposed Christian converts Abu and Hassad, are praying in the courtyard, either on rugs or on bare ground.

Burkett starts toward his module, but Nick grabs him by the elbow, silently reminding him to take the long way around. It would be an insult to walk in front of the men during their prayers.

'I thought Abu and Hassad were Christians,' Burkett says when they've passed out of earshot.

'Followers of Jesus,' Nick corrects him.

'So why were they praying like that?' he asks. 'Have they gone back to Islam?'

'Of course not,' he snaps. 'Prayer is more than bodily position or even words.'

Burkett seems to have touched on a sensitive topic. He decides not to pursue it further, but later that evening, after dinner, Nick stops him outside the bathroom.

'Hassad and Abu are followers of Christ, but that doesn't mean they don't still live in a strict Muslim culture.'

'Sure,' Burkett says. At the moment he is more interested in urinating and taking a Xanax than in hearing a lecture from Nick on the cultural practices of Christian converts.

'All I'm saying is that you're right to question it,' Nick says.

'It's really not a big deal.'

'I don't want you to think I can't see where Owen was coming from. In order to follow Christ you have to give up everything. Jesus said, "If anyone comes to me who does not hate his own family, then he cannot be my disciple." That's all well and good but my opinion is that the separation has to come more gradually.'

Hate. The word follows him into the bathroom. He locks the door and places his shaving kit on the counter and takes out the vial of Xanax – which is nearing its end faster than he might have hoped. He swallows a pill and stares at himself in the mirror. Was he hated by his brother? Was it hatred that drove Owen so far from home? He wonders if he'll ever understand what his brother actually believed.

The sign over the herbalist's store features a snake coiled around the stem of a goblet. On the shelves are mason jars full of herbs, spices, or animal specimens. Snakes and lizards float in murky fluid.

The herbalist, who wears a light blue lab coat, speaks no English but understands the terms 'Xanax' and 'Valium'. From behind the counter he peels open a Tupperware box to reveal four red and white packages of generic alprazolam. The expiration dates are long past, which Burkett expected.

'What about Valium?'

The herbalist shakes his head without apology.

'I'll take them all,' he says. Thirty in each package, one hundred and twenty pills. He unfolds a stack of banknotes and the apothecary takes his share, the equivalent of twenty dollars.

He pauses on his way out. 'What about *siddique?*' he asks.

The man motions for him to wait, and disappears into a smoke-filled room. Through the open door Burkett notes a pair of middle-aged men hunched over a *hookah*. The TV shows an empty bedroom through a gap in a shuttered window – probably bootleg footage from a surveillance drone. A woman passes into view, but only for a moment.

The herbalist returns with a plastic bottle, approximately twenty ounces. Burkett eyes the fulvous liquid and unscrews the cap, the smell alone probably strong enough to inebriate a child.

'Do you have any more?'

The herbalist says something in Arabic.

'Any more?' Burkett asks again. He holds up five fingers. 'How about five – five bottles?'

He waits while the herbalist retrieves two additional bottles. Perhaps supplies are low. He decides it isn't worth the trouble to complain.

'How much?'

The herbalist opens his palms in a manner of helplessness, perhaps apologizing for the high cost. Burkett lays a couple of five-hundred-khandar banknotes on the counter, totaling around fifty dollars. The man crumples one of the notes into his pocket and slides the other back across the counter. To Burkett it seems like a discount after what he paid at the hotel in the capital. That concierge either ripped him off or sold him a product of much higher quality. He wonders if he'll go blind drinking from this cheaper batch.

He thinks he knows a shorter way back to the clinic. The streets in the village are quiet. He passes the site of last week's suicide bomb, but all that remains is a black tattoo where the explosion scorched the pavement.

It starts to rain, but his face and bare arms feel numb to it, as if he were covered by an invisible membrane. He's struck by the notion that he could take a blade to his own skin and hardly feel it. A kind of intrinsic anesthesia, as if his consciousness, his soul, had somehow become detached from his nervous system.

Eyes bore into him: two young men on a weed-infested tennis court. They stride toward him. Nimbly one of them hops over the sagging net. From their jeans and tee shirts, their cleanly shaven faces, he knows they aren't Islamic militants, but there are plenty of others who would harm an American. In the capital he heard warnings about foreigners beaten and robbed. After what happened to his brother, he is perhaps a fool to have left the compound by himself, even if Nick does it on a daily basis. Nick might insist that divine forces render bodyguards unnecessary, but he also has the advantage of being a former Navy Seal.

Burkett imagines lying in the gutter in the rain while hands search his pockets and satchel. No doubt they'd make off with the *siddique* and the expired Xanax – his wallet as well.

The young men are jogging now. They will overtake him in a matter of seconds. He considers running, the smartest option, but something keeps him from doing so. His heart races, but more from anger than fear. His muscles flex as if to fill a surrounding void.

As far as he can tell, they are unarmed. He imagines fighting, two against one. He is stronger than either of them, perhaps stronger than both of them combined. An old saying comes to him: *Once a wrestler, always a wrestler.*

He stops and turns. He grips the strap of his satchel, thinking he'll use it as a weapon. The combined weight of two books and sixty ounces of *sid* could do real damage to a man's face.

They are close now – not men but boys. Teenagers just past puberty, not even old enough to shave. The desire to fight leaves him as fast as it came, and to his relief they run past him to take shelter from the rain under the awning of an empty café. One of them meets Burkett's gaze and offers a polite nod, making him feel foolish for having ever seen them as a threat.

Back in his module he opens the packages and lays out the foil-lined cards. The pills sit in their little domes, prisons from which they await release, but these have waited too long: the most recent expiration date is two years past, the oldest nearly three.

He puts the cards in his shoulder satchel and jogs through the rain to triage. In the top drawer of the desk he finds the key to unlock the safe. The exchange is easy: the expired tablets for those in the safe. He hopes no one will find it strange that all four boxes of Xanax have been opened or notice that the tablets have changed color. These are risks he'll have to take.

8

Burkett has been at the clinic almost three weeks when news arrives of Abu's murder, his body found hanging from a tree just outside town. In a handwritten note, the Heroes of Jihad accused Abu not only of converting to Christianity, but also of collaborating to sterilize Muslims at the medical clinic.

It is past noon when Nick returns from the police station. He embraces his wife but hardly speaks. Burkett and Hassad stand in the courtyard hoping for more information, but Nick turns from them and slouches alone behind the modules. They can see him sitting in the shade at a picnic table he built himself and recently painted bright red. Nearly half an hour passes before Burkett, against Beth's wishes, goes back and sits across from him.

'Tell me what happened,' Burkett says.

'He was killed,' Nick says, his face blank.

'I heard they found him hanging from a tree.'

Nick looks away. Even if he'd prefer not to discuss it, Burkett has no choice but to ply him for details: the murder feels too close to Owen's.

'A man in the image of God,' Nick says.

Burkett waits and asks, 'What did they do to him?'

'Gouged out his eyes, castrated him.'

'Was he still alive?'

'I don't know,' Nick says. 'They killed him by cutting his throat.'

Burkett feels a horror verging on nausea, but he tells himself he needs to know everything Nick does.

'What else did they do to him?'

'His genitals were discovered in his mouth.'

Maybe he shouldn't be surprised by the spectacular cruelty of it – he could find similar atrocities in stories of religious conflict the world over – but still it shakes him to the core. Such evil, pure and absolute.

Through his mind drift images of blood and skin, the resistance of flesh against a blade. The surgical terms seem outrageously inappropriate: enucleation, orchiectomy. But what is torture if not a ghastly caricature of surgery? The torturer if not the demonic inverse of a physician? The privileged access to the body, the concern with pain: it's an analogy he can't bear to make, the very idea an affront to his profession and all he stands for, but he has no control over the movement of his thoughts. *Do no harm* means nothing unless one is also capable of doing harm.

How does a man become a torturer? What happens in his mind? Is it the result of some monstrous event in childhood – some kind of abuse? Burkett wants to write it off to a kind of insanity, but if he were to find Owen's killer, when would doing harm become torture? Is it only a matter of degree? He would have no qualms about harming that man, causing prolonged pain, but how far would he be prepared to go?

Compared with Abu, Owen hardly suffered. Burkett is struck by the inconsistency. Did Abu's murderer just happen to be more of a sadist? Or do these different methods of execution reflect some difference in their crimes? Perhaps the Heroes have a system of justice that demands specific penalties for different Christian activities. While evangelism calls for death by gunshot, apostasy warrants mutilation.

In the late afternoon Hassad unlocks the gates for a black Mercedes to drive in. Through the window Burkett watches Nick and Beth shake hands with three men in business suits, two of whom carry automatic weapons. The shortest and oldest of the three must be Walari, their putative protector, here to discuss his recent failure in the case of Abu.

Burkett is annoyed not to have been summoned for the meeting. He crosses the courtyard while the driver, barely visible through the tinted glass, turns the Mercedes so that it faces the open gate. Burkett expects some kind of challenge from the henchmen guarding the door of the clinic, but without a word they step aside to let him pass. One of them even nods in greeting. Perhaps they were expecting him. Or perhaps it's simply inconceivable that a threat to their boss could have white skin and western clothing.

Nick and Beth sit with Walari at a folding table normally used for triage. Nick rises and introduces Burkett. Walari shakes hands with a limpness typical of Khandarians, but still unexpected in a warlord, and the clamminess of it gives Burkett a momentary urge to wash his hands. There is nothing in the man's appearance to support the rumors of brutality. He supposedly built his fortune during the interregnum, the chaotic decade before the Behemoth took control.

'Mr Walari personally knew our friend Abu,' Nick says. 'He's here to express his condolences.'

'Will there be increased security after what happened?' Burkett asks. 'Tell him we need somebody standing by, a twenty-four-hour guard.'

'That's what we've been discussing,' Beth says, 'but apparently it's going to cost us. For this *upgrade* we have to get approval from IMO.'

After an exchange in Arabic Nick says: 'He questions what Abu might have confessed – under pressure. If, say, we had Bibles here, the Heroes of Jihad would have reason to raid the clinic.'

'All the more reason to have round-the-clock guards,' Beth says, looking at her husband.

'I worry that the presence of armed guards would undermine our ministry,' Nick says. 'Shouldn't we look to God for protection?'

'We have,' Beth says, 'and he's delivering armed guards.'

Husband and wife lock eyes and in a moment of silence, as Burkett imagines it, replay a years-old dispute before Nick concedes by looking away.

'What if this is a scam?' Burkett asks. He glances at Walari, just to make sure he understands no English. 'How do we know it wasn't his people who killed Abu?'

'No way,' Nick says.

'Ryan has a point,' Beth says. 'Do you remember that road construction project? Supposedly he was behind the very attacks that made it necessary to hire him in the first place.'

Nick shakes his head. 'That was hearsay, and this is small beans by comparison. The torture – and mutilation.' He shakes his head in sadness. 'It's just not his style.'

Walari speaks gently, looking at Beth, and Nick interprets: 'Until the issue of payment is resolved, Mr Walari will have someone drive by the clinic every hour.'

'That's very kind of him,' Beth says.

Burkett wonders if sarcasm sounds the same in both languages, but Walari seems sincere as he bows and places his hand to his chest.

They file into the parking area and say their farewells. The portable operating unit sits dormant just outside the gates. It is too large to fit inside. What, if anything, keeps the fanatics from blowing it up? Or the clinic itself for that matter? The wall and gate would tear like tissue with a large enough car bomb.

Burkett watches Nick shake hands with Walari. First Owen, now Abu

– and still Nick would question the need for armed guards. At what point will he acknowledge the risk? When the bomber shouts *Allahu Akbar*? Maybe Nick is suffering from some kind of delusion. Beth at least can offer an element of pragmatism – pragmatism being a relative term and perhaps unsuited to circumstances as decidedly unpragmatic as a Christian mission in the Muslim world.

'I want out,' he says as Hassad closes the gate behind the Mercedes.

'Why don't you give it a week,' Nick says, 'to let the dust settle?'

An image comes to mind: that swollen, infested foot. He would have operated this morning if Nick hadn't closed the clinic to all but emergencies.

'Call the patient with Madura foot,' he says. 'I want to do the amputation this afternoon.'

'It's too dangerous,' Beth says, nodding toward the portable unit outside the gate.

'I'll do it in one of the examining rooms.'

'The patient has to be nil by mouth for eight hours,' she says.

'Then we'll do it first thing in the morning.'

'What about a two-stage operation?' she asks. 'Owen had talked about doing a guillotine first and letting the wound drain for twenty-four hours.'

'It's not unreasonable,' he says, irritated not so much by Beth as by his brother – his brother still second-guessing him even from beyond the grave. 'But this is an indolent infection. I'd only start with a guillotine if he were septic.'

It occurs to him that his professional value is greatest where he's most likely to be killed. Perhaps he'll join Doctors Without Borders and work somewhere in Africa, as far as possible from lunatic jihadists. Would they take a surgeon with a suspended license? No doubt something could be arranged.

'When is the next car to the capital?' he asks.

'Pierre from IMO is visiting next week,' Nick says. 'You can ride back with him.'

Burkett goes to his room and swallows a pill with a shot of *siddique*. He recalls a moment last month in Atlanta, maybe a week before he left, but he hasn't thought of it again till now. Some time in the night he woke on the couch of his apartment. The lights were on so he could see himself clearly reflected in the plate glass of the sliding doors. What woke him? Some presentiment he couldn't explain at the time, a feeling hardly mitigated by any pill. Only now does he realize it could have been the exact moment of Owen's death.

The next morning, the patient, whose name is Sabib, sits on the padded table in a gown that snaps in back. His diseased foot looks like a lump of clay stuck to the end of his leg. Beth gives him a pair of red tablets, which he swallows with a thimbleful of water.

'What are those?' Burkett asks.

'Xanax,' she says.

The long expired tablets are unlikely to have any effect. He considers telling her, but it would require some kind of explanation, no doubt leading to lies upon lies. The open packages might already have started her on the path of suspicion. Then again, how much does the patient actually need Xanax? Without it, he might have trouble sleeping through the operation, but there shouldn't be any difference in the pain he experiences.

'How about giving him Versed IV as well?' Burkett suggests.

'We don't have it,' Nick says, having just returned from the portable unit with another bag of supplies.

Beth pulls open the man's gown, exposing his bare back, and runs her

78

fingers down the bumps of his spine. Since an amputation requires only regional anesthesia, Burkett doesn't need the mechanical ventilator in the portable operating room. An orthopedist would use a peripheral nerve block, but Beth, who has extensive experience in obstetrics, is something of an expert in epidural anesthesia.

Burkett watches while she sponges betadine onto the patient's lower back and numbs the skin with lidocaine. She inserts a needle and attaches an air-filled syringe and taps the plunger while driving the needle into the epidural space. Burkett is impressed: it takes skill to distinguish muscle from fat by resistance in a needle. She threads a tiny catheter through the bore and after removing the needle she tapes the catheter to the skin.

Last night, after they scrubbed the examining room, Burkett for a third time watched the surgical video his brother had left in Sabib's file: a DVD of a below-the-knee amputation. Afterward he couldn't help but replay the operation in his mind from start to finish. He had to take an extra dose of Xanax to keep himself from going through it yet again. This was always one of his problems in medical school and residency: the endless mental repetitions that would distract him from daily tasks and rob him of sleep.

'Do you feel that?' he asks as he pokes Sabib's skin with a scalpel. A simple question of pain – Nick doesn't need to interpret. Sabib smiles at Burkett, as if to assert himself against the useless Xanax, but just as quickly, thanks no doubt to the Fentanyl, he falls asleep.

The bulbous, encrusted foot – perhaps even more grotesque with the sheen of betadine – lies on a cushion of sterile blue drapes. A loose tourniquet encircles the thigh, not yet inflated. Burkett finds the pulses of the arteries: popliteal, anterior and posterior tibial, and peroneal. With a felt marker, he outlines the path of his incision.

'Aren't you getting a bit close to the induration?' Beth asks.

'It's fine,' he says without looking at her.

Her question – which she probably wouldn't have asked if the surgeon were Owen – is all the more annoying for touching on his own doubts, his discomfort with an operation he's never actually performed. But he resists the urge to explain the basic principles, that for whatever length of bone he wants to preserve, he'll need an even longer flap of skin to cover it.

He makes a circumferential incision. Blood seeps despite the pneumatic tourniquet, so he singes the edges of the wound with electrocautery. He uses a blunt probe to tear free the skin, exposing the moist tissue underneath. He begins plucking away the fibrous layer covering the greater and lesser saphenous veins, which cling like vines to the surface of the gastrocnemius muscle.

'Light,' he says, prompting Beth to adjust the lamp.

It's taking him far too long to locate the tiny sural nerve, especially when compared to the expert in the video who found it in no time at all. He's tempted to abandon the search, to simply amputate the nerve along with the rest of the leg, but as a sensory nerve it could cause chronic pain, so he presses on till he finds it, and when he does he cuts it as close to the knee as possible, high above where he plans the stump.

He notices the trembling of his hands, the first sign that he needs his pills. As if his hands were sentinels, the first warning of a progressive tremor – a tremor that will spread through his nervous system, from the outside in, till it reaches his brain and renders him frantic with anxiety. In less than an hour, he'll be able to think of nothing but the pills.

This morning he took a single Valium instead of his usual two. He skipped the dose of short-acting Xanax. He thought he needed his mind clear for this unfamiliar operation, but now he sees that he made a mistake.

'You all right?' It is Nick, standing across from him in a matching gown and mask. With a wad of gauze he pats the surgical field. Beth sits on a wheeled stool, easing Fentanyl through the patient's intravenous line.

'I need a bathroom break,' he says, tearing off his gown and gloves in a single motion.

Nick and Beth stare in surprise. The patient sleeps, the prongs of a cannula resting in his nostrils.

Burkett hurries back to his room, where he takes another Valium, along with a Xanax and a shot of *siddique*. He is aware that his craving is worse now than during his fellowship just a year ago, when he could last eight hours on a single Valium. This depressing thought is eased by the taste of the *sid*, the knowledge of those pills dissolving in his stomach.

Nick, Beth, and the patient remain exactly as he left them. On the blue-draped table, Beth has placed a new sterile gown and pair of gloves on top of the forceps, probes, needle-drivers, clamps, and retractors. Only after he snaps on his gloves and knots his gown does he realize that he does in fact need to urinate.

An amputation below the knee. It seems simple enough: cut the tissues, control the bleeding, and cover the stump with a flap. But even the simplest procedures have nuances that can only be learned through experience. By merely watching a video, he couldn't possibly prepare for every contingency, but the hands of that anonymous surgeon seem almost interchangeable with his own as he ties off the vessels and saws through the tibia and fibula, smelling even through his mask the crisp, dry bone dust. After cutting the last strand of muscle, he nudges the severed foot off the table and it strikes the floor with a thud.

9

He seems to have overslept. Last night he finished the *siddique* from the capital, so if he wants his usual shot he'll have to settle for what he bought from the apothecary. He uncaps one of the bottles, but the fluid inside seems more turbid than he remembers. He's heard stories of *siddique* causing blindness, a side effect of methanol contamination. Maybe before drinking it he should test it on one of the stray dogs.

The sink runs dry, as it often does, so he uses bottled water to wash down his pills. He swipes his armpits with a stick of deodorant and puts on the Penn State tee shirt and a pair of scrubs.

He had a dream he can't recall – only that it was suffused with bitterness, as if the dream had no content other than a disconnected feeling. If this dream featured characters, landscapes, or sounds, he has no memory of them now. All that remains is the aftertaste.

Pausing at the door, he reconsiders the *siddique*. He opens the bottle and brings it to his lips. It tastes no different from the previous batch. A local word comes to mind: *inshallah*. As God wills. It is the shrug of fatalism, the nearly comical resignation of so many of his patients. If he goes blind, so be it. He follows the first small sip with a larger one.

He crosses the courtyard toward triage, thinking he needs to check Sabib's wound and send him home. In the two days since the amputation, the patient has been sleeping on an air mattress in the clinic. After Burkett leaves at the end of the week – he's arranged for his trip back to Atlanta two days from now – Nick will have to visit Sabib's home to remove the skin staples.

The clinic is unusually quiet, at least for this hour of the morning. It might be a Muslim holiday. Normally a line of patients would be waiting outside the door, but the only patient he sees is an old man at the gate limping away from the clinic. Even from a distance Burkett can make out the open sore on his leg. The bandage meant to cover it is wadded in his hand, as if he'd left in such a hurry there was no time for putting it on.

He is running from something, Burkett realizes. The other patients must have fled as well.

The parking lot is empty but for a spavined American station wagon, parked in such a way that he doesn't see it till he turns the corner at the entrance to triage. The roof of the station wagon has been sawed open to accommodate a mounted machine gun. The driver's door squeaks open to reveal a teenager in a police uniform. A Kalashnikov, pointed skyward, rests in the crook of his elbow as he gestures with his free hand for Burkett's phone. The boy must be too young for policework – fifteen or sixteen at the most – but perhaps age limits are waived when a militant switches sides. Or maybe the boy simply stole the uniform.

He pockets Burkett's phone and conducts him into the clinic's small anteroom, where Beth and Hassad face another gunman. This one wears a police uniform too, but with a red turban and full beard. Burkett's eyes fall to the man's flip-flops and thick, discolored toe-nails. Toe-nails like horse's teeth: a severe case of onychomycosis, a chronic fungal infection.

'Weapons aren't allowed here,' Beth says, jabbing her finger toward the gunman's face. Hassad doesn't bother interpreting, and his silence seems like a comment on the pointlessness of her statement.

The man aims his rifle at Burkett and barks a question.

Burkett stares. Was it you who killed my brother? Do you look at me and wonder how Owen came back from the dead?

His Kalashnikov is indistinguishable from the boy's, at least to Burkett's eye. Worse than dying by the same gun would be to die by the same gun and not know it. If only he could be granted the satisfaction of that final symmetry. But if these were Owen's killers, surely they would betray some reaction, some flicker of recognition on seeing the twin brother.

'He asks if you're here to spread Christianity,' Hassad says.

'Absolutely not,' Burkett says. 'Tell him we're doctors, we're here to give medicine—'

The man thrusts the gun barrel against his chest. He staggers backward, reeling with pain. He rubs his sternum, half expecting an unnatural depression or loosening of bone. An image flashes before him: a textbook skeleton labeled in elegant calligraphy. The segments of the sternum are called *manubrium* and *gladiolus*, handle and sword. He always appreciated the use of metaphor in anatomic names, but for the first time finds himself wondering about the incorporation of weaponry. Did the early anatomists, when considering the bone closest to the heart, have more in mind than its vague resemblance to a sword?

'He wants to know where are the Bibles,' Hassad says.

'We don't have any Bibles,' Burkett says.

Abu told them, no doubt, and why shouldn't he? This is the way it is with torture, Burkett imagines. You tell them what they want to hear, whatever you can say to stop the pain. Surely Abu would have told them about the hidden compartment under the floor of the supply closet. Did they force him to renounce his faith as well? On that one issue perhaps he refused to yield.

The man in the red scarf is speaking directly to Hassad. Burkett recognizes the word *Amrikee*, American.

Hassad nods toward Burkett and says, '*Tabib, na'am*.' Doctor, yes.

Another policeman, also in flip-flops, emerges from the back room, pharmaceutical packages loaded in the front of his shirt. Burkett recognizes the sky blue label of Xanax. He feels a twitch of shame, but now that the worthless pills are in the hands of jihadists, he dares to wonder if some good might come of his ruse. Perhaps some suicide bomber will come up short on the dose needed to blunt the fear of death.

'He can't take those,' Beth says. 'That's medicine for our patients.'

After a brief exchange, Hassad says, 'It's the religious tax.'

'Religious tax?' Burkett asks.

'The government provides uniforms and guns,' Beth explains, 'but no paycheck till they've been vetted by Khandari special forces. That could take up to a year, so in the meantime they collect a "religious tax" to support themselves.'

He hears the sound of another car in the driveway, probably Nick returning from his rounds.

'Please tell me he went out with one of Walari's men.'

'What do you think?' She is pinching the front of her tee shirt, or perhaps the cross she wears tucked behind it.

By the time Nick steps into the clinic, he has somehow managed to keep his phone from the boy, but the gunman in the red scarf pries it away and strikes him in the abdomen with the butt of his rifle. Despite the awkwardness of the blow, Nick grunts and bends at the waist and lowers himself to the floor.

Beth kneels beside him. Nick has his eyes closed, his head bowed as if praying, but Burkett realizes he is actually listening to the conversation among the spurious policemen.

'What are they saying?' he asks.

'We're going to be all right,' Nick says. 'They only want us for ransom.'

'Ransom? We're being kidnapped?'

'As soon as we're gone,' Nick says to his wife, 'call Mark Rich, describe the car.'

'I'm going with you,' she says.

'Unlikely,' he says. 'They'd see it as shameful to take a woman.'

Before she can object, he says, 'Once you've talked to Mark, call Pierre at IMO.'

She nods. 'Where will they take you?'

'South, probably.'

At gunpoint they are led outside. The boy stands in the back of the station wagon and sights them with the mounted machine gun, but it seems like an empty threat since his compatriots too would fall in the line of fire. The one in the red scarf walks to the edge of the lot and surveys the road.

'They want us – to lie in the back of the vehicle,' Hassad says, clearly wishing the *us* were a *you*.

'I'm sorry about this,' Nick says to Burkett. 'It's not what you signed up for, and just two days before you're scheduled to leave.'

'Maybe we'll get it resolved by then.'

'Maybe.'

But the doubt in his voice reminds Burkett of kidnappings that have lasted weeks or even months. He can't help but smile wryly at the absurdity of it. The word that comes to mind is 'godforsaken': a word for himself and his brother and this entire island.

Strange that he isn't more afraid. Curiously enough, his heart rate would suggest a state of panic, but he feels abstracted from himself – the way he felt the second time he was arrested for drunk driving, when his cuffed wrists seemed to belong to someone else. He isn't drunk at the moment, not even close. But if he hadn't taken the pills and the shot of *siddique*, he'd probably now be begging for his life.

'Make sure they see you crying,' Nick mumbles to his wife. 'Cry like you've never cried before.'

Her weeping seems authentic as she embraces him under the watchful gaze of the jihadist policemen.

'Why do you want her to cry?' Burkett asks.

'They'd be less inclined to kill a man supporting a family.'

'Can she cry enough for the three of us?'

He meant it as a joke, but of course no one is laughing. Beth, seeming to take it to heart, drops to her knees with her fists clenched and face contorted as she howls in wordless entreaty. The display seems unnatural – like an American trying to imitate the funereal ululations of the local women – but she carries on even as Burkett, Hassad, and Nick climb into the back of the station wagon.

The vehicle lacks any kind of back seat, so they have to make use of the wood planks on either side of the mounted machine gun. Their captors force them to lie down in order not to be seen through the windows. As the car passes through town, Burkett can see the tops of cinderblock and mud brick walls, the occasional tree. Brown dust rises when they leave the paved road. The legs of the gun jab into his back as the car bumps over the uneven surface. He is relieved when they finally come to a stop.

'Where are we?' he asks after they've climbed out.

'South of town,' Nick says.

Their captors drape the station wagon in camouflage mesh. Two women, fully covered in burqas, are plastering the walls of a hovel with what looks like a mixture of mud and straw. A cow stands tethered in the yard, dipping its snout in a bucket. Out of the hovel limps an old man with seashells braided into his long beard. He speaks to the gunmen, while the boy walks to the far side of the building and starts the engine of a decrepit Buick sedan.

'Shouldn't we make a run for it?' Burkett whispers.

'Beth's calling in the cavalry,' Nick says, shaking his head and looking toward the sky for some sign of military or perhaps heavenly rescue.

'I agree with Dr Burkett,' Hassad says. 'I have an uncle who lives nearby.'

The two older gunmen follow the bearded man into the hovel. From the Buick the radio blares as the boy searches for reception.

'This is as good a chance as we're likely to get,' Hassad says. 'This is the time to run.'

'Look at the terrain around here,' Nick says, sweeping a hand across the empty fields. 'We'd be sitting ducks.'

Hassad locks eyes with Nick. 'A white man would bring a high ransom,' he says, 'but me, a Khandari from a poor family, they will kill me first.'

'The best way to get yourself killed is to run.'

But Hassad turns and sprints into the stretch of scrub and stone, toward a copse of trees in the distance. Burkett looks at Nick, who glances back toward the hovel. It is a question of risk, a window of opportunity – and perhaps for Nick a concern for his ministry, a fear of being perceived as a coward – but Burkett has already made his decision, and he is glad when Nick starts running as well.

Behind them now the boy is shouting, honking the horn of the Buick. Hassad is still at least twenty yards ahead of them when they hear the first gunshots.

Burkett feels in his ear a change in pressure, the hum and press of what can only be a passing bullet, and that very instant a cloud bursting from a nearby rock showers particles into his face and eyes. All he sees is black and he wonders if the bullet in fact has penetrated his skull and severed his optic nerves, but when he drops to the ground he finds his vision again in the flood of burning tears.

The sharp cracks in the air seem to grow ever closer, but then there is a pause in the gunfire, and from somewhere off to his left he hears Nick shouting in Arabic. Burkett risks a glance over his shielding rock. Nick is walking toward their pursuers with his hands raised. Perhaps he is trying to create time for the others to escape. Burkett wonders if he should make a run for it, but when he looks again, that red turban is only a few feet away.

The boy guards Burkett and Nick while the others pursue Hassad. They sit in the back seat of the sweltering Buick, irritated as much by the safety mechanism that blocks the windows from fully opening, as by the boy outside who circles the vehicle and occasionally taunts them with his Kalashnikov for no reason beyond the pleasure of startling them, or perhaps imagining what it would be like to strafe the glass and metal and flesh inside.

Nick regrets running – 'Stupid, stupid,' he says – but it might have given Hassad the extra seconds he needed. And if someone heard the gunshots and called the authorities, then maybe at this very moment the hovel and the Buick are pictured on a screen in some military control center. It seems to Burkett that every minute of delay should improve their chances of rescue. But there are no helicopters or special forces, only the boy and his gun, and the old man who emerges from the hovel to give them all a drink from a canteen of water. It is less than an hour before the jihadists return. Hassad is nowhere in sight – which could mean either death or escape – but Burkett can tell from their downcast expressions that they haven't found him.

Within minutes they are driving south in the Buick. Burkett and Nick are given scarves to cover their heads – disguise enough for the casual observer. Burkett sits in the middle of the back row, Nick in the front passenger seat, both of them staring straight ahead in silence as they travel deeper into the barren country. They turn off the main thoroughfare and continue on a dirt road. Mountains loom in the distance ahead but never seem to get any closer. Near sundown they pull off in the scrub. The jihadists unfurl rugs and pray while Burkett and Nick walk a short distance to a rock outcropping.

'Stay where they can see you,' Nick warns.

Burkett turns his back to the car and scans the horizon while urinating in the dirt.

'Hassad knows the Buick,' he says as he zips his pants. 'Maybe there are drones tracking us at this very moment.'

'You're on edge,' Nick says. 'You need to relax.'

'I'm fine.'

'When you're jumpy they're jumpy, and they're the ones with the guns.'

Another two hours pass before they arrive at a small house made of stone and mud brick. They park beside a dented Ford SUV with rope and wire holding the rusted bumper in place. Their captors, who for the last hours have been completely silent, shout praises to Allah when a group of bearded men, no doubt fellow jihadists, file from the house. It is a mixed group – both Arabs and Khandari tribesmen.

The owner of the house, an elderly farmer, greets Burkett and Nick as if they were invited guests, introducing them to his teenage grandsons and offering them millet cakes and tea, which they gladly accept. Inside they eat and drink, sitting on the floor with the others in a loose circle around a tea kettle and propane burner. Against the wall are uncomfortable-looking pillows adorned with fragments of mirror and colored glass. When the old man begins to speak, the others fall silent.

'What is he talking about?' Burkett whispers.

Nick waits a moment for the old man to finish. 'He was there when Mullah Bashir, the jihadist leader, put on the cloak of Muhammad.'

'What kind of cloak?' The sharpness of his voice draws glances from the others. 'They actually think they have clothes worn by the Prophet?'

'Take it easy,' Nick says.

'Assuming the mullah didn't buy it in a consignment shop, how is Muhammad's cloak supposed to have ended up in Khandaros?'

'Legend has it that in the early seventh century, islanders heard about the Prophet and traveled to Mecca to meet him. He was dead by that time, but that didn't stop them from collecting mementoes: his dagger, chalice, and cloak. All that remains is the cloak. Supposedly, when Mullah Bashir put it on, those in the crowd who were sick or lame were healed.'

'Do you believe that?'

'No.'

'But you would if the cloak had belonged to Jesus, or if it had happened in a church rather than a mosque.'

'I have to assume that most people who believe in miracles do so in the context of a single religious tradition.'

Nick seems on the brink of smiling. That smug, axiomatic style of disputation: Burkett finds it all the more irritating for being expected – for being so typical of Nick. Why does he all of a sudden find Nick so annoying? His voice is like an allergen that prompts a stronger reaction with each exposure.

'If God has the power to stop suffering,' Burkett says, 'why doesn't he go ahead and do it? Why doesn't he cure all sickness and heal all pain?'

'You're asking why suffering exists at all.'

'How can you believe in a God who would allow it?'

'Because he himself experienced it at its very worst.'

92

He has an answer for everything, Burkett thinks: I'm the only one in this room who knows the feeling of doubt.

He looks at his hands, the tremor worse by the hour. Recognizing the symptoms of withdrawal does nothing to mitigate them. What he needs is a Xanax, or at least a drink, neither of which he has any chance of finding here.

After the old man retires and the lamp is put out, Burkett and Nick lie down, sharing a single blanket. He could make a list of the things keeping him awake: the mildew stench of the blanket, the rustle of the plastic sheet in the window, the chorus of snoring, Nick and his theological certainty.

Burkett yearns to take a shower, or at least to wash the layer of grime from his hands and face. Earlier he saw a water tank on the roof, so there must be a working bathroom, but so far they've only gone outside to urinate. His sudden fastidiousness surprises him. He's been kidnapped – possibly by the very men who killed his brother – and all he wants is to get drunk and take a shower.

The door at the far end of the room, which leads deeper into the house, seems off limits to all but the old man. Perhaps there are women, the old man's wife or daughters – the daughters hidden from the world of men, protected from sinners like Burkett. He imagines a fragrant bedroom just beyond the wall. He sees himself getting up, gingerly stepping past the snoring heaps, the stacked flip-flops, and Kalashnikovs.

But the vision takes him instead down a carpeted hallway, a place from his memory. It is the lake house where many years ago he and his brother spent a weekend with friends.

While the others were out in the boat, Burkett and Amanda, his brother's girlfriend, found themselves alone in the house. It seemed to be a random encounter, but in truth each of them had stayed back in the hope of being alone with the other. Over the preceding months a kind of tension had developed inside of Burkett and when they kissed in that hallway it seemed like the final snapping of a cord stretched to its limit.

That night Owen and Amanda, being Christians, slept in separate rooms, so Burkett got up and tapped on her door and she let him in. This was a night of firsts: her first time having sex, their first irrevocable betrayal of Owen. They swore it wouldn't happen again, but in the weeks that followed their efforts to avoid each other only fueled the attraction. Since she and Owen never slept together, Burkett gravitated to her dorm each night as if the vacuum left by his brother were abhorrent to nature. One twin by day, the other by night: did she try to pretend they were the same person? Burkett wishes he could blame alcohol, but at the time he drank neither more nor less than the typical off-season wrestler.

Amanda broke up with Owen two weeks after that trip to the lake. Since Owen seemed to have no concept of the antecedent betrayal, she and Burkett, in an attempt to make their affair seem legitimate, concealed the overlap by staging a careful escalation. Burkett took it as permission granted when Owen agreed that Amanda looked like she could use some company, that it might be a good idea for him to spend time with her. But how could Burkett have been such a fool? How is it that he failed so completely to appreciate the pain his brother must have felt on merely seeing the two of them together?

When Owen's clavicle healed after the national championship, he needed to train for the Midlands wrestling tournament as well as the Olympic trials. Burkett had no such ambitions and would have preferred at that point, the spring of their senior year, never to set foot on another wrestling mat, but still he woke every morning at six a.m. to train with his brother in the wrestling room. Owen worried about reinjuring his clavicle, so they began slowly, easing over days and weeks back into their former vigor.

Burkett and Amanda were spending more time together, and Owen had retreated into the fold of his Christian friends, so the brothers rarely interacted except during those morning sessions. Burkett began to sense a kind of rage in the way his brother wrestled. Each bout felt like a relentless assault, far beyond the intensity level anyone would reasonably expect in a practice setting. Morning after morning, Burkett left the wrestling room sore and bruised, knowing it was only a matter of time before he sustained the injury that would free him of any obligation to continue.

A month before graduation, Owen came down on Burkett's knee with the clear intention of tearing ligaments. Burkett saw it but allowed it to happen, even while knowing such an injury could end any prospect of future competition. And when he suffered no more than a sprain – enough still to spare him another month of brutality – he realized Owen must have pulled back at the very last moment.

Owen found another drill partner and went on to win the Midlands tournament and become an alternate on the US Olympic team. Burkett sat with their father in the bleachers at both tournaments. It was during the finals at Midlands that the old man with tears in his eyes said, 'I have a son who wrestles like a god.'

Only after the brothers had moved to different cities for medical school could they sustain a fiction that nothing had come between them. There was never any kind of apology on Burkett's part or, as far as he knows, any forgiveness on Owen's, but isn't this how it is between brothers? Is rivalry not essential to the relationship? Like wrestlers, each man pushing against the other. Perhaps he most feels the loss in the sudden absence of that opposing force. He's off balance, reeling without purchase. There is no one now to envy, betray, or forgive – no one with whom to compete.

10

In the morning they set out on foot, following a dry creek bed into the hills. Their original captors having returned north, Burkett and Nick now find themselves under the watch of three Arabs and two native Khandaris. The tribesmen wear hoops in their ears and shells woven into their hair. Two of the Arabs carry large framed backpacks with stuffed pockets and dangling tools and canteens. It is the third who seems to be the leader – he walks in front and shows the least interest in Burkett and Nick. The striking thing about him is that, in addition to the standard Kalashnikov, he carries a scimitar against his back and a large, ornate dagger at his waist.

The crumbling ruin of the Khandarian Wall stretches across a valley, disappearing into the hills on either side. Kings built the wall over a thousand years ago in defense against the native Khandaris, who were viewed by the Arabs as barbarians. Once as high as thirty feet, with periodic guard towers, all that now remains of the wall are remnants of its foundation, with jagged projections like a row of broken teeth spanning the width of the island.

Just south of the wall they rest in the shade of a carob tree and eat its chocolate tasting legumes. Nick speaks to their captors in Arabic, which surprises them and no doubt causes them to wonder what they might have inadvertently revealed. Burkett considers it a mistake for Nick to show his hand, even if it earns him a measure of respect, even if that respect could spill over to Burkett as well.

'The leader is Safiullah,' Nick says when they've resumed walking.

'What else did you find out?' Burkett asks.

Slowing his pace, Nick turns and speaks under his breath: 'There will be ransom negotiations when we reach our destination.'

'Where is that?'

Nick looks away without responding, perhaps regretting how much more they could have learned by simply eavesdropping.

'When do we get there?' Burkett speaks loud enough for the others to hear. This is his way of pointing out the uselessness of Nick's information.

'About two days,' Nick says in a defiant whisper. 'Apparently it's a large house with running water and electricity, and room enough for all of us to sleep. They say we'll be comfortable.'

'Great, tell them I'll take a non-smoking room with two queens,' Burkett says. 'And preferably a minibar.'

A path takes them through a verdant forest whose canopy breaks the afternoon sunlight into slanted beams. On a large boulder someone long ago had chiseled the eye and teeth of Samakersh, and the lichen crusted eye seems locked on Burkett as he passes.

He lags behind till he feels a nudge against his back, the last of the jihadists urging him forward with the barrel of his rifle.

Kidnap, he thinks: to nab a kid. Perhaps for him the better term would be *abduct*. Duct, for lead. To lead away – farther and farther away.

By the time they leave the cover of the trees, he wants nothing more than a glass of wine – red wine, then rest. Wine is the thing that will enable him finally to relax, to sleep. One glass and he would be able to sleep even while walking. If he collapsed, they could leave him behind or carry him. He'd be fine either way.

He realizes what has made him think of red wine: the faint odor of pinot noir. The most likely source is the Arab walking a few paces ahead, the bladder dangling from his shoulder. It looks to be made of lambskin or leather, some material porous enough to allow the smell to seep through. And how appropriate that the spout is plugged by a cork.

They scale a sunlit talus, staggering their positions to avoid the small avalanches created by those above.

'Can I have a drink?' Burkett asks when they reach the top. They look at him, confused, till he pantomimes drinking. One of the Arabs opens his backpack and offers him bottled water.

'No,' he says pointing to the Arab's canteen. 'I'll just take some of that.'

'Drink this,' Nick says. He sips from the proffered bottle of water before passing it to Burkett. 'They brought the bottles for us. They don't want us to get sick.'

'But they have wine,' Burkett snaps. More calmly he says, 'I just want to know why they're carrying wine.'

'There's no wine,' Nick says.

'Just ask,' he says.

'Why would you think they're carrying wine?'

'Can you not smell it? Just ask him if it's wine.'

Nick hesitates, then asks, and it's clear from their expressions that the answer is no. Alcohol is forbidden. But the Arab with the canteen must be lying. He's obviously trying to hide his drinking habit from his fellow Muslims.

Burkett and Nick finish the water. Nick hands back the empty bottle, which one of the tribesmen tosses into the brush.

Again they set off, Burkett trailing that canteen, the smell ever stronger. After about half an hour (he can only guess at the passing time from the position of the sun and the length of his shadow) he stops the Arab with the canteen and again asks for a drink. As before, one of the others produces a bottle of water, but Burkett insists on the canteen.

Nick stands a short distance away, gazing toward the sky yet radiating disapproval. Burkett through long exposure feels immune to moral scorn. His impulse is to guzzle the entire canteen, but as he takes the bladder and removes the cork he decides to restrict himself to just a few sips.

He spits it out – nothing but water. Only the wine he imagined could have pierced the dryness in his throat.

He drops to his knees and retches. A band of saliva hangs from his lower lip, a liquid connection to the dust. He must not be so parched after all.

Inside him is a void and there are separate versions of himself falling through it. One version is responsible for the tears brimming in his eyes, another for his desire to keep hold of his dignity. Why is he crying? He doesn't remember the last time he cried – never in his adult life, not even the day he learned of his brother's murder.

'Stop,' Nick says. He grips Burkett by the elbow and drags him to his feet. 'They see your crying as shameful.'

'I don't care how they see it.'

'It's easier to kill a dog than a man,' Nick says – probably some local proverb.

Safiullah and the others watch from a short distance ahead. Burkett half expects to be prodded from behind, but the solitary gunman bringing up the rear has settled into a squat, his rifle at a vertical beside him. Burkett wonders why they are waiting. Is his breakdown the excuse they needed to rest? More likely they're simply enjoying the sight of an American making a fool of himself.

*

Now what he smells is blood. It must be something in the soil – iron or copper perhaps in the small stones that clatter on the path. This was the source of his earlier mistake. The smell of wine so closely resembles the smell of blood – he can't think why he'd never noticed till now.

It transports him back to the operating room: an open appendectomy, perhaps. He sees the slick intestinal coils, feels the heat of the abdominal cavity. Sutures feel taut as guitar strings as his fingers flutter through one-handed ties. His steps on the path fall in cadence with the heart monitor.

On a downhill track they encounter a herd of about twenty goats, each with a tin bell at its throat. The men and animals file past in opposite directions, and Burkett runs his palm over the fur, feeling their spines. Behind them climbs an elderly goatherd, his hands clasped at his back, his torso bowed almost as low as his wards. A rifle hangs from his shoulder. He doesn't speak or in any way acknowledge the party, even when Nick greets him in Arabic.

At the bottom of the slope is a small stream, where the men drink and fill their canteens. Burkett and Nick are given a bottle of water to share, but Burkett, after only a sip, leaves the rest for Nick.

Safiullah stands over Nick, berating him for reasons at first unclear, at least to Burkett. The goat bells are still audible, so Safiullah, despite his anger, is keeping his voice to a whisper. Burkett watches his hand as it moves from the dagger to the belt buckle and back again. Nick opens his mouth to speak but falls silent when Safiullah slaps him across the face. Safiullah then turns and scowls toward the path, as though wishing he could slap each of the goats as well. And all at once Burkett sees the problem: Nick shouldn't have spoken to the goatherd.

They follow the stream through a narrow defile with high rock faces on either side. Nick has to walk near the front where Safiullah can keep an eye on him.

101

Shaded from the afternoon sun, Burkett rubs his arms against the cold. He wonders if he has a fever on top of the nausea. This is withdrawal, he thinks: his body revolting against him. *I would give it to you if I could,* he wants to say to his stomach, to his trembling hands.

It is dusk when he stops and vomits. To support himself he grips the weeds of an embankment, his arms outstretched as if tied for whipping. The others hardly break stride. It's getting late, and there is nothing surprising in a westerner's gastroenteritis. He falls back into line, the penultimate spot, but almost immediately vomits again, this time onto the stones of the creek bank. He hears the jihadist chuckling behind him but doesn't bother looking back.

At a place where the water pools, their captors unroll mats and kneel in prayer, silently touching their foreheads to the ground.

Burkett sags against the trunk of a tree. One of the Kalashnikovs lies within easy reach. He could simply pick it up and open fire on his prostrate captors. What are his chances, one against five – or two against five, if Nick could grab a weapon as well?

Nick seems to guess what he's thinking. He shakes his head, silently warning him away from the gun. Burkett follows his eyes up to the ledge and realizes it would be futile to make a run for it in this narrow pass. For miles they'd be trapped in the open, with no place to hide. Besides, he can already feel the nausea returning. Sick like this, he'd probably make easy prey on any terrain.

After praying, Safiullah orders Burkett and Nick to collect wood for a fire. It is their first chance to speak since this morning.

'You look horrible,' Nick says.

'Probably something I ate.' His hand trembles as he reaches for a stick.

'That old man back there could tell we were American,' Nick says. 'Maybe there's a military outpost somewhere near his village – maybe he'll report what he saw.'

An unlikely prospect, but Burkett remains silent. There's no point arguing a matter of faith, or belittling Nick's interaction with the goatherd. A pointless act of courage: he'd admire it more had it been for courtesy alone.

For dinner, their captors pass out retort packets that read 'US Government Property'. It seems the American military sells not just drones, but also MREs, or Meals, Ready-to-Eat. Burkett doubts his government would do business with terrorists. The MREs have more likely come all this way through some black market transaction or misplaced shipment, or even a convoy attacked and looted.

Nick knows how to use the flameless heater to warm their meals – beef stew, mashed potatoes with gravy. Burkett's had nothing all day but flatbread and a handful of nuts, but nausea keeps him from enjoying more of the MRE than the crackers and peanut butter. He doesn't mind giving the so-called entrée to Nick.

The temperature drops after dark. The five jihadists sleep on mats around the fire. Burkett and Nick again have to share a single blanket, but after a short time Nick removes himself, complaining of the blanket's smell.

Burkett hovers on the edge of sleep. He's vaguely aware of Nick building a fire. Some time later – minutes or hours, he doesn't know – he wakes to the sight of a figure. A woman. He's standing ankle deep in the stream. He must have walked in his sleep. She's silhouetted by fire, a black figure like a tin cutout. It's someone he knows. Véronique could have followed them, but that seems implausible for even the most intrepid reporter. Who is she? He steps gingerly on the smooth stones but his ankle rolls and he collapses in the shallows. When he recovers she's gone. All he sees is Nick, who plods into the stream and helps him to his feet.

*

They are walking again. The slender path disappears in a field of stones and forms again at the base of a steep hill. The path takes the form of switchbacks, and Burkett keeps his eyes on the ground to avoid the stares of those ahead of him.

At the top of the hill he sits down on an outcropping of rock, even though it's clear the group has no intention of stopping.

He's tired, but that isn't why he needs a break. He pulls up the frayed, dirt-covered hems of his jeans, and examines the skin underneath.

Since early morning he's been plagued by insects. At first they seemed to confine themselves to his ankles, but in the last hour they've become more aggressive, working their way higher up his legs.

But now that he looks, he can find no trace of them. He sees the red marks where he's clawed at bug bites, but he can't discern the bites themselves.

Perhaps these are microscopic insects. Perhaps they burrow under dermal layers to lay their eggs. Could this be the earliest manifestation of Madura foot? He remembers the amputation he performed at the clinic, the indurated gourd at the end of that man's leg. With the image comes a shot of guilt: the man had to go through surgery with expired benzodiazepines.

He feels the bugs tickling inside his shoes and wonders if the infestation could have something to do with the fact that he's not wearing his socks. By last night his socks had become so dirty he had to rinse them in the stream. All morning he's carried them dangling from the waistband of his pants. Now that they're dry he sits down and puts them back on, though he isn't sure if they'll stave off the bugs or trap them inside.

He's startled by a hand on his elbow – one of the gunmen ordering him to stand and walk. Burkett drops a shoe and nearly falls from his perch on the rock. As the jihadist bends to pick up the shoe, Burkett notes the holstered pistol at his waist. The man seems to be inviting him to make a grab for it, but it's Nick who supposedly knows how to fight. Burkett at this point, starved and exhausted, swarmed by invisible insects, isn't sure he could keep his hand steady enough to aim or pull a trigger.

Nick kneels beside him. 'You all right?'

'Fine,' he says.

Without asking permission, Nick takes Burkett's wrist and feels his pulse. 'You're tachycardic.'

'Just tired and thirsty,' he says.

'You feel warm,' he says. 'Do you have a fever?'

A creek bed takes them across a valley of stones. There has been no breakfast, no lunch. Each man is given a small bag of peanuts, the type distributed on airplanes. Burkett feels weak and hungry but the first of the peanuts sits nauseously on his tongue till he spits it out. He stuffs the bag into his pocket and keeps walking.

Not till that evening, when they make camp, do the insects begin to explore the territory above his knees.

A word comes to mind: *Formication*. The tactile hallucination of ants. It is so typical of withdrawal that he should have recognized it from the earliest tingles.

They seem most active when he rests, and now they feast on his thighs, crotch, and torso. All his scratching does little good except perhaps to mask the prickles with self-inflicted pain.

While the others sleep he lies on his back and stares into the night sky. He has his hands in his pockets, his body rigid as he tries to ignore the needling bugs.

He has a vision of his brother on the ground beside him. The bullet holes in his chest bubble with pulmonary air. A bloodstain spreads in the dirt, and as its edge nears Burkett, he sees that it isn't blood but a swarm of ants.

He stacks his palms against his brother's sternum and counts a series of compressions. Ribs crack under his weight. With each thrust, more ants erupt from the bullet holes. They appear on Owen's lips as well, and within moments they are spilling from his mouth and nostrils. Burkett tries to breathe into his brother's mouth, but the airway is clotted with ants. Ants form heaps at every orifice, mounds that rise and come together to form a black shroud that vaguely conforms to the shape of the body underneath.

The ants form sleeves up Burkett's arms. When they cover his face, he pauses his chest compressions to swat them away from his eyes and mouth, but the moment he clears a swathe more ants flood into it. He feels them inside his ear canals. He keeps his lips clamped shut, but it doesn't take long for the ants to find their way through his nasal passages and down to his throat.

When he reaches again for his brother's chest, it is nowhere to be found in the thick darkness that he realizes will kill him as soon as he tries to breathe. At the last moment he has a view of himself and his brother from above, and all he sees is a pair of black mounds.

11

Burkett wakes in some kind of cell, a straw mat cold against his skin. He aches with thirst. Nick sits against the opposite wall, between them a rectangle of light cast by a small window. Without being asked, Nick passes him a bottle of water.

'Where are we?' he asks after emptying the bottle.

'In the mountains,' Nick says. 'Near Allaghar, I think.'

'Where is Allaghar?'

Nick shrugs. 'About a hundred and fifty miles from the capital.'

This jars Burkett. He remembers boarding an SUV with a new set of captors, but of the rest of the journey he has no memory.

'You had a seizure,' Nick says.

'When?'

'Yesterday,' he says.

They were wearing burqas at the time, so Nick doesn't know where in his body the seizure began, nor how long it lasted. It only became apparent when he bucked off the seat and jostled the others in the car.

He turns over his hands. He notices a tremor, ever so slight. Could this be an after-effect of his seizure? Or perhaps a sign of more to come? It persists even as he reaches down and pinches the edge of the blanket. In surgery he always prided himself on his steady hands. If the steadiness doesn't return, he'll have to find ways to adapt, like that ophthalmologist at Emory who managed brilliant feats of microsurgery despite rattling instruments. If he survives this experience, he doubts he could get away with popping Valium before every operation. 'To be honest,' Nick says, 'I can't say I expected—'

He holds back the rest of the sentence, what he *can't say*. A seizure. The truth is, Burkett wouldn't have expected it either. It dispels any doubt he might have had about being an addict. The cause is probably the benzos more than the alcohol. He estimates he's been drunk, on average, four to five days a week for about ten years. For some that might qualify as alcoholism, but he's known plenty of medical students and physicians, men and women alike, who could match him drink for drink. His real problem – which he recognized before even losing his medical license – was the daily use of Valium, morning and night, usually supplemented by short-acting doses of Xanax. He wonders if the medical board would accept Islamist captivity as an alternative to one of their treatment programs.

No doubt he has diminished in the eyes of Nick, starting with the regrettable episode of crying, from a competent surgeon to a groveling alcoholic. He doesn't know what Nick thought of him before – nor for that matter does he particularly care – but it seems Nick could only hate him now for wearing this face, for doing such dishonor to Owen by looking exactly like him.

He shivers even though they've been given blankets. There is a painful throbbing in his head. He imagines his brain as a pulsing muscle, squeezing fluid in deranged mimicry of his heart. The pressure steadily builds inside his skull. He lifts his hands to his head but seems to lack the strength of counter-pressure.

The headache pursues him into sleep, and in a dream he realizes that ants have entered his skull and begun eating his brain. When he next wakes, Nick is watching him from the other side of the chamber. Burkett winces at the stench of urine. He notices the dampness of his clothes, the stickiness down the leg of his pants.

On the floor is a package of bottled water. Seeing it makes him aware of his thirst. He drains one bottle in gulps, imagining his body absorbing the water like a dry sponge. Only after he's finished does it occur to him that water might be in short supply, but Nick doesn't seem to mind. He tosses the empty bottle into the corner at the foot of his mat. He can tell from the pile of trash there that Nick has consumed several MREs since their arrival.

'How long has it been?' Burkett asks.

'We've been in this room almost four days.'

'Have they not let us use the bathroom?'

'There's a septic pit,' he says. 'It's easier to wash you here than there.'

Do their captors understand the nature of his sickness? The natives expect food poisoning in a westerner. If they recognized alcohol withdrawal, it would only confirm their general opinion of Americans as decadent and corrupt, and what difference would that make?

They expect us to be addicts, he thinks. He is proof of Christianity's failure. But why should he, an agnostic at best, be expected to represent Christianity? Perhaps the jihadists would go easier on him if they understood his position. Or would his lack of belief only cause greater offense?

Burkett senses Nick's stare but refuses to return it. He picks up another water bottle and turns it in his hands, pretending to study the label, though he can't read it in the dim light. When he finally looks over, Nick is facing the opposite wall, probably asleep.

*

The door bangs open, toppling an open bottle he'd filled last night with urine. A bearded Arab, well over six feet, stands there smiling, amused perhaps by the spill. He leads them into the courtyard and orders them to sit at the base of a dry fountain, whose centerpiece has been smashed and partly buried in sand, the fragments suggesting a life-size horse and rider.

Burkett must have seen this courtyard when they arrived, but he has no memory of it. The enclosure is formed by a low-slung, horsehoe-shaped building accessible by rows of doors painted in bright colors. Graffiti marks every available space on the otherwise stark white walls – Qu'ranic verses in the same brown paint. Jihadists with machine guns scowl at them from the shaded part of the courtyard. Those who brought them here are nowhere in sight.

A boy of around twelve strides toward them. A man follows, keeping a hand on the boy's shoulder. The Kalashnikov looks almost comical in the boy's small hands, at least till he points it at Burkett. The boy seems to brace himself to fire. Burkett extends his arms, palms out, and says, 'No, wait,' but the boy doesn't pull the trigger. He begins shouting, gesturing with the gun. Burkett flinches when it sweeps past him. He glances at Nick, who keeps the boy locked in an impassive stare.

'Is he going to shoot us?' Burkett asks.

'I don't think so.'

'You don't think so?'

The boy presses the gun against Burkett's cheek, forcing him back against the low wall of the fountain. The tirade goes on, with prompting from the man beside him, who mumbles at every pause. Other jihadists stroll over to observe what is beginning to seem like some rite of passage for the young boy.

Is he to become a man by killing an infidel? Surely Burkett is worth too much in ransom to die at the altar of someone's coming-of-age experience.

He imagines an orderly delivering the message to his father. Ryan died as well – the same ones who killed Owen. His father stares, perhaps confused, or perhaps too far gone even for that. It is a small mercy that he no longer recognizes those names.

Pain bolts through his head. He hasn't been shot, only jabbed with the gun, but still his fingers search his brow for a wet hole. A blaring tinnitus drowns out the boy's voice. He tries to keep eye contact, but his vision blurs from the pain or welling tears, perhaps both.

An image comes to mind: that woman he glimpsed at their campsite. All at once he knows her. Or his mind paints her silhouette with someone he knows – Amanda Grey, the one he stole from his brother. He hasn't spoken to her in years, but knows she's in Nashville working as a forensic pathologist. It occurs to him that of all people she alone might mourn his death.

Did she mourn Owen? Does she even know that Owen died?

The boy spits, first on Burkett and then on Nick. The spectators seem particularly impressed by the glob of viscous saliva that oozes down Burkett's cheek.

12

The next morning the same guard wakes them by again kicking the door. He seems to enjoy startling them, as if he expected to catch them trying to escape. Along with the usual Kalashnikov, he carries a rucksack and a camera case.

Burkett props himself up on his mat. He can barely see through the slit of his left eye. He reaches up to touch it, imagining how he must look with his facial bruising, vomit stains, and trembling hands – a man near death – but the truth is, he feels better than he did yesterday.

Nick interprets the Arabic. The guard, whose name is Nibras, laughs about the shame they suffered at the hands of that boy. He insists on palpating Burkett's swollen eye, chuckling as he mashes the bruise with his thumb. At first Burkett refuses to wince, but the pressure increases till he has to push away the hand. Nibras makes some joke about how they would have wet their pants if they hadn't already relieved themselves in a bottle.

'Is he part of the Heroes of Jihad?' Burkett asks.

'Probably,' Nick says.

'Does he know who killed Owen and Abu?'

'How would you suggest I go about asking that question?'

Burkett stares at the smiling Nibras. 'He seems jovial enough,' he says. 'Just ask him.'

The guard squats, looking from one to the other as if waiting for an interpretation, but Nick remains silent.

'At least tell him I'm not a Christian,' Burkett says. 'Tell him I've always admired the beauty of Islam and would like to learn more about it.'

Nick's silence carries a hint of condemnation, but Burkett has no qualms about seeking a neutral ground between religions. He tells himself that the truth is more important than solidarity among prisoners. He wishes he could speak the words himself rather than depend on Nick to translate. To distance himself from Christianity is to distance himself from Nick, and perhaps it's cruel to ask him to interpret, but when the time for violence comes, Burkett has no interest in suffering for beliefs he doesn't hold.

Nick begins speaking in Arabic. Burkett manages a partial smile when Nibras turns to face him.

'He also thinks it's a beautiful religion,' Nick says. 'No surprise there.'

From his rucksack Nibras takes a roll of duct tape. Burkett imagines himself gagged and bound by the wrists and ankles. But the only purpose of the tape, it turns out, is to hang a bedsheet from the wall.

They pose for pictures with yesterday's *International Herald Tribune*. Nibras is dissatisfied with the lighting, so he extinguishes the bare bulb and repeats the process. He opens the door to augment the natural light from the window.

'Why not just take the picture outside?' Burkett asks.

Through Nick Nibras explains that the CIA can deduce information from background detail – even the grains of sand and direction of light.

Nibras turns the screen of his camera so that they can see the pictures. He asks them to choose their favorites, as if doing them a courtesy, but to Burkett he seems more like an artist seeking affirmation. Burkett's face seems to twitch with the shuffle of images. The swelling all but buries his left eye. At random he selects one of the pictures, but Nibras prefers another.

'He keeps saying you have a distinctive American face,' Nick says.

'What does that mean?'

The jihadist provides notepads and ballpoint pens that bear the logo of the Aljannah Hotel. He instructs them to write letters to their families. With his gap-toothed, jaundiced smile, he apologizes for the need to exaggerate the hardships of captivity. It's important for ransom purposes that they give the impression of extreme discomfort, daily threats to their lives. But not to worry, he says. They aren't Muslims, so he isn't committing a sin by asking them to lie. In fact, their lies are in keeping with Allah's will, since the financial gains will support Jihad.

His eyes brighten with sudden realization: Burkett's bruises will lend credence to their claims of suffering. Perhaps the kids can doctor Nick's picture to look more like Burkett's.

'Kids?' Burkett asks.

Nick seems confused by his translation as well, but after another exchange in Arabic, he says, 'Their computer experts are kids.'

'Our friend from yesterday?'

'Probably.'

Burkett imagines a chamber here devoted to information technology, servers managed by twelve-year-olds. It comforts him to recognize the social phenomenon of kids knowing more about computers than their elders. Not that Nibras would qualify as an *elder*. He can't be older than thirty, but what's the average life expectancy for a jihadist?

Nibras and Nick fall into conversation. Nick agrees to something, but reluctantly. He stands, his fists clenched at his sides. Nibras sets down his rucksack, raises his fists, and punches Nick in the face. Nick stands still, eyes closed, while Nibras examines the trickle of blood from his lip.

Nibras gives him a consoling pat on the shoulder, and the two men position themselves for another punch. This time Nick staggers backward and places a hand against the wall.

'You all right?' Burkett asks.

'I'll survive,' Nick says, dribbles of blood trailing down his chin.

Nibras has him hold the newspaper for more pictures.

'Tell him to come back in an hour,' Burkett suggests. 'Your face needs time to swell and bruise.'

Nibras seems to think it's a good idea. As soon as he leaves Nick starts writing to Beth. Burkett stares at his own blank sheet. Will they actually mail the letter, or is this merely a way of gaining personal information for ransom negotiation? He'd rather not supply them with any more detail than absolutely necessary.

But to whom should he write? His mother is long dead, his father in a state of senile oblivion. The cousins in Cleveland he hasn't seen in over a decade.

He considers friends from medical school and residency. Robert Crook, now a dermatologist in Boston. Elliot Spears, who no doubt just completed his fellowship at Emory. He hasn't spoken to either of them since being cast out of the program in plastic surgery.

All of his recent social interactions – outside his moonlighting job in the ER – revolved around drinking and sex. With some of those women, he could make an argument for a genuine connection – Ellen and Mary, perhaps Carol Ann – but he can't even remember their last names.

How could he subject some hapless friend or former girlfriend to the stress of being contacted by the Heroes of Jihad?

A name comes to mind: Véronique, the intrepid journalist. She'd probably appreciate the prospect of ransom negotiation.

You might not remember me, he writes.

He tears off the page and crumples it into a wad.

There is always Amanda, though he hasn't seen her since medical school. He's kept track through mutual acquaintances, but his information has been spotty at best. He only recently heard about her divorce, probably a year after the fact. He wonders what was worse for her, the divorce or the break-up with Burkett. Selfishly, he hopes for the latter. Or perhaps she suffered most when she broke things off with Owen – the virginal college romance that under Burkett's influence spiraled into a drama of betrayal and deception.

Burkett's relationship with Amanda lasted longer than his brother's – four years compared with three. She came with him to Atlanta, where they shared a small apartment, and she matriculated at Emory two years after he did. Why did she and Burkett stay together so long? Somehow their relationship dragged on even when there was nothing left to sustain it but guilt. No doubt it would have lasted even longer if not for his chronic infidelities She could forgive him only so many times.

In his memory she sits with a friend in a crowded bar. She hasn't seen him yet. He hopes to slip out before she notices the scantily clad undergraduate who keeps whispering in his ear. He smiles at something the girl says, urging her toward the exit, and just at that moment, still smiling, he meets Amanda's cold stare in a mirror behind the bar. Other memories flash through his mind: when she found incriminating text messages from another woman, or the following year when he tried and failed to seduce her away from the classmate she would later marry. But it's the thought of her face that night in the mirror that makes him quail with shame.

The blank page rests on his thigh. A ransom plea is no way to re-establish contact with an old flame, but for all his sins, he has no doubt Amanda would devote herself entirely to his release. But how could he ask her to take on such a burden, when he hasn't spoken to her in years, when he's already caused her so much undeserved pain?

Better just to write to his father, who would neither understand nor care. He'll ask them to send it to the US embassy in the capital. If they insist on an address, there's no reason not to give them the name of that nursing home in Atlanta. It's almost comical to imagine his father trying to communicate with some jihadist through the barriers of language and dementia.

Of course the best candidate for such a letter would have been his brother, his perennial 'emergency contact'. By impulse he pulls the collar of the Penn State tee shirt over his nose, but the foul odor is entirely his own.

'You need to write something,' Nick says, neatly folding the page he's filled.

'Will they kill me if I don't?'

'Just write a note to your father,' he says.

'I don't want them to know where he lives.'

'You can use the IMO address.'

'I'm not writing anything.'

When Nibras returns, he seems pleased enough by the swelling in Nick's upper lip to take more photographs.

'*Jayyid jiddan.*' Very good. He magnifies the swollen lip on his view screen.

Nick's letter to Beth fills both sides of the page. Nibras doesn't seem surprised when Burkett hands him the blank notepad. After less than ten minutes, he returns with an older man they've only seen from a distance. Some kind of commander, he wears an eye patch with a thick scar crossing behind it. He holds out the notepad and taps the empty page with what remains of his index finger. As far as Burkett can tell, he's lost all or part of every finger on his right hand.

Burkett shakes his head. 'I have nothing to say.'

The old warrior grips Burkett by the wrist, lays the ballpoint pen in his hand, and again taps the notepad.

'Just make something up,' Nick says. 'If you want, I'll tell you what to write.'

Nick turns and speaks to them directly, taking the notepad and pen, no doubt promising to get a letter out of Burkett.

'Tell them I'll write a letter as soon as I find out who killed my brother.'

Nick hesitates before interpreting, but when he does, he speaks longer than would seem necessary and in a tone far more conciliatory than Burkett intended. He hears *min fadlak*, or please, and imagines Nick politely arguing that the sickness of grief keeps him from writing, that the best treatment would be knowing who killed his brother. The old man listens with a thoughtful expression, as if he were considering the offer – a letter, potentially worth thousands of dollars, in exchange for some small piece of information.

'The old man says he's never heard of your brother,' Nick says. 'But if you don't write a letter, you will shortly join him in Hell.'

13

The next day they're permitted outside – perhaps a reward for the letters. The courtyard is a welcome escape from that cell and their own fetid odors. Burkett sits alone in the shade and watches as masked men pose for photographs with a grenade launcher.

He ended up writing the first thing that came to mind:

> Dad, I'm being held captive, possibly by the same men who killed Owen.
> Unharmed so far, but give them whatever they ask.
>
> All the best,
> Ryan.

As an afterthought he wrote, *I love you*. Of course he wouldn't have said that under normal circumstances, not ever to his father, but his captors might be less inclined to torture and murder him if they see him as a loving son.

A completely ridiculous letter, he thinks. His father at his prime would have found it laughable, an embarrassment. But he doubts the letter will actually reach him.

They've been given clean clothes: baggy, brightly colored shirts and pants down to their calves. Sitting in the courtyard, Burkett slips off his running shoes. Without socks it's only a matter of time before he develops athlete's foot.

Nibras and several others have gathered under the awning. The boy who struck Burkett has set up a laptop on a crate. The grenade launcher, momentarily forgotten, lies in its foam-lined case. Burkett looks across the courtyard, where Nick stands with the single other prisoner, Tahir, a lawyer from the capital apparently being held because of his family's political influence.

Nick too seems to have noticed the grenade launcher. But what can be done? The prospects are bleak for a single missile against twenty Kalashnikovs in a walled compound.

Cheers draw Burkett's attention back to the group. They are watching some kind of video on the boy's laptop. His eyes find Nibras, who lifts a hand inviting him to come and watch.

With Nick he wavers at the periphery of the huddle. The video depicts a series of suicide bomb attacks, with a soundtrack borrowed from some action movie. Graphics enhance the shaky footage – a circle or red arrow marking the suicide bomber or targeted Hummer. The Islamists shout praises with each explosion.

Nick turns and walks away. Burkett should follow, but he stays, even for the grainy magnification of a severed arm – probably belonging to the bomber himself, but that doesn't seem to diminish the glee it inspires in the jihadists. The video concludes with a glossy montage culled from some Hollywood film – Muslim swordsmen slaying Christian knights.

One of the jihadists is wearing Burkett's Penn State tee shirt.

'That's my shirt,' he says.

Nick isn't there to interpret, but it is clear the man understands. He must have gone into their room and found the shirt in the pile. Begrimed and threadbare, it has little value. Perhaps he sees it as a token of conquest. Or maybe he meant the taking as provocation.

He's old enough for a beard the length of a fist, the way the Prophet Muhammad wore his. He points his Kalashnikov at Burkett's chest.

'Keep the shirt,' Burkett says, raising his hands and backing away. He shouldn't have said anything – at least not so soon after the movie, the heroic murders fresh in the man's mind.

Nibras comes over and talks his friend out of pulling the trigger. Burkett notices Nick at the door of their chamber and realizes he must have witnessed the entire exchange.

An execution takes place the following day. Burkett and Nick hear the gunshots from their cell. Later in the courtyard they recognize the severed head of Tahir, the lawyer from the capital, propped on a sheet for photographs. The body hangs upside down and drains into a bucket. It is Nibras who dips a brush into the bucket and adds to the scriptural graffiti covering the walls.

Just yesterday, Nick says, Tahir had described a recurrent dream – the dream – in which he was summoned by a bearded man in a white robe. It is the same dream Christian missionaries have encountered all over the Muslim world.

'He's with Jesus now,' Nick says.

At this hour the massive pine trees outside the wall cast the entire compound in a pleasant shade, but today Burkett and Nick prefer their dim chamber. They prop open the door to ease the stench, which has grown worse by the day.

'Would they ask us for letters if they planned to kill us?' Burkett asks.

'You shouldn't be afraid of death.'

Burkett hears nothing in this beyond smug condescension. He resists an impulse to lash back. Of course he's afraid of death, of being decapitated on video.

An image flashes before him – the barrel of a Kalashnikov, that boy in the courtyard. Why did the boy choose Burkett rather than Nick? Perhaps even he could see the difference between them. Perhaps he recognized in Nick a fellow fanatic buoyed by the promise of everlasting bliss. What then did he see in Burkett? A coward? It is easier to kill a coward – easier to kill a dog than a man. Maybe this is the advantage of a child soldier. He is old enough to use a Kalashnikov but too young to know the difference between cowardice and a reasonable fear of death.

How did his brother face the final gun? He fought to the end: that much was obvious from the bruises on his hands, the fractured metacarpal – the so-called boxer's fracture. But what happened between the fighting and the shooting, when he lay incapacitated by the blows? Perhaps he was unconscious, dying from shattered ribs and a collapsed lung, so that the bullets came as a relief, if he felt them at all.

From somewhere comes a verse: *To die is gain*. Perhaps those were the last words in his brother's mind.

Owen would have wanted to stare into the eyes of the man killing him. Did the man look away? Or did those criminal eyes take in the very last light of Owen's life and then resume their interactions with all the meaningless light from elsewhere? How unjust that the person least deserving should carry the memory of Owen's last moment. Perhaps it is one of the soldiers outside, even the jocular Nibras. If only Burkett knew the man. If only the eyes were marked somehow by what they had seen.

Nick bows his head and faintly whispers, but Burkett can't discern the words. They are sitting against the back wall, as far as possible from the door and Tahir's body outside.

'Are you praying for our freedom?' he asks.

'No,' says Nick, opening his eyes.

'Then what are you praying for?' He's unable to keep the irritation from his voice. 'Do you *want* them to kill us?'

'I'm thinking about James and Peter when they were imprisoned.'

'What happened to them?'

'An angel opened the prison doors and led Peter out into the street.'

'What about the other guy?'

'James,' he says. 'He was put to death.'

Burkett's nose in a glass of bourbon would block the growing stench of Tahir's blood. He imagines pouring three fingers, neat. He would take a moment to breathe it in before the first sip.

He turns to Nick. 'Do you smell the blood?'

'What blood?' Nick gives him a skeptical look. 'From all the way across the courtyard?'

Burkett wonders if it's another hallucination, or perhaps the aura preceding a seizure. He looks at his crotch, half expecting to lose control of his bladder. But of course he wouldn't be conscious of it till afterward.

'Are you all right?' Nick asks.

'No,' he says.

A flurry of nausea sends him bounding for the door. What little he's consumed – rice, bread, water – surges from his mouth. Kneeling in the doorway, he is aware of the headless body maybe fifty feet away, but he refuses to look at it.

'Feel better?' Nick asks.

Burkett drags his forearm across his mouth. With a reeking sigh he slumps against the wall. He can no longer smell Tahir's blood, so his answer to Nick, if he cared to give him one, would be yes, he feels better.

14

Nibras is ranting against the western news media – the anti-Muslim bias, the obscene photographs. Just this morning, an American reporter and a photographer were given a limited tour of the compound while Burkett and Nick sat bound and gagged in their cell. Nibras would have killed the journalists, or at least forced their godless newspaper to pay a crippling ransom, but their escort, a relation of Mullah Bashir himself, had sworn a vow of protection – a vow that would have obligated him to die before letting his guests come to harm.

'Even a prophet's family has fools,' says Nibras, who suspects that the journalists were in fact CIA operatives searching for the American prisoners or scouting the compound for a planned raid. They were blindfolded for the journey, their phones and computers left behind, but their camera might have held some tracking device. The prospect of a rescue operation might have given Burkett hope, but he remembers the Aljannah disaster, the helicopter in the pool, and feels almost relieved when Nibras announces the plan to transfer him and Nick to another location.

For the trip they wear blindfolds under burqas and ride in the back of a Chevrolet SUV. Burkett's blindfold, an abrasive scarf that smells of human sweat, slides low enough that he can see through the mesh window of his burqa. Nibras sleeps in the passenger seat while the driver navigates a series of unpaved mountain roads, passing ramshackle huts and slowing for mule carts and livestock.

When they stop at an abandoned farm for a meal of beef jerky and bottled water, the jihadists' phones chirp with news of a drone attack on the compound – a bombing within hours of their departure. There were no survivors. Nibras and the driver beat their chests and tear their tunics while swearing revenge.

Burkett and Nick have been permitted to remove their burqas and blindfolds. It is a relief from the heat, but their uncovered faces only stoke the rage of their captors, who reflexively blame America for the problem of drones. Nick provides a running interpretation as the jihadists consider the retaliatory justice of killing their prisoners. Even if Djohar's cowardly soldiers flew the drone and pressed the button to drop the bomb, is it not the US that props up his secular regime – that supplied it with that very drone and so many others just like it? The driver, probably in his early twenties, shoulders his rifle, but Nibras urges restraint: the millions in ransom would far outweigh the pleasure of killing these Americans.

The weapon pointing at Burkett has the look of something other than a Kalashnikov. An M-16 perhaps, not that it matters, for in the end there are only two types of gun: one aiming at him and one that is not. It is a binary code, he thinks, a dash or a period. No, not a period: with the vertical sight, the end of the barrel looks more like an exclamation mark.

!

The man shifts his rifle from Burkett to Nick and back again. Only after firing a skyward round does he set aside the weapon. He leans against the SUV in the attitude of a man spent, as if pulling the trigger had been the necessary release to an exhausting urge.

Another SUV pulls into the clearing, smoke roiling from its hood.

Nibras mutters praises to Allah as three Arabs emerge. The jihadists greet one another by name and embrace with somber affection, the new arrivals obviously aware of the recent bombing. One of them has a scar that distorts his face, creating a pinkish gap in his beard. He is the shortest of the three, and also it seems the least sociable, but the scar lends his reticence a quality of battle-hardened seriousness. While the others talk, he inspects the smoking engine, pouring a bottle of water into the coolant tank.

Burkett and Nick help transfer the crates of bottled water and MREs from one vehicle to the other. Burkett has no particular attachment to the gregarious Nibras, but for some reason this new set of jihadists gives him a sense of foreboding, particularly the one with the scar. He wonders if he and Nick have been sold to another faction, perhaps more militant. Or maybe these men merely represent another cell of that larger organization calling itself the Heroes of Jihad.

Once again in burqas, they travel east with their new captors. They have been spared the discomfort of blindfolds, perhaps an oversight on the part of their new handlers, but Burkett can't imagine any strategic advantage in knowing the monotonous scenery. They drive nearly an hour without passing a single building or landmark that could feasibly serve as guidance in any future attempt at escape.

The vehicle lurches nauseously on dirt roads till they reach an isolated compound about half a mile from a tiny village. The house sits on a steep incline, and the tilting wall around it gives an impression of inevitable collapse despite a diagonal array of makeshift support beams on the downhill side.

Akbar, the one with a scar on his face, orders Burkett and Nick to carry supplies into the compound, the bottled water, MREs, blankets, and cans of petrol. The largest room contains a fire pit and a gas lamp, which Akbar lights even though it's not yet dark out. A narrow passage gives way to another room with gaping holes in the ceiling and some kind of mural on the plaster wall, a rudimentary depiction of green hills, a pair of robed figures by a meandering stream. Off the hallway is an alcove where bags of rice are stacked under a wooden counter.

Burkett and Nick are assigned to a basement chamber with stone walls and a dirt floor. They've grown accustomed to the lack of running water, but in their previous compound they at least had electricity for some portion of each day, a bare bulb to illuminate their cell. This place offers nothing of the sort – although the cans of petrol raise the possibility of a gas generator yet to arrive. They seem to have undergone a staged withdrawal, a weaning from all modern amenities.

Yet another deprivation comes later that evening, when they are forced to relinquish their shoes. Burkett's soles have begun to detach, but he could have repaired them with the duct tape he noticed among the supplies in the SUV.

For their waste, they are given a plastic bucket that, judging from the smell, others have used for the same purpose. A proper toilet sits in the cowshed, though disconnected from any pipe or water supply, perhaps left there by some former occupant whose plumbing endeavors never came to fruition.

The next morning they sit in the courtyard and watch their two guards wrestle in the dust. The third, the one who drove, seems to have left sometime during the night. Burkett recognizes the style of wrestling, their movements like an echo from his past. They wrestle at the level of decent high school competitors. His own muscles twitch in occasional sympathy. Sajiv, the tall one, looks at least ten pounds heavier, but Akbar makes up for the difference with speed.

Sajiv has Greco-Roman tendencies, exposing his legs as he positions himself for unlikely headlocks and upper-body throws. Burkett remembers working as a coach at a wrestling camp one summer during college. He would encourage the boys to stick to the basics – what he called 'high percentage moves' – but the less experienced wrestlers could hardly resist the brutal appeal of a hip throw, the kinetic beauty in the rise and fall of an opponent's body. How rarely physical reality allows the perfect move, but Akbar's rigid, linear style – his head-on attacks and delayed counters – might give Sajiv just the leeway he needs to pull off one of those flamboyant throws.

'Watch his hips,' Burkett calls to Sajiv, unable to resist even if neither of them can understand. And yet the comment draws Sajiv's attention, as if he knew it was meant for him. He turns to Burkett, distracted, and Akbar takes the opportunity to dive for an ankle. Burkett almost smiles at the awkwardness of it, the moment of imbalanced wrestling when one man stops while the other persists. It reminds him of his brother, how he always made a point of ignoring the boundary and the sound of the whistle, how he'd keep wrestling till he felt the hard gym floor or the referee's hand on his back. Burkett in contrast felt safest when skirting the edge of the ring, his back to the edge, such that any attack by his opponent would carry them out of bounds.

Now the wrestlers are sitting upright, Sajiv's hand on Akbar's shoulder, the look on his face asking, *Do you hear that?* Both men stare at the sky, waiting and listening. And then Burkett hears it too: a distant buzz. He realizes he could hear it even before they stopped wrestling – it's been getting louder – but still Akbar and Sajiv listen with strained expressions, as if doubting the sound's very existence. Akbar doesn't seem to hear it at all, not yet. Perhaps they've suffered auditory damage from overexposure to guns and bombs – or perhaps it is the rush of blood from wrestling, their own panting breath. And finally the buzzing sound brings them to their feet, and they herd Burkett and Nick down the stone staircase and into their basement cell.

While they wait, an image of Akbar's face lingers with Burkett: a look of complete terror. That buzzing sound, almost like a taunt, a harbinger of destruction. The sound that so frightened Akbar, that seemed to make his very eyeballs tremble. But why must a drone make noise at all? Are the surveillance drones not notorious for stealth, for hovering in silence outside windows? He thinks of the Phantom gliding like a fish through water. Perhaps it is too expensive to equip the long range bombers, the high flyers, with stealth technology. Or perhaps it is merely a form of intimidation, psychological warfare: perhaps the government in the north sends out noisy drones for the sole purpose of instilling fear.

Where is the drone now? Could its ordnance be aimed at this very house? There is no reason to think Akbar and Sajiv, mere foot soldiers, would qualify as high value targets. But how would he know? After the destruction of the last compound, a satellite or drone could have tracked them all the way here, perhaps mistaking Burkett and Nick for jihadists, or in their burqas as the wives of jihadists.

High value target: a phrase he no doubt picked up from the news media, like *collateral damage* or *surgical precision*. This last he finds particularly absurd, his profession a metaphor for killing. A profession that is anything but precise: he thinks of all the complications he's seen, all the collateral damage from surgery. Postoperative infections, disfiguring scars, and bowel obstructions. And all the mistakes – the inadvertent clipping and slicing, the wrong-sided operations.

Who was the high value target in that last compound? The old man with missing fingers? Certainly not those poor 'kids' working the computers, not the twelve-year-old with the Kalashnikov. How close Burkett and Nick came to becoming collateral damage – an hour, two at the most. Is it possible that the drone waited for them to leave before dropping the bomb? Far more plausible is the explanation of chance – simple luck they left when they did.

Nick has his eyes closed, probably in prayer. Perhaps he is preparing for the bomb, preparing his soul for a fiery release. Burkett imagines the collapse of the roof and walls. He would rather die in the initial explosion than bleed out or starve under a heap of stone. The minutes pass in silence, and finally the sounds from upstairs – Akbar and Sajiv all but laughing in relief – announce the passing of danger. Nick lifts his eyes to the ceiling and smirks. Burkett sees in his face not just resignation but also disappointment, as if death from above were their best hope of escape.

15

Akbar and Sajiv sit near the cowshed, cleaning their teeth with twigs. A battery-powered radio plays the Arabic version of Voice of America. At the news of a suicide bombing in Israel, ten dead, they stand and shout praises. Akbar turns to Burkett and Nick, as if suddenly offended by their presence, and orders them to say the words *Allahu Akbar*. With a shrug Burkett complies, but all Nick will say is, 'God is great.' Even after Akbar slaps him across the face, Nick utters the English version.

'Why not say it?' Burkett asks. 'I thought you said your God and his had the same name in Arabic.'

'They'll take it as praise for theirs,' Nick says. 'Which in itself doesn't matter, but they won't see our faith – my faith – as having value unless I'm willing to suffer for it.'

It seems like pointless bravado, even a contradiction: Burkett remembers Hassad and Abu, how Nick approved of their Muslim rituals despite their Christian beliefs. Akbar seems prepared to strike him again, but a knock on the door stays his hand.

Someone outside, another human being: the first in the week since their arrival at this remote outpost. Burkett's mind churns through the possibilities – a goatherd asking for directions, more journalists on a guided tour. He steels himself for the inevitable gunfire. Could this be the final raid, the incompetent rescue operation that will culminate in death for all of them? Would the raid begin with an innocent knock?

Sajiv slides back the shutter and peers through the slit in the door. He has to wait while Akbar digs a key from his shirt. Akbar makes a point of checking the aperture for himself before unbolting the door. Burkett wonders how it was decided that Akbar would keep the key, that source of authority, when he seems the less intelligent of the two. Perhaps it has something to do with the scar, a higher rank earned through combat.

A teenage boy carries in a large stainless steel pot by both handles. After lowering it to the ground, the boy stares curiously at the barefoot Americans sprawled against the wall. Behind him stands a figure in a burqa, perhaps his mother or sister. In silence she turns and disappears behind the doorframe. Only after the boy is gone does Burkett notice the lidded basket she left on the threshold.

The pot contains lamb stew, the basket flatbread and apples. Also in the basket is a handwritten note which Akbar and Sajiv burn after reading.

Sajiv hangs the pot from a gambrel over the fire, but before the stew has time enough to warm, they begin scooping it directly into their bowls. To Burkett it tastes bland, in need of salt, but after a week of nothing but MREs he savors the feel of the stringy meat and soft carrots on his tongue.

'The boy and the woman live in the neighboring house,' Nick says, listening to Sajiv. 'It's about a half mile to the north.'

'How often will they bring us dinner?'

'They're supposed to come twice a week till the rainy season.'

'The rainy season? When is that?'

'Two months away. But he says we'll be long gone by then.'

Burkett sets aside his bowl. He moves closer to the fire and prods the embers with a charred stick.

'Can they not give us something to read?' he asks. Nick directs the question to Sajiv.

'He'll send a message,' Nick says.

'Tell them I'd love to read the Qu'ran if they could get me an English translation.'

'*La!*' barks Akbar, who till now has remained silent.

'Why not?' Burkett asks.

'It would be unsuitable for you to touch the Holy Qu'ran,' Nick interprets.

'But how am I to learn about Islam?'

Akbar and Sajiv discuss the question.

'If you want to read the Qu'ran,' Nick says, barely concealing his amusement, 'you would have to wear gloves while touching it, or listen to an audio edition.'

'No problem,' Burkett says.

'And your reading would have to be supervised, in case you had plans to desecrate the book by urinating on it or throwing it in the fire.'

The idea of such desecration causes Akbar to moan and beat his fist against his own chest. The others watch in silence.

'Does he honestly think I'd do that?' Burkett asks.

Akbar scowls at the fire, as if searching there for smoldering pages.

Sajiv tries to ease the tension by smiling and patting Akbar on the shoulder. He sloughs past the fire, stepping over the stack of dirty bowls. He delves into his rucksack and produces not a Qu'ran but a box of polished wood. He removes the lid and unfurls two strips of intricately embroidered fabric. On the fabric he sets out clusters of wooden pawns, each crafted in the shape of a different type of fish. The largest pieces, one black and one white, are cycloptic sharks – the god Samakersh in his dual forms of good and evil. Sajiv explains that the game pieces have been in his family for many generations. The game is called chaupar.

At first Akbar is reluctant to participate in a game with pagan tokens and a board in the shape of a cross. Formed by the intersection of the two embroidered strips, the cross seems to bother him far more than the draftsmen, but Sajiv convinces him that chaupar pre-dates Christianity.

Within minutes Akbar is staring at the pawns in deep concentration. Burkett and Nick watch while their captors play. The room is silent except for the crackle of the fire and the tap of the ivory dice against the stone floor. Toward the end of the game Nick gets up and lights the gas lamp.

It is Akbar who asks Burkett and Nick to join in, the game being better suited to four players than two. This was likely Sajiv's intention all along, but Akbar needed to come to the realization on his own.

Nick picks up the game far more quickly than Burkett, as if remembering it rather than learning it. Burkett isn't surprised to be a slower learner – he refuses to feel embarrassed. Having never been one for games, he would certainly avoid this one if there were any reasonable alternative.

As they play into the night, the others disappear into the game. Where is the appeal? It's as if they see in it some mystery – a puzzle demanding to be solved. More likely, the difference lies in Burkett himself. As he's known since boyhood, he lacks something of that competitive urge possessed by most men. He is in the minority here: the three of them bend so far over the board that their heads nearly touch.

His aversion to games is yet another difference between him and his brother, who in college could spend hours playing cards. It dawns on him that beyond the superficial resemblance Owen had more in common with Nick than with his own twin. Did Owen and Nick think of themselves as brothers, in a religious sense? Perhaps 'brethren' would be the more appropriate word.

How could such close companions in youth become so distant as adults? Owen might have begun the process of estrangement – by winning the greater share of their father's love, or by being the better wrestler, or even by turning to Christianity, but Burkett has greater cause for guilt. Sleeping with Amanda Grey created a chasm between him and his brother that could never be bridged.

He should have put a stop to it that weekend at the lake house – not when he got up and went to her room, but earlier that same day, before the not quite accidental encounter in the hallway that led to their kissing. Better yet he should have stopped himself months or years earlier, at whatever point they began to joke, even affectionately, about Owen behind his back – laughing at his moral rigidity, his seemingly obsessive-compulsive work ethic. Burkett should have seen the different paths laid out before him. He was the spitting image of the man she loved, but without that exhausting expectation of holiness, without that unique gift Owen had for making the people around him feel inadequate. Long before that perfidious consummation they forged a bond under Owen's very nose, convincing themselves all the while that they weren't morally deficient after all, that in fact they had advantages over Owen – advantages of insight and wit and world experience. And Owen's obliviousness to their developing attraction was yet another example of that naïveté they found at once so endearing and so annoying.

Burkett slept with her even when he knew his brother truly loved her. It was all so long ago, yet he had half expected to find among his brother's belongings some memento of the woman who came between them.

During the game, Burkett's eyes keep drifting to the single wall decoration, a photograph pinned up where Akbar sleeps: a masked Islamic militant pointing a rocket-propelled grenade toward the sky. He's studying the hand-drawn decorative border when he realizes the others are waiting for him to roll the dice.

'One of his friends?' he asks, nodding to the photograph.

Nick's interpretation obviously does away with the sarcasm. He speaks of the photograph in an admiring, even fearful tone. Akbar nods, clearly pleased with his photograph, but it is Sajiv, impatient to go on with the game, who has to tell them that the masked warrior is Akbar himself.

The following week, when the boy and the woman return, Burkett and Nick are sifting the tiny stones from a bag of rice. An old newspaper keeps the rice out of the dirt. Akbar, who is out hunting, has meticulously blotted all human faces from the advertisements and pictures.

The boy has a new pot of stew, the woman another basket. Burkett glimpses an edge of the burqa just as Sajiv shuts the door.

From the basket Sajiv takes a scrap of paper with a few handwritten lines. This method of communication seems remarkably primitive given the Heroes' reputation for clever cyber attacks. Locked in a metal box in the cowshed is a satellite phone – Burkett saw it when they unpacked the car – but for now the jihadists seem to prefer passing notes, any of which could mean death: *Kill the Americans. Photograph their heads.*

But Sajiv refuses to share the contents of the latest missive. He folds it into his pocket, dismissing their pleas with a shake of his head and a half smile. Nick presses him with questions. Any news on the ransom negotiations? What about their request for books? When will they be released? Sajiv shrugs. He knows nothing. All he can do is promise to tell them immediately if they're to be killed or set free.

Burkett takes little comfort in this. If the death order comes, he'll fight his way out of this place. He tells himself it is better to die fighting. Besides, Sajiv would expect him to fight. It seems to Burkett that Sajiv would either refrain from telling him or kill him at the very moment of receiving the order. So what good is the promise?

For now, Sajiv assures them, negotiations are in progress. The ransom must be agreed upon. But with whom are the jihadists negotiating – IMO? How much would IMO be willing to pay? To afford the ransom, no doubt exorbitant, would they have to lay off workers? Shut down some medical clinic? Burkett regrets his lack of connections, a wealthy donor to make a contribution on his behalf. It wouldn't be unreasonable for IMO to stall: they'd gain time for raising money, time for the ransom to drop. Two men cost more than one: surely IMO would prioritize Nick over Burkett. Would they purchase freedom for one and not the other? Would they hold out for an execution?

Akbar announces his arrival by tossing a gutted marmot on the floor near the fire. It seems he expects Sajiv to prepare the animal for cooking, but since their neighbors have provided stew, there's no point in taking the trouble, at least not tonight. Akbar only recognizes this after setting aside his rifle and dousing his face from a bucket of water. They have no freezer, no salt for preserving meat. He glares at the pot of stew, and for a moment seems ready to kick it over. Instead he takes the unappreciated marmot and hurls it over the wall of the compound.

Burkett and Nick have formed sketchy portraits of their captors: Sajiv, who worked as a bricklayer on an American-funded project but turned to jihad when the government in the north humiliated his family by filming his younger sister with drones. Sajiv on the whole seems less interested in wielding a gun than simply studying the Qu'ran. His hardbound volume, given to him by his father, is adorned with intricate tessellations of gold on a background of dark blue. He hopes one day to teach in a madrassa, which doesn't strike Burkett as much of an aspiration, since Akbar seems to have graduated from one without knowing how to read. At least that's what they gather from his audio version of the Qu'ran, and his request for Sajiv to read aloud when the player runs out of batteries.

Akbar's surly detachment falls away when he's given a chance to boast of singlehandedly killing over a hundred members of the Khandari special forces in six different battles. Burkett and Nick are skeptical, even if the facial scar adds an element of authenticity. It seems odd for such a great warrior to be relegated to guarding prisoners. On the other hand, the guarding of prisoners might not be such a menial assignment if he were expected to torture and murder them as well.

16

Burkett lies on his back with his eyes closed. The silence in the courtyard must resemble that of a monastery. He is attuned to the faintest scrape of stone or snapping twig in the woods outside the wall. Scissors snip from across the courtyard, when Akbar begins trimming Sajiv's beard. It is about time for Voice of America, but Sajiv's radio has run out of batteries.

He envisions an operating room. On blue-draped tables gleam the rows of instruments he needs for a laparoscopic gastric bypass. Yesterday it was a cholecystectomy. His mind seems to be working on parallel tracks: one listing the steps of the operation, the other recreating the sights and sounds. But today he has trouble sustaining the dream. To keep himself focused, he introduces a series of complications – unexpected bleeding, a cardiac arrhythmia (which in reality would be managed by an anesthesiologist), and a malfunctioning bovie that sets the drapes on fire.

Maybe he should feel guilty for having so much useless time, when time has been cut short for his brother. Or furious that these fanatics would turn what time he has into a means of torture.

He abandons the surgical conflagration when he hears Nick beginning his daily push-ups. Burkett sits up and watches, irritated by Nick's rigid technique. The way he keeps his body straight and times his breathing, he could be a fitness instructor in a video. When he finishes the first set, dirt clings to his moist skin at the hairline. It reminds Burkett of their captors after prayer.

A month has passed since they arrived at this moldering compound. At first, when Nick began his workouts, Akbar in particular found much to ridicule, but today he spares only a glance from the delicate work of clipping Sajiv's beard.

Between sets Nick leans against the wall with his eyes closed and his head bowed. Whatever the benefits of prayer, perhaps for Nick it serves also as a means of avoiding conversation. How can the two men, in such close quarters, go so many days saying so little? Burkett waits for the mumbling devotions to fail, the performance to fall apart. At some point, Nick will have to open his eyes and face the reality of their situation.

What could he possibly be saying? A problem with prayer would be the difficulty of composition, not having enough to say. Or perhaps Nick merely sits there repeating himself. Perhaps he recites the Lord's Prayer over and over again. Or something shorter, simpler: *Lord be with me, forgive me, be with me, forgive me.* Perhaps God hears the intentions rather than the words.

When Nick resumes his push-ups, Burkett does a set of his own. He strains to reach thirty, well aware of the sloppiness of those final repetitions – his body angled at the waist, his head too shallow. During the break that follows, Burkett expects some comment from Nick, but no words pass between them. Nick doesn't even acknowledge Burkett's exertions, except to do him the courtesy of lengthening the period of rest. But it's still not long enough for Burkett: the next set, he fails to reach even ten.

How he's weakened over the years, the muscles atrophied to fat. A hundred push-ups came to him so easily when he was a wrestler. It was part of his daily warm-up before practice.

'In college we used a deck of cards,' he says.

Nick nods. 'We did that, too.'

'Face cards and aces twenty.'

'We counted the aces as twenty-five,' Nick says.

'That's impressive.' He should leave it at that, but he goes on: 'It was something we did on our own, above and beyond the two daily workouts with the team.'

Such boasting, it seems childish even as he speaks, and more so in the silence that follows. Who knows what Nick endured as a Navy Seal? Whatever the hardships of college wrestling – the incessant workouts, starving to make weight – at least no one was trying to kill him.

In the following days, Burkett finds in push-ups another way of passing the time, creating noise. But they serve yet another purpose, one he doesn't immediately recognize, and when he does he keeps it to himself. What he wants is to wrestle them – either Akbar or Sajiv, but preferably both, though once he beats the first he's unlikely to have a shot at the other. Akbar is the one he'd like most to manhandle – first Akbar, the warrior, and then if possible Sajiv, the intellectual. He doubts either of them actually murdered his brother, but the circumstances seem designed for revenge: that these particular jihadists would happen to be wrestlers.

In his mind he sees the two of them at the roadside with their Kalashnikovs, watching Owen bleed to death.

He can't imagine entering the ring in his present condition. It's been years since he last broke a sweat from physical exertion. He'll never again know the strength of a college wrestler – not at this age, not without the driving presence of his brother.

It takes him six days to match Nick's two hundred push-ups in thirty minutes. Another week and they add sit-ups and squats, and later wall-sits at one-minute and eventually five-minute intervals. For endurance they resort to jumping jacks and imaginary jump rope. Their endless laps in the courtyard draw outright mockery from Sajiv and Akbar. The Americans running in circles like dogs chasing their tails. Burkett would like nothing more than a long distance run, but their few daily excursions outside the compound are limited to the noisome pit where they relieve themselves, or the stream where they bathe and fill buckets.

Inevitably each tries to outlast the other – two men in their thirties trying to validate the training of their younger days. The ex-Navy Seal versus the ex-college wrestler, each with his own repertoire of brutal exercises, such as Burkett's one-legged wall-sits or Nick's flutter-feet. The mindless strain permits a kind of escape, at least from the boredom, and while he likes Nick well enough – on some level even respects him – he's beginning to realize that exercise is the only thing keeping his chronic irritation at bay. If nothing else it creates a point of shared interest. Something to talk about for two men who otherwise have nothing in common.

Aside from the occasional buzz of a drone, the threat of violence has become almost abstract. It's been only two months since they witnessed a man's severed head. Burkett has to search for the name. Tahir, a lawyer. The head seems to have receded into a haze of memory, an image that comes uninvited, a lolling orb with pale lips and bared teeth. The rest he can't bring into focus – not even the eyes, if they were open or closed. He'd ask Nick, the only one he could ask, but the question would come across as ghoulish or perverse. Why would anyone want to remember such a thing?

If Nick is any indication, Owen must have spent countless hours in prayer, but Burkett never witnessed a single moment of it. Or maybe he did without being aware of it. He tries to imagine how his brother looked while praying. Did he take on the same posture and expression as Nick, who sits Indian-style with his hands resting on his knees, with his eyes closed, head tilted back, and lips twitching inscrutably?

He recalls those words from his brother's notepad: *Grant me the words to pray as You'd have me pray.*

He hopes a memory of Owen in prayer will come back to him, a moment forgotten, but the strangeness of seeing someone in prayer isn't something he would forget.

Owen tends to appear when Burkett's thoughts are elsewhere, as if the memory were jealous for his attention. There are innumerable memories of Owen, but separate from those memories is an idea of him, a presence that seems to operate of its own accord. Like a spirit coupled to Burkett's mind, tampering with it, shuffling memories like playing cards, and saying *Remember this* not as a question but as a command.

A day comes when Burkett feels prepared to wrestle. He's lost weight from the exercise and meager diet. His body has hardened, lean and agile, and in his limbs and trunk he recognizes hints of that old strength. For the first time in years he thinks he could hold his own against his former self.

Akbar and Sajiv face each other shirtless and barefoot. The distance between them widens then narrows again with grunts and slaps. Knees dip toward the ground, hands fumble for purchase. Moments of tense equilibrium are punctuated by bursts of activity.

After watching for a time, Burkett approaches and asks for a bout. He pantomimes by bending his knees and gripping an imaginary opponent, even while Nick interprets the request. Sajiv seems to consider it, but Akbar takes obvious offense, turning away and spitting in disgust. Constant sin has left Burkett unclean, as evidenced by his foul odor and even rumors of seizures. The taint of sin might infect them like a disease, and cause them to suffer epileptic fits in this life and who knows what deprivations in the next. On the day of reckoning, Akbar would hate to give up any portion of his reward just because he'd agreed to wrestle with some infidel.

Sajiv brings up another point: given the blackness of Burkett's soul, and Islam's mandate to destroy sin, could they justify fighting him without intending to kill him? To wrestle Burkett would create a moral dilemma they would rather avoid. Burkett catches a glint in Sajiv's eye, a hint of amused sarcasm, but in Akbar's grim expression he finds nothing to match it.

'Come on,' Burkett says, almost pleading. 'You think you can beat me?'

Akbar reaches for his Kalashnikov before even hearing Nick's interpretation.

'All right,' Burkett says, backing away.

For the rest of the day he sequesters himself in the basement chamber, emerging only for food and a trip to the septic pit. Nick goes about his usual exercises, but Burkett refuses to participate. After dinner, when Nick tries to coax him into a game of chaupar, he says he'll only play when Sajiv and Akbar agree to let him wrestle. But he can't follow through on his threat. Since the game calls for either two players or four, a boycott on his part would have the effect of excluding Nick, who enjoys the game more than any of them.

That night his brother appears to him, a face hovering in darkness. Burkett begins to speak, to offer him the promise of revenge, but all of a sudden it strikes him as ridiculous, this idea of vengeance through wrestling. What does he hope to accomplish? Does he think he can catch Akbar in a stranglehold and choke him to death before Sajiv intervenes? Will scoring back points or takedowns ease his brother's suffering in death?

His brother reaches for him but the space between them begins to widen. *Come back*, Burkett says, but realizes he is the one drifting away. His brother recedes into the distance till all he can see is a pinpoint glint from the ring on Owen's finger, the ring that was stolen, either by the ones who killed him or the ones who handled his body.

Burkett was there when Owen discovered that ring on a creek bottom almost twenty years ago. They were jogging in the woods near their high school when Owen stopped and knelt by the shallow water. Burkett remembers the mud seeping away to reveal the silver in Owen's palm. A sign, Owen called it, apparently having prayed for one just as the gleam caught his eye.

He had the ring inscribed with a verse from the Bible. Burkett can't recall the words – something from Genesis, when Jacob wrestled with God. Or was it an angel? That story always had great importance for Owen: wrestling as a collision of the human and divine. He seemed to think of himself as a man wrestling with God.

Lightning flickers in the high window on Nick's side of the chamber. Rain patters against the corrugated roof of the cowshed. He's heard about the wet season, ponderous and unceasing: over a hundred inches of rain. They'd expected to be released before the start of the monsoon. It was over three months ago that they were taken – he never imagined their captivity lasting this long – and with the rains limiting travel, especially in the mountains, they probably won't be leaving for another month at least.

Boredom never came easily to him. His entire adult life – which is how he thinks of his years after wrestling – he's devoted almost all his waking time to sex and work – and the invariable problem of keeping himself drunk enough for the former and sober enough for the latter. But now there is nothing: a void of meaningless hours. Till now he's operated under the assumption that he would return to his former life and simply pick up where he left off. He'd accept the required rehabilitation, reclaim his medical license, and take a job in private practice. Now he wonders if anyone is even negotiating for their release. He could spend years in this intellectual vacuum, gradually regressing, forgetting. How long would it take to lose his skills as a surgeon? To become officially incompetent? He wonders what he's forgotten already.

If a man is defined by his work, then what is Burkett becoming? A master of push-ups and chaupar, a practitioner in the science of boredom. Even if they released him tomorrow, he suspects he would return home a different person. He sees his life as a succession of identities: brother, wrestler, and surgeon. Now he is none of those things. He is a captive, nothing more. Who will he be when he re-enters the life he knew?

17

It is the second week of near constant rain. Burkett sits shirtless at the fire picking mud and carob seeds from his beard. The bones of a rabbit, Akbar's latest kill, lie in the embers, the head still impaled on the gambrel.

The rain hasn't prevented Akbar from hunting. Quite the opposite, his excursions have become more frequent since the basement flooded and the four of them began sleeping in the same room. Almost every day he goes out with his cherished hunting rifle, which he keeps sheathed in plastic, presumably till he finds something to shoot.

For the third day in a row, Nick is trying to convince Akbar to take them on his next hunt. They need fresh air, which is to say they need a break from the damp walls, the cramped quarters – and the growing tension not just between captors and prisoners but also between each man and the other three. They have another reason as well, one they have no intention of sharing: they want to get the lay of the land. It's becoming clear that sooner or later they will have to escape. They have no plan as yet, but with each passing day a successful ransom has begun to seem less likely.

Akbar makes the same arguments he made yesterday and the day before that. The third time around Burkett can almost get by without translation: hunting requires silence and deep concentration. It is a solitary endeavor, a form of prayer. The Americans would block prayer with their sacrilegious conversation, and even if they were able to keep quiet, their stench alone would warn away any game.

Akbar's face discourages anyone from taking his last point for a joke. And it's probably true that the Americans must bear a greater portion of blame for the odor, that rank combination of mold, dampness, and stale sweat. Part of the problem is their continued insistence on daily exercise even in the mud and rain. Every afternoon they bathe in the stream, but weeks have passed since their last bar of soap ran out.

Sajiv, who typically remains silent during Akbar's arguments on hunting, suggests that the smell of the Americans might serve as an advantage. The animals might mistake them for potential mates.

'Why not take them with you?' Sajiv asks.

'Do you not appreciate having meat in your stomach?' Akbar says.

'Of course I appreciate the meat.'

'If you want so badly for them to experience hunting, why don't *you* be the one to take them? You can bear responsibility for them in the wilderness.'

'I have no interest in spending all day in this downpour.'

'What if Tarik came and found no one in the compound but you?'

Akbar falls silent and looks at Nick as if suddenly aware of the ongoing interpretation. It occurs to Burkett that Nick's knowledge of Arabic probably adds to the stress of the crowded conditions – at least for Sajiv and Akbar. For four men sharing fifty square feet – and much of that space taken up by the fire pit – a language barrier might have offered a modicum of privacy.

But when Akbar speaks again, his voice is louder, his words slower, as if he were attending to the need for interpretation – as if he wanted the Americans to understand.

'Suddenly your real motive is clear,' he says.

'And what might that be?' asks Sajiv.

'You want to be left alone with your pornographic magazine.'

Here Sajiv looks at the Americans and says, 'I have no such magazine.'

'You would multiply your sin by lying about it?'

'You're the one who is lying.'

Sajiv goes outside and walks through the rain to the woodshed and returns with a plastic bag. He pulls out a glossy magazine entitled *Hollywood Extra!*, the text a mixture of Arabic and English.

'Is this the magazine you call pornography?'

Akbar gasps at the cover, which shows the actress Jennifer Aniston in a bikini and Angelina Jolie and Scarlett Johansson at some movie premiere. After staring for a moment, he averts his eyes, spits in the fire, and says, 'Filth.'

Sajiv displays the magazine not for Akbar, but for the Americans. He flips through the pages, offering glimpses of actors on red carpets, stills from popular movies. He gives an uncomprehending shrug, as if to ask, *Does this look to anyone like pornography?* Unlike the newspapers reviewed by Akbar, none of the photographs in the magazine have been defaced.

Women in gowns and bathing suits: is it pornography or not? Both Akbar and Sajiv seem now to await a verdict from the Americans, as if they were experts on the subject. Clearly it isn't, not by Burkett's standards, but the challenge faced by Nick is how to phrase it without causing offense.

'Best not to say one way or the other,' Burkett says.

Nick thinks for a time before diplomatically suggesting that many of the women are in fact dressed in revealing outfits.

But this isn't enough for Akbar, whose eyes twitch side to side as if searching for some means of expressing his outrage.

'What if Tarik saw this vile material?' Akbar asks.

'That name again,' says Burkett. 'Who is Tarik?'

'No idea,' Nick says.

Akbar stands and kicks the leather sack that holds Sajiv's chaupar set. The tokens scatter, at least one bouncing down the stairs and landing with a splash in the basement.

'Didn't you come here to escape the temptations of the world?' Akbar asks Sajiv. 'The internet cafés and whorish American women? What today a man tolerates, tomorrow he accepts and the next day embraces.'

Sajiv goes down to retrieve his game piece from the ankle-deep water.

While he's gone Akbar opens the magazine to a random page and what he sees there, a woman in a bathing suit, prompts him to cast the magazine into the fire. When Sajiv returns, he shows no surprise at the sight of the burning pages. Akbar, perhaps feeling guilty for what he's done, helps him collect the remaining game pieces.

It is past midnight when the boy, who they now know is called Asadullah, arrives from the neighboring compound. They haven't seen him or the woman since the rains began. Though out of breath and soaking wet, he shows no interest in drying himself by the fire. The words come in frantic bursts. Burkett catches *saa'idni* and *mareedh*. Help me, sick. Nick fills in the details: a baby with vomiting, fever, and bloody stool.

'How old?' Burkett asks.

'Six months,' Nick says.

'What color is the vomit?'

'Bilious,' Nick says. 'You think it's volvulus?'

'I don't know,' he says. 'Maybe intussusception. We should go there.'

Sajiv begins lacing his boots, but Akbar makes no move to leave. He sits there watching, his eyes bouncing from Nick to the boy. He seems to be withholding a decision even though there is nothing to decide. A baby is sick – how could they not help? Perhaps Akbar suspects a conspiracy between the Americans and this teenager. It would be no less plausible than the escape tunnel he occasionally searches for under their bed mats.

Akbar declares that Burkett must see the baby while Nick stays behind. To treat the child Burkett needs Nick to interpret, but there is no point in arguing: Akbar would never betray such weakness as a change of mind.

So Nick interrogates the boy, who is clearly impatient to return. The symptoms began mid-afternoon, perhaps twelve hours ago. There were only two episodes of bloody diarrhea, but the abdominal pain and tenderness seem to have become worse.

'Was the stool watery?' Burkett asks.

The boy shakes his head.

'Was it like jam?' he says.

'Jam?' Nick asks.

'Just ask him – like cherry jam.'

The boy nods.

'Does he feel better after throwing up?'

'It's a she,' Nick says. 'She felt better at first, but now she's inconsolable.'

'And still vomiting.'

'Yes.'

'Did she have a recent infection?'

'No.'

'No diarrhea or vomiting before today? Maybe an upper respiratory infection?'

'No.'

'Why can't they take the child to a hospital?'

'They tried,' Nick says. 'The girl's parents left this morning, but there was a bridge.'

'The bridge was flooded?'

'I don't think so,' says Nick. Again he questions the boy and says, 'The bridge was destroyed – bombed.'

'Isn't there another way?'

'It would take three days by mule cart. The parents thought the best thing was to come home.'

It is Sajiv who accompanies Burkett to the neighboring compound. Following the boy, they move at a brisk pace despite the rain and mud – a half mile in ten minutes.

The mud brick walls of the compound have a foundation of piled stone. Burkett and Sajiv stand in the rain while the boy fumbles with the door. Not a sound from inside: the silence is a problem. If there is a sick baby, they should hear it crying, even over the patter of rain.

In the main room Burkett counts twelve people, standing women and seated men. The crowd would account in part for the warmth – not unpleasant after the rain – and that same ammoniac smell which seems to exude from anyone who spends long enough in these mountains, Burkett himself included, but so much stronger here in this concentration of sweating adults.

The women wear burqas, but not Asadullah's sister, the mother of the sick child, who wears a headscarf and a loose fitting shift over what looks at the ankles and wrists to be a bright red sweat suit. Burkett sees at once what he couldn't have seen on her visits to their compound – that she is attractive, perhaps even beautiful. Or is this merely an effect of her eyes in the firelight, the glow of her tears? Whatever the case, he should stop staring, even if this is the first female face he's seen in over three months. A moment passes before he even notices the baby, her daughter, lying in a crib.

Sajiv joins the four men who sit on a rug as far as possible from the crib and its feminine penumbra. The men are puffing on the rubber tubes of a *hookah*.

Burkett washes his hands with a rag in a bowl of warm water. No one speaks as he nears the crib. He looks at the mother, who nods her consent.

The baby is dying. He suspects intussusception, a condition where the walls of the bowel roll inward to form an obstruction. He feels the racing pulse and taut abdomen. The child is dehydrated and possibly septic as well. He bends close to the skin of the child's belly and draws its scent into his nose. In an extreme case of bowel necrosis he might detect a faint odor of putrescence – it would imply a dire prognosis – but here he smells nothing of the sort.

One of the women hands him a white plastic box, a first aid kit. Inside he finds a cracked tube of Neosporin, a stack of gauze, several bandaids, and a syringe of epinephrine. None of this can serve him here. He might have come up with a creative use for the epinephrine if it weren't expired by over a year.

The fire pit has a wall to contain the cinders. Smoke escapes by means of a metal pipe, a kind of makeshift chimney attached by brackets to the mud brick wall. One of the women stokes the fire with an old-fashioned wooden bellows.

The bellows give him an idea, perhaps ridiculous and even irresponsible. And yet he can't help but wonder: could he reverse the obstruction by pumping air into the child's colon, the very method used by surgeons in any American children's hospital? Those surgeons of course have the advantage of imaging guidance and pressure control. Burkett couldn't hope for a bellows with a check valve or pressure gauge – he might as well ask for a fluoroscope. And he can tell by just looking that the wooden spout would be too large for the child's anus.

But some kind of lubricant could make the difference – animal lard or soap, perhaps. Worst case, he could use water. He reckons that a mere anal fissure would be an acceptable risk, a small price to pay.

He picks up the bellows, drawing curious looks from those faces he can see. An air enema. Of course it also carries a risk of perforation – a significant risk, given the lack of pressure control – but the child will most certainly die if Burkett does nothing at all.

He wishes Nick were here to interpret. He looks at the child's mother and tries to explain the problem of bowel obstruction. The typical metaphor for intussusception is 'telescoping bowel'. He stands in the space between the men and the women. With his hands he tries to pantomime the enfolding colon, increasingly aware of an unbridgeable gap between hand gestures and bowel anatomy, and when the mother lifts one of the baby's hands and gives him a questioning look, it occurs to him that she thinks he's trying to describe some defect in the child's fingers.

An old man, the grandfather or great-grandfather, says something, and others flash skeptical glances. Sitting beside him, Sajiv looks for a moment like he might come to Burkett's defense but instead wraps his lips around one of the tubes of the *hookah*.

'It's a matter of plumbing,' Burkett says, but of course none of them understand. He speaks from habit, a rote metaphor to explain problems of stool, urine, and blood.

A matter of plumbing. It suddenly strikes him as odd how much of human physiology can be reduced to substances moving in tubes.

He tries for a simpler pantomime, the motion of writing, the fingers of one hand scribbling against the palm of the other. This prompts obvious confusion and even vexation among the family members, until one of the women produces a leather-bound book and ballpoint pen. He can tell from her arthritic hands that she is old. The book is a diary of some sort, with pages of calligraphic script running right to left.

Three women in burqas face him like a row of pawns on a chessboard. Only moments have passed, but he couldn't even say which of them gave him the diary – the one in the middle? He flips to a blank page at the end and begins drawing. He kneels to rest the pages against his thigh. For his rune-like infant, composed of lines and circles, he receives quiet nods of understanding. He adds a coil of intestine and points to his own abdomen and says, 'Bowel.' Lower on the page he draws the sinuous ileum merging with the larger, sack-like colon.

The men in the corner have gotten to their feet, leaving Sajiv alone with the dubious grandfather. The boy, Asadullah, watches in silence as Burkett again draws the same segment of bowel, the ileocecal junction, but the ileum, now massively distended, protrudes into the colon and tapers to a point.

Burkett shows what he's drawn to the baby's mother. She turns to Asadullah, who takes the book and begins explaining. Burkett can tell from the way the men nod and whisper among themselves that the boy is known in the family for his superior intelligence. The boy displays the book for the others, his finger tracing the intestines. He holds his breath and inflates his cheeks. Burkett might have doubted the boy's interpretation, but he sees the puffed cheeks as a hopeful sign, perhaps an analogy for obstruction: the distention that results from downstream blockage.

When the boy finishes, he turns to Burkett with a look that seems to ask, Now what?

Burkett stands over the crib with the bellows and tries to convey the idea of an enema, gesturing between the spout and the baby.

'Do you understand?' he asks the boy.

He sees he doesn't, so he takes the notepad and flips back to his first drawing. Between the stick legs he jots a triangle for the bellows and an arrow for the direction of air.

The boy studies the illustration and with a nod turns to address the others. Burkett has no way of knowing how much he actually understands. But then one of the women retrieves a clay jar from another room – a lubricant of some kind, similar to petroleum jelly. The concept of lubricant far exceeds what Burkett could draw or sign, but somehow this woman recognized his need for it. He nods his thanks toward the screen of her burqa. Ever so slightly the burqa tilts: a nod in return, or perhaps he imagined it.

The boy smears jelly on the spout of the bellows. Burkett takes one of the infant's flaccid wrists and feels for the pulse, but it is so weak he has to palpate the neck instead. The heart rate is well over a hundred beats per minute. Babies tend to have elevated heart rates at baseline, and Burkett is no pediatrician, but what could this be if not septic shock?

He turns over the child. The mother shifts the head from left to right. To face Mecca, Burkett realizes: a Muslim should face Mecca when she dies.

He spreads the buttocks and studies the anus, the tiniest hole, smaller than he expected. Even with lubricant, the spout of the bellows is just too large. The damage would be far worse than a fissure.

The hardest decision for a surgeon, the decision to do nothing: but now that bacteria have infested the blood, now that the child is sure to die, why subject her to the trauma of the bellows? Why risk a painful treatment for a condition she might not even have? There is no question of bowel obstruction – but caused by what? He can't be certain of intussusception. She could have some kind of mass or, as Nick suggested, a volvulus, a twisting of the bowel.

Intussusception. Perhaps he was too easily convinced by the jam-like stools – words he himself proposed. Perhaps he's committed the error of molding the evidence to fit the diagnosis. He heard only what he wanted to hear. Even the bellows, so appealing for their novelty, seem to have reinforced his diagnosis of choice.

Asadullah is kneeling between Sajiv and the old man. The old man listens, nods, and with a curved dagger slices one of the rubber tubes from the *hookah*.

It is a good idea. There is no reason the length of hose couldn't be used for an enema. The boy tugs on the rubber segment to prove its strength and elasticity. The relatives mumble their approval, clearly impressed by the boy but uncertain why Burkett isn't convinced, as if the doubt in his face were connected solely to this particular piece of tubing and not the entire course of treatment.

He wishes the boy would forget the bellows and the rubber tube. A harebrained treatment, he thinks: more likely to perforate the colon than bring any relief to the child. By adding pressure to an already distended system, Burkett risks killing the baby faster and more painfully. But the enthusiasm of Asadullah only kindles the general sense of hope, the notion that Burkett has the power to make things better. Before his arrival, most if not all of the relatives had accepted the futility of the case, probably even the mother, but now they have the bellows and tubing, tangible objects to which their hopes can attach. They have intestinal doodles and ideas of plumbing.

After the child dies, will they keep his drawings? Will they cling to them out of hatred, grim mementoes of that arrogant American who made a diagnosis, proposed a treatment, and then did nothing? He must remember that these people, some of them at least, are in league with the Heroes of Jihad. The baskets of food, the handwritten notes: this compound represents a link in that chain of communication and supply. He wonders if his treatment of the child could have an impact on his captivity. His actions tonight might make it easier for someone down the line to kill him or set him free.

The boy, having partially submerged the tube, begins blowing bubbles in the bowl. One of the men pats the boy's shoulder and mutters some comment of praise that prompts chirps of agreement from the burqas.

But not from the mother: she remains silent. Staring at Burkett, she offers little more than a nod, and when he meets her eyes, he sees the despair he would have expected, but also something else, perhaps a kind of rage. He can understand why she would be angry, why she would even despise him for hesitating to save her child. She could easily take a cynical view of his reluctance, seeing it not as overly careful medicine but as a cold bargaining tool, perhaps a means of hastening his release or gaining some advantage from his captors. Or even worse, she could accuse him of withholding care simply out of spite. Could she even imagine such a thing? Would any human be capable of that kind of cruelty, using the life of a baby as a tool for vengeance?

He reminds himself yet again: the baby will die either way.

The tube fits easily over the spout of the bellows. He lubricates the other end and slides it into the infant's anus. Without being asked, Asadullah squeezes the buttocks together to keep the tube from slipping free.

'You should think about medical school,' Burkett says, even though no one understands.

Very slowly he compresses the paddles. When he removes the tube, gas squeaks from the anus, followed by a spurt of blood and mucous. Again he inflates the bellows and inserts the tube. Drawing together the paddles this time he feels a greater resistance but of course there is no way to check his progress. All he can do is imagine the length of colon on fluoroscopy: the gas inside pushing against that knot of mucosa, a gentle unfolding till all at once the blockage disappears.

Afterward, when he turns the baby onto her back, he feels no change in the distended abdomen. It is impossible to know if he perforated the colon or reduced the intussusception – if there was an intussusception at all.

He sits on the floor by the crib. His eyes meet Sajiv's, who remains seated on the far side of the room with the old man, the grandfather now asleep.

Women pass in and out of an adjacent room. Through the open door, Burkett can see curtain partitions, a bare mattress separated from the dirt floor by a sheet of plywood.

The mother of the child jerks free when one of the men tries to lead her away from the crib. It must be her husband, wanting her to come to bed. Burkett can guess the nature of the dispute: if she wants to stay with her baby – and keep the baby near the doctor – she'll have to spend the rest of the night in the same room as a man from outside the family. It is bad enough that Burkett has seen her face. In the end the husband goes to bed – rather selfish, Burkett thinks – while two of the other women lie on wool blankets by the fire. It seems their purpose in staying is to ensure the virtue of all present, particularly the young mother. Would she otherwise suffer the wrath of her husband? From the way he grabbed her wrist and tried to pull her away from the crib, Burkett suspects she will suffer his wrath no matter what.

Now he faces that ancient task of the physician. He must serve as a witness to death. Having exhausted all means of treatment, he will sit here till the child dies.

Sajiv disappears into a separate part of the house with Asadullah and the grandfather. Burkett lies on the floor and tries to sleep. Whenever he opens his eyes the mother is seated in the same place, both hands draped through the bars of the crib. After perhaps an hour, he walks over and checks the baby's pulse and presses the abdomen. Nothing seems to have changed, but he takes that as a good sign. He would have predicted death by now.

At the bustle of morning prayer, the mother is holding a wet rag, dripping water through the baby's trembling lips. The pulse is stronger. There is a new warmth to the fingers and toes. Burkett can see now there is no longer any need to turn the child's face toward Mecca.

On the walk back he and Sajiv pass a coffee tree recently struck by lightning. The crown is nearly bisected, charred limbs on one side and green leaves on the other. It must not have taken long for the rain to extinguish the fire. Despite the persistent downpour, Sajiv takes the time to gaze at the tree from different angles. Burkett doesn't understand what he's saying till he forms an imaginary camera with his hands. Sajiv wishes he could take a picture of the half-burnt tree.

18

Sajiv wakes Burkett before sunrise. By flashlight they climb the stairs and pass through the room where last night their game of chaupar lasted into the late hours. Sajiv and Akbar's mattresses are stacked neatly against the wall. Outside he can hear Akbar in whispered conversation, but the other voice he doesn't recognize.

Down the corridor light seeps from a curtained doorway. Burkett wonders what waits for him there, in the largest room of the compound. With growing fear he envisions spotlights for a video production, an online decapitation. They'll demand that he read some statement on the secular government in the north, or perhaps American foreign policy, but he won't give them the pleasure. He will wait for his death in silence.

A grumble in the distance at first sounds like one of the drones. Or a chainsaw, for cutting off his head.

Akbar has to prod him along. Almost against his will his thoughts take the form of prayer: *Be with me, give me strength*. But whom is he addressing? How illogical to believe in God simply because you think you're about to die. And yet he prays: *If I live through this, I'll believe in you*.

Sajiv pulls back the tattered curtain to reveal a man at a table, the room illuminated by an electric lamp. No Islamic flag, video camera, or masked gunmen. An extension cord leads out the window. The grumbling sound,

Burkett realizes, must come from a power generator.

The man at the table – in his late twenties, Burkett would guess – is writing on the lined page of a leather-bound journal. Burkett studies the hands, half expecting the amputation stumps of a bomb-maker, but the man's fingers are intact. Burkett stands behind an empty chair, waiting while the man finishes whatever he's writing.

'Forgive me,' the man says. He rises and places his right hand to his chest.

'No problem,' Burkett says. Now that he's dodged a video execution he can hardly resist the lure of sociability.

'Call me Tarik,' the man says.

Tarik: he remembers the name. This is Akbar and Sajiv's superior. The neatly trimmed beard, the prayer cap and wire-rimmed glasses, slightly crooked, remind Burkett of those clerics in the news, the ones who inspire terrorists, although his western attire – khakis and white oxford shirt – and knowledge of English suggest worldly experience beyond the usual madrassas and militant training camps.

A *high value target*, he thinks as he sits in one of the injection molded plastic chairs.

'It's a pleasure to make the acquaintance of a fellow physician,' Tarik says.

'You're a physician?' Burkett asks, stunned.

'Internal medicine,' he says, with a slight bow, as if to say, *At your service.* 'But Allah willing, I will some day have an opportunity to train as an endocrinologist.'

Burkett stares, making an effort to keep the smile from his lips.

'Where did you do your training in medicine?' he asks.

'A perfectly reasonable medical school and residency program, I assure you.'

Is he actually a physician? What could possibly be the advantage of such a lie? No, he thinks: the name is a lie but the profession is real.

'How is your stay with us?' Tarik asks. 'Have you been comfortable?'

He hands Burkett a Snickers bar with English writing on the wrapper. 'Have you been well provided for?' he asks.

Burkett shrugs and tears open the Snickers and bites off the top third.

'When can we go home?' he asks through the mouthful of candy.

'That's precisely why I've come,' Tarik says, as if struck by the coincidence of their shared interest. 'Yes, I'd very much like to arrange for your safe and joyful return to – Mejidi-al-Alam? America? Where is home for you, Dr Burkett? Online it says you are a fellow in plastic surgery in Atlanta, but this information seems out of date.'

Burkett flinches at the thought of his truncated fellowship, though now it seems like a distant memory.

'I'm in transition,' he says.

'The perfect time for a visit to our beautiful island,' Tarik says with a smile.

The tone is off-putting: sarcasm in the form of sympathy. Burkett focuses on the man's brown eyes, slightly magnified by the lenses.

'What about you?' Burkett asks. 'Do you practice medicine – or does jihad take up too much of your time?'

'I've had to put my career on hold,' he says, taking the question at face value. 'You're right, though, with all this ...' A weary sweep of the hand seems to indicate not just Burkett but also Sajiv, who sits just outside the door, as if together the two of them embody the stress of the whole enterprise – the ransom negotiations, the management of prisoners and guards.

'When this is over,' Tarik says, 'I hope to advance my training.'

'A fellowship in endocrinology,' Burkett says doubtfully.

'Why not?' he asks. 'I've done quite a bit of research on diabetes.'

'Terrorism might not look so good on your CV.'

'Call it what you will,' he says with a shrug. 'Our goal is to gain independence for the Islamic Republic of South Khandaros. When that happens we will put aside our weapons, beat our swords into plowshares, as they say.'

'I'll believe it when I see it.'

Tarik's face suggests that he doesn't care whether Burkett believes it or not. He smoothes a sheet of paper on the table and takes a moment to study what looks like a typed list of names with handwritten notes in the margins.

'And who is Véronique?' he asks, attempting the French pronunciation.

Véronique. The sound of it, that dip of the middle syllable, brings to mind an image of her pale thighs on either side of his. With the memory comes a spark of desire, quickly suppressed by the sound of Tarik clearing his throat.

'Your few other phone contacts include the first and last name, but for this Véronique, you used the first name only. Why is that, Dr Burkett?'

'I never learned her last name,' he says. 'She was a woman at my hotel.'

He tries to remember how many names he had programmed into that phone. Surely no more than four or five – he'd only just bought it at the airport.

'Did you and Véronique enjoy a roll in the straw?' He expands this last word as if to make room for both humor and disapproval.

'It's hay,' Burkett says. 'The expression is *roll in the hay*. If you want to know her last name, call her and ask. You have her number.'

'Is this woman a spy, Dr Burkett?'

'No,' he says. But of course there's no other answer he could give. If she *were* a spy, she certainly wouldn't have told Burkett.

'Are *you* a spy, Dr Burkett?' The smile that accompanies this question seems isolated to Tarik's mouth. His eyes retain an air of detachment, as if he were looking not at Burkett but considering the possibility of a diagnosis.

'How could I be a spy?' Burkett says. 'Do you think I came here to collect data between appendectomies?'

'The CIA has been known to use medical personnel to procure DNA and other forms of biological data. Perhaps you're part of a covert operation to sterilize Muslims.'

'Surely you don't believe that?'

'No, I personally do not, but there are many intelligent, godly men who do.' He nods toward the doorway, where the curtain exposes a sliver of Sajiv's foot with its cheap sandal of plastic and foam.

'You can see how this idea would have appeal, Dr Burkett, can you not? Muslims being emasculated by Christians? Here is this occupying force, these crusaders, not just invading our very homes on a daily basis, but also depriving us of the very means of creating a home.'

'There is no occupying force,' Burkett says.

'I seem to see white faces everywhere I look.'

Burkett thinks of Captain Rich. 'The few Americans are here as advisors and nothing more.'

'And what do you think of this fleet of drones? That is the real occupying force. Through the stupidity of Djohar and his secular advisors, our island now plays host to an army of foreign robots. The Khandari special forces might think they control these robots, but of course there is an override switch in the Pentagon. These are CIA drones first and foremost.'

Such idiocy, Burkett thinks, and from a physician no less. But he shouldn't be surprised: he's heard equally moronic conspiracy theories from paranoid doctors in the States.

Tarik goes on: 'South Khandaros, you must realize, is a sovereign nation, at war with a so-called Republic whose military has been usurped by foreigners – namely the CIA with its drones. Do you not see how these drones not only kill but cause shame by invading people's very homes?'

'You're talking about a democratically elected government buying products from legitimate businesses and other democratically elected governments. If you have a problem with the drones, why not ask your representative to write laws that limit the government's power of surveillance? If he won't do that, then vote for someone else, or run for office yourself.'

'Democratically elected, you say? A better description of the government in the north would be *democratically engineered*. The majority of those in parliament were installed by enemies of Islam. The Khandari special forces have been infiltrated by foreigners, secular cowards who would prefer to use robots to fight their battles.'

Burkett's eyes drift over the mural of paradise, the green hills and blossoming trees. There are gashes in the plaster where Akbar took his hunting knife to the pair of human faces.

'But there is reason for hope,' Tarik is saying. 'Let me show you.'

From his satchel on the floor he takes out a laptop and turns the screen toward Burkett. Camcorder footage shows the rooftops and streets of the capital from a high vantage, probably a minaret. The camera zooms in on a line of traffic, and a red circle highlights the middle of three SUVs with tinted windows.

'This was yesterday,' Tarik says. 'The president of North Khandaros sits in that car.'

A policeman steps between concrete barriers as if to cross the street. Burkett has seen enough of the *fedayeen* videos not to be surprised by the explosion that engulfs the SUV and the policeman. After a caption in Arabic, there is a slow-motion replay of the officer approaching the vehicle. An instant before the explosion, Burkett notices a twitch in the cluster of pixels at the end of the policeman's arm – perhaps the thumbing of the detonator.

'It still needs editing,' Tarik says, as if Burkett's disgust were purely aesthetic. 'A triumphant soundtrack.'

'I'm curious about something,' Burkett says. 'If someone in your family were to die, would that person be buried or cremated?'

'Buried, of course.'

'Why is that?'

'In Islam it is forbidden to burn the body, which is the seat of the soul.'

'So how is it that your suicide bombers can justify incinerating themselves? Is that not a form of cremation?'

'You're falling victim to the fallacy of legalism. There is religious law, and then there is Allah's law. Usually these things are in harmony, but not always. Allah's law always trumps ideas of morality. Look at the hero in this movie. A strict legalist might accuse him of the sin of lying. He dressed as a policeman, did he not? But when Allah commands that something be done, then by definition it is impossible for that action to be sinful. It was the same when he commanded Abraham to sacrifice his son Ishmael. When Abraham lifted the blade, intending to kill, was he a murderer or a righteous man?'

'A lot of people think they know the will of God.' Burkett nods toward the laptop. 'If that's his will, then he's not the kind of God I'd want to believe in.'

'Does Allah care what you want to believe? Is Allah some politician who would change his character in order to win your vote?'

Burkett doesn't reply. It's pointless arguing with someone who sees intransigence as a divine virtue.

'When will you let us go?' he asks.

'It depends on IMO,' Tarik says. 'I expect it will happen a week from Monday, when our representative meets theirs. On that day, if all agree to the terms, you will be released.'

'What are the terms?'

Tarik's fingers patter against his keyboard. So far from internet access, Burkett wonders what he could possibly be typing. Or it could merely be a way of ending the conversation. Without looking up, Tarik summons Sajiv, who draws back the curtain.

Burkett turns on his way out and says, 'Do you know anything about my brother?'

'He was killed for spreading Christianity.'

'Who killed him? I'd like to know the individual responsible.'

'Had I been directly involved,' Tarik says, closing his laptop, 'you might have paid a ransom instead of attending a funeral. I've argued many times, regarding missionaries and journalists, that killing them is hardly profitable.'

'Whoever killed him stole a ring from his finger.'

'Probably what you'd call foot soldiers – men acting on their own, certainly not on orders from me or anyone else. But what do you expect? Your brother was spreading Christianity, trying to convert Muslims. To my mind that is worse even than castration or rape.'

'I'd like to know the names of the foot soldiers. They stole his car and laptop as well.'

'How should I know which man shot him, or which man searched his pockets or took his silver?'

'How did you know the ring was silver?'

He shrugs, his irritation obvious. 'Men make the mistake of killing an American rather than holding him for a ransom, but Allah provides financial rewards in the form of a ring, a computer, even a vehicle.'

'Where is the ring now?'

'Perhaps it was sold on the black market. Silver has great value these days.'

Sajiv holds his AK-47 by the barrel. It would take him precious seconds to aim and pull the trigger, by which time Burkett could have Tarik in a choke hold. Perhaps Sajiv would refrain from firing, for fear of hitting Tarik by accident. But how long would it take to kill a man by strangulation? Too long, Burkett thinks. Sajiv would have enough time to cross the room and shoot him point blank.

'Dr Burkett,' Tarik says, 'I almost forgot.'

He lays a ziplock bag on the table and pushes it toward Burkett.

'What's this?'

'I understand you were very sick on your arrival. You even had a seizure?'

Burkett steps closer. In the bag he counts twenty round pills.

'Diazepam, ten milligram tablets,' says Tarik. 'Enough to last until your release. I'm happy to offer you this, one physician to another, as a gesture of hospitality.'

Burkett's fingernails scrape the table as if he were sliding downward and searching for some purchase. The bag crumples in his fist. He glances at Tarik's blank eyes and courteous smile, and suppresses an impulse to thank him.

Tarik has brought an elderly companion. Sajiv and Akbar call him *Maalim*, teacher. Their first lesson takes place in the courtyard, the very spot where most days at this hour they would probably be wrestling. Burkett and Nick go about their usual calisthenics, drawing harsh glances from Akbar and Sajiv, who seem to regard push-ups as the height of impropriety in the presence of such distinguished guests. Burkett and Nick have no qualms about causing offense, and the teacher even vindicates their exertions with a point on physical fitness in Islam.

'A strong Muslim is a good Muslim,' Nick interprets between isometric rows.

Just then Akbar answers a question incorrectly, and Maalim slaps him across the face for the third time in an hour. Sajiv, for his part, has yet to be slapped, but his kinship with the teacher – apparently they are cousins of some kind – would suggest an element of favoritism.

'He's quoting the Qu'ran,' Nick says, releasing the broomstick. '*Man was created weak and impotent.*'

They rest their backs against the base of the wall, pretending not to realize they are the topic of discussion, but Tarik, who squats alone with a book, watches them with a knowing expression.

'Without discipline and effort,' Nick mumbles, 'men are slaves to their desires.'

Akbar is obviously distracted, repeatedly glancing at the sky for fear of drones. Is Tarik aware of the danger implied by his visit? Perhaps he even takes pleasure in his status as a high value target. For the moment Burkett too finds himself searching for a black speck against the clouds.

'We bear what he calls the seal of obstinacy,' Nick says, still immersed in the words of Maalim. 'Which essentially means we are incapable of righteousness.'

'So there's no point in even trying,' Burkett says.

'Wait, he's quoting another verse: *There is a veil over their ears and their eyes, and a painful torment awaits them.*'

'Another set?' Burkett picks up the broomstick.

'To them we have hardened hearts,' Nick says, reaching for the stick, 'like Pharaoh in Exodus.'

'What do you mean?'

'When the Israelites were slaves in Egypt, God demanded their freedom, but at the same time hardened Pharaoh against setting them free.'

'Why would he do that?'

'There was a series of plagues, each worse than the last, and finally God killed the firstborn son in every Egyptian home.'

They face each other, with legs interlaced, and pull the broomstick in strained mimicry of rowing.

'What kind of God would kill children?' Burkett asks, his arms trembling from the effort.

'You have to see it in context.' Nick's back tilts toward the ground as he pulls the broomstick against his chest.

'Is there any context that makes it okay to kill children?'

'The Egyptians,' he says between breaths, 'had a policy of killing every male baby born to the Jews.'

'So this was a form of revenge?'

Nick doesn't speak till they've completed the set. 'The Egyptians were killing *all* male infants. God's decision to kill only the firstborn could be seen as merciful.'

'Merciful? To me it sounds completely insane. You're telling me God hardened Pharaoh's heart, kept him from freeing the Jews, just so he could avenge the Jews by killing untold numbers of Egyptian children?'

'Not necessarily children – just the firstborn male in every household. Not all households had a firstborn male. There's no way to know the exact number, but given the high infant mortality rates —'

'Do the numbers even matter? One household or twenty, murder is murder.'

'Before Christ, justice came only through revenge. God took on that burden by sending his destroying angel.'

'Is revenge a burden when you're all-powerful, or when you can't be hurt in return?'

'God could, and did, allow himself to be hurt in return – in the person of Jesus Christ.'

'There's an obvious difference between allowing your son to be killed for some greater good, and having your son murdered in his sleep.'

'Do you think the creator of the universe is subject to the very laws of good and evil that he himself created? Or that he isn't capable of ensuring perfect justice – in this life or the next – for every last human life? You see death as the greatest evil, which is perhaps natural for a physician, but the death of the body is inevitable.'

'So what you're saying is that God will murder each and every one of us.'

'No,' Nick says, 'we are immortal, each and every one of us.'

'That's the sort of idea that makes it easy for people to kill and die in the name of religion,' Burkett replies.

Brushing away sweat, Nick leaves a streak of mud on his forehead.

'There is little so honorable as dying in God's name, but nothing worse than taking others with you.'

Burkett glances at their captors, who seem to be eavesdropping. It is a kind of reversal: the speakers have become the listeners, with Tarik in the role of interpreter. How long has Nick been aware of it? Was he speaking to them all along? Perhaps he sees all of this, his abduction and imprisonment, as an opportunity to evangelize – a mission field all his own.

That night Burkett lies awake thinking how much easier he could sleep with the help of the diazepam. He begins to draw the bag from its cleft, but the sound of crumpling plastic stops him. He can't bear the thought of waking Nick and having to explain himself.

He drapes his arm across his eyes, as if to block out the darkness. He summons the face of his father. What comes to him, from some deep recess of memory, is a face contorted by grief: his father kneeling before his mother. 'I'm sorry,' his father says. It is a scene from Burkett's childhood, a moment he never remembered till now. His father reaching for his mother's hands and his mother snatching them away in disgust.

Why would this memory visit him now, uninvited, so many years later? Would a dose of Valium send it back where it belongs? Would Valium protect him as well from this new vision, an image of Tarik pointing a Kalashnikov down at Owen's dying body, or the thought that at that very moment Burkett himself lay half drunk on a couch in Atlanta?

He remembers how he and his brother, in the wake of their mother's death, were convinced of a supernatural connection unique to identical twins – that the ghost of the one who died first would have to linger till the other died as well. When he has an urge to reach for the pills, he can almost feel his brother's hand gently restraining him.

19

After Tarik and the teacher leave, Sajiv affirms the promised ransom and release, scheduled for next Monday. Burkett can tell that Sajiv and Akbar also yearn for an ending. They too are captives in a way, no doubt bored out of their minds. As freedom nears, Akbar and Sajiv dispense with friendly banter, even during the nightly games of chaupar. It makes Burkett wonder if the two of them have anything in common beyond chaupar, wrestling, and radical Islam.

But the day of their promised release passes without any sign of action, as somehow they knew it would. Akbar and Sajiv receive no word to suggest any progress in the ransom negotiations, if any such negotiation has even occurred.

That night Burkett opens his stash of diazepam. He works carefully to keep Nick from hearing the crinkle of plastic. Two pills he swallows dry, but he feels nothing, so an hour later he takes two more. He begins to wonder about the expiration date, the efficacy of these unpackaged pills, but then it seems that his very blood has the lightness of a cloud. He closes his eyes and thinks: *This should get me through the night.*

In the morning he has to fight the urge to take another. Just at night, he tells himself, to help him sleep. Given the short supply, only twenty pills, he needs to pace himself. Four in one night was too many. The problem is resistance – he needs a relatively high dose to feel the effect. But the next night he fares better, managing to fall asleep after two pills, but now he has only fourteen left.

Seven nights, he tells himself. He sees in the pills a new countdown to freedom. It is simply unimaginable that his captivity would outlast his supply of drugs. One way or another he will leave this place before he runs out of diazepam.

He and Nick have long considered the possibility of escape, but now their speculation takes the form of planning. Nick is confident he can keep them alive for as long as it takes – the days or even weeks they'll need to reach a friendly town or military outpost. They'll head north, following the stream as long as possible and avoiding people at all costs. By language alone Nick might pass for a local, but his blue eyes and reddish-blond beard would betray him at any distance close enough for conversation.

How to break out of the compound? Akbar and Sajiv, their only guards, leave their weapons unattended while wrestling. The key to the front gate stays with Akbar, connected to his wrist by a lanyard, but when he wrestles he leaves it under one of his sandals. They could try to steal it, but the closer they come to Akbar, the greater the likelihood of physical conflict.

'I've never killed a man,' Burkett whispers as they walk down to the stream, 'but how hard could it be? Collapse the airway, break the neck, pinch off the carotids.'

'You won't be killing anyone.' Nick glances back at Sajiv, who has knelt to pet the mangy fur of a stray dog and feed it a scrap of flatbread.

'You don't think I've handled it very well,' Burkett says.

'Handled what?'

'The loss of my brother.'

'I can't be a judge of something like that.'

In the short silence Burkett feels the weight of judgment. What Nick should have said was, *There's no right way to handle it.*

'I probably sound like I'm the first person who ever suffered,' Burkett says, 'but that's the thing about pain: it makes you so self-centered.'

No, he thinks: what you sound like is a bad self-help book, some dime store guide to coping with grief. Why are you trying to impress Nick with your attempts at psychological insight?

Behind them the hungry dog shambles toward Akbar, who gives it a vicious kick and then shoots it in the flank. The gunshot still rings in Burkett's ears as he and Nick, under Akbar's watch, drag the carcass to the septic pit. Burkett wonders why they don't skin the animal and cook it for dinner – the very idea, he realizes, being a gauge of his hunger – but it seems Akbar and Sajiv would rather starve than eat a dog.

Burkett and Nick return to the bank, take off their clothes, and step into the stream. During the monsoon it rose as high as Burkett's waist but today it comes only to his ankles. The new package of soap left by Tarik contains only two small bars, so to conserve it Akbar has all but banned its use – at least for the Americans – and he refuses now to make an exception, even though Burkett has blood on his hands from the dead dog.

'I won't be a part of any plan that involves causing harm,' Nick says.

'What, are you a pacifist?' Burkett asks.

When Nick doesn't answer, he says, 'You're kidding me. I thought you were a Navy Seal. You killed people – presumably.'

'My faith has evolved.'

His silence on past killing seems to confirm it.

'How can you preach non-violence while paying off a warlord?'

'Ex-warlord,' Nick says, as he climbs out of the water and sits on a stone to dry. 'And that was for the protection of others in the clinic – our employees and patients.'

'But God himself caused harm,' Burkett says, using mud from the creek bottom to scour his hands. 'All those plagues in Egypt, the killing of the firstborn sons.'

'You're talking about another dispensation, human history before Christ.'

'But how can such a violent God then turn around and command non-violence?'

There seems to be no point in discussing religion with Nick, and yet the following morning Burkett has a memory from his days of Catholic school. It feels like just the argument he needs to change Nick's mind. 'Didn't Jesus say something about a sword?' he asks. 'A sword rather than peace?'

'*I bring not peace but a sword*,' Nick says. They are sitting in the shade of the courtyard, under a tarp meant to hide them from satellites and drones. Burkett's eyes follow Akbar and Sajiv as they wrestle.

'That verse is often taken out of context,' Nick says. 'Jesus was warning his apostles about the violence and hatred they would suffer for his sake.'

'How do you know? You could just as easily see it as a command to take up your sword and fight.'

Nick shakes his head. 'Read the chapter, Matthew 10. He's telling them to walk away from persecution, shake the dust from their feet.'

'My brother wasn't a pacifist —' Burkett stops himself from adding *was he*? He knows it for a fact: he has the evidence of bruised knuckles and a fractured metacarpal.

'Owen believed in just war,' Nick says. 'The possibility of it, I mean.'

Burkett imagines the two of them, his brother and Nick, talking over these questions late into the night. At the moment Burkett can't remember ever talking with his brother about anything other than wrestling.

'Just war,' he says. 'That's just what I'd like to give that guy Tarik.'

Only a few yards away, their captors roll in the dirt. They have worked themselves into a tangle, each gripping the other's leg as their bodies writhe together like some deformed beast in the throes of death. Akbar is the better wrestler, even if their grappling has devolved into a kind of mechanical routine in which neither can gain an advantage. It is the very problem Burkett and his brother faced in college: having wrestled each other so often they were essentially neutralized by familiarity.

All that day the question of escape lingers in Burkett's mind. Even if he managed to get the key by stealth rather than force, Akbar would notice it gone before they had a chance to use it. Maybe the best option would be to take one of the rifles while the men wrestle and shoot them dead, both of them. A simple enough task for a Navy Seal, perhaps, but Burkett has never held a Kalashnikov, much less fired one. He has an image of himself fumbling for the safety catch while Akbar picks up the other rifle. Would Nick just stand by and watch while their chance slipped away?

So what is left but to wait out the ransom or make a *non-violent* escape? Rather than bother with the key they could climb to the roof of the cowshed and jump from the eastern wall – its lowest point but still as high as fifteen feet. They could make a rope from their blankets, but the only place to tie it would be the old antenna bolted to the northeast corner. To reach the antenna, they'd have to traverse the top of the wall, which is barnacled with shards of glass.

Another possibility: they could simply flee the next time they're allowed outside the wall, whether to bathe or fill buckets or use the septic pit. That way they wouldn't risk injury by jumping from the wall. But it's during those forays outside that they're under the closest scrutiny. If they slipped out during the night, whether by stealing the key or climbing the wall, they'd have a three- or four-hour head start, which could make all the difference.

Judging from the marmots he kills, Akbar is something of a marksman, or at least a reasonably accomplished hunter. As they discuss their options that night in their keep, it is Akbar's cherished weapon that concerns Nick – an L96 sniper rifle favored by the British military, accurate at great distances even without the telescopic sight. Akbar knows the terrain – he'll expect them to follow the stream north. All he has to do is get them within shooting range. Perhaps they could find a way to sabotage his rifle without his knowing.

'The firing pin or the bullets,' Nick says. 'It's not a bad idea. But if he catches you near his stuff—'

Burkett remembers how Akbar didn't hesitate to shoot that dog. 'So it's the roof of the cowshed,' he says. 'We drop from the eastern wall and hope not to get hurt.'

'We have to put as much distance as possible between ourselves and Akbar's rifle.'

'What if I wrestled him?' he asks.

'What good would that do?'

'I could take out his knee.'

'What do you mean, take out his knee? I told you I'm opposed to any kind of violence.'

'How do you define violence?'

'Violence I define as intentional harm.'

'Wrestlers get hurt all the time.'

'But not intentionally.'

'Think of it this way. I'm causing a minor injury to keep us from being shot.'

'The degree of injury makes no difference.'

'So if someone were about to shoot a child in the head, you wouldn't try to stop him?'

'Ideally I'd do everything in my power to stop him without hurting him.'

'Why do you say ideally?'

'Because I've been known to give in to lesser impulses. If someone I love were threatened, I probably wouldn't handle it very well.'

'You said you paid the warlord to protect others.'

'A precautionary measure.'

'A compromise, even if no one was hurt. If you hire men with guns, you have to allow for the possibility of someone getting shot.'

'In the States, I benefit from police protection, even if I oppose their use of firearms. I see the bodyguards as no different – a police-like deterrent for the protection of those working at the clinic.'

'You're basically permitting the use of physical force. That's what I'd call a compromise.'

'More like a strategy.'

'Think of this as my protection. A *strategy* for the protection of someone else.'

'I can't agree with it, but no more can I stop you.'

'I just need your help convincing them to let me wrestle.'

In the silence that follows, Burkett listens for the sound of Nick's breathing, which seems to have a different rhythm during prayer. Or so he imagines: it comforts him to believe he can tell exactly when Nick is praying. In truth he has no idea.

He'll wrestle Akbar – he'll take out the knee. And during the night, while their jailers sleep, they'll climb the wall and head north. A simple plan, but with so many potential problems. The wrestling is the part that worries him least. It won't be difficult to injure Akbar's knee, at least he doesn't think so: it's a matter of using his shoulder as a fulcrum. The greater challenge lies during the night, in sneaking out to the courtyard without waking their captors.

He pokes his finger into the crack in the wall. What if he drugged Akbar and Sajiv? He could grind the remaining diazepam into powder and mix it into their food or drink. There's more than enough to knock out two men. The problem is he rarely handles their food after it's cooked. Though he and Nick often have the task of separating small stones from the rice, it is always Akbar who ends up cooking it.

As for the water, he can't imagine gaining access to both of their canteens at once. He could spike the water he brings up from the stream, but the buckets hold at least a gallon, and even if he could concentrate the solution without arousing suspicion, there is no guarantee that both Akbar and Sajiv would drink from that particular supply.

Quietly he opens the bag and presses two of the pills against his tongue. Only eight remain – still enough, he tells himself, to sedate their captors. He would expect a relatively low tolerance in a devout Muslim. Akbar and Sajiv are unlikely even to have tasted alcohol.

He wonders where the use of drugs would fall in Nick's pacifist scheme. At what point would sedation qualify as poisoning? Nick would need to know about it – he'd have to be warned of any contaminated food or water, but Burkett has yet to tell him about the stash of diazepam. Would Nick believe him if he lied about the original number of tablets? It is a conversation he would prefer to avoid.

20

It is late afternoon. Akbar and Sajiv circle and feint, gripping each other by wrist, elbow, or neck – coming together and backing away, again and again till Akbar makes a lunge for Sajiv's knee, tall gangly Sajiv, who turns away, prying at Akbar's locked hands in the rising dust.

As Burkett nears the edge of their imaginary ring, he's keenly aware of Nick's eyes at his back. Today might be his last chance to wrestle Akbar before Tarik comes back. It was three days ago that they learned of Tarik's impending return, but not till now have Akbar and Sajiv taken the time for one of their grappling sessions.

The challenge now is convincing Akbar. If Nick refuses to make the argument, Burkett will have to resort to some sort of provocation, a shove or a leg attack. No question, Akbar is the sort to respond to brute force. The language barrier hardly matters when picking a fight, but Burkett must strike a fine balance, since picking a fight with Akbar could get him shot. Better to reason with them, and for that, he needs Nick.

When Akbar and Sajiv notice him on their side of the courtyard, they break apart and glance toward their guns.

'Let me wrestle,' Burkett says.

They stare, uncomprehending. Placing his hand to his chest, he speaks the Arabic word for wrestling: '*Sura'a.*'

Sajiv says something Burkett doesn't understand, drawing a rare laugh from Akbar.

'He's making fun of you,' Nick says. 'The words for 'wrestling' and 'seizure' sound similar, more so with poor pronunciation.'

Akbar is no longer laughing when he speaks. 'It would be unwise to wrestle an epileptic,' he says with Nick interpreting. 'The condition results from demon possession, and the demon could pass from one body into another.'

'My seizure wasn't caused by a demon,' Burkett says.

Akbar smiles with self-satisfaction and says, 'Drug addiction is itself a kind of demon possession.'

'But when a man's faith is strong,' Sajiv says, 'he should be able to fight demons without fear of possession.'

Akbar scowls in the silence that follows. Now that it's a matter of faith, he can't easily refuse without admitting spiritual weakness.

Perhaps Burkett shouldn't be surprised to find common cause with Sajiv. Have he and Nick not privately referred to him as the ironic Islamist, as the movie fan? He remembers that burnt magazine. Perhaps by trapping Akbar in a theological quandary – and bringing him down a notch as a wrestler – Sajiv hopes to have his vengeance for all those bikinis and sequined gowns lost to the flames.

'Why can't you be the one to wrestle the American?' Akbar asks.

'Because you're the better wrestler,' Sajiv says. 'A man doesn't go into battle with his practice sword.'

Akbar gives a reluctant nod. He has no choice but to agree.

After a pause, he takes a different tack. 'It is far too dangerous,' he says. 'Tarik would be furious if the American were hurt or killed.'

'Does a great wrestler not have the skill to refrain from hurting or killing someone?'

C. E. SMITH

'Shouldn't I wait for Tarik?' Akbar asks.

'Why not now?'

'Tarik will have a camera,' he says. 'If I'm going to humiliate the American, we should film it and put it on the internet for Muslims all over the world to see.'

'Perhaps it would be best to keep it private,' Sajiv says. 'While our brothers in jihad might be encouraged to see you make a fool of him, others might see it and think of you afterward as unclean.'

'The only opinion that matters is that of Allah.'

'That is true, but you should consider your prospects in marriage. What man would risk exposing his daughter to filth and disease?'

'I will die in battle long before I take a wife in this world.'

'There won't always be a battle for you to fight,' Sajiv says. 'Now that so many of the politicians opposed to us are dead, it is only a matter of time before we have achieved our goal of independence.'

'I will travel across the sea. There are always infidels to fight.'

'You've never left Khandaros in your life,' Sajiv says. 'Wrestle him today, and let his defeat be the stuff of tales rather than spectacle. Did the Prophet need video recordings to spread his message?'

'I won many matches in America,' Burkett says, 'where the wrestling is the best in the world.'

Sajiv laughs at the claim. 'Arabs are the best wrestlers,' he says. 'Persians second.'

'It disgusts me to touch him,' Akbar says. 'Physically as well as spiritually, he is unclean.'

'If you're worried about hygiene,' Burkett says, 'I'll make it easier for you by bathing with soap.'

At this suggestion Sajiv smiles and unlocks the cowshed. He retrieves one of the precious bars of soap and tosses it to Burkett. The four men

189

walk down to the stream, which during the night has risen as high as Burkett's calves. Nick too leaves his clothes on the bank in order to take advantage of the rare availability of soap. Burkett lies on his back in the running water, his lips and nose breaking the surface when he needs to breathe. He keeps his eyes closed and his ears submerged, and it feels like genuine solitude. If all goes as planned and tonight they escape, the one thing he might miss is the stream.

They are back in the courtyard. Burkett offers his hand, but Akbar ignores it and without warning dives for his ankle. Burkett should have expected a fast start. He shrugs off the leg attack, and another that immediately follows – both of them sloppy and ill-conceived.

In Akbar he senses the panic of one who realizes he's outmatched. Akbar seems oblivious to Sajiv's commentary, whether advice or ridicule. Burkett recognizes the word 'American'. No doubt they're surprised this middle-aged American knows how to wrestle.

Their arms locked, Burkett observes the predictable shifts and compensations. He feels the old thrill of near effortless control in the face of an opponent's exertions. It puts him in mind of the Penn State wrestling room, when he'd go against one of the high school recruits: so easy for him, almost playful, yet such a challenge for the recruit. And of course, back then, he never meant any harm. Not till now has he ever wrestled with the desire to cause injury.

While Akbar flails he can almost relax, expending strength only where necessary. He could score at will, but he's waiting for the perfect moment.

In order to take out the knee, he needs Akbar's weight on the left foot, the toes rotated outward. He tries different combinations of taps and drags, and even when he finds just the right set-up he rehearses it yet again. It is perhaps a minute into their bout – by now Akbar is gasping for breath – when Burkett drives his shoulder against that knee. The sound of snapping ligaments – two ticks in rapid succession – reaches Burkett's ear like a secret signal tapped on a wall and meant only for him.

When Burkett wakes he has no recollection of being struck in the head by Sajiv's Kalashnikov. He might have doubted Nick's account, but how else to explain the swelling in his scalp? Or the fierce headache, unrelenting and even audible, as if he could actually hear the razor blades scraping the inner surface of his skull. He holds a hand before his eyes to make sure he isn't seeing double.

The way Nick tells it, the otherwise taciturn Akbar lay there writhing in pain, shouting obscenities (Satan would defecate on Burkett's grave) while Burkett made unconvincing apologies. Sajiv ordered Burkett and Nick to kneel with their hands behind their heads while he tended to Akbar. Sajiv palpated the knee and tugged on the ankle despite Akbar's obvious pain with even the slightest movement. Burkett, apparently, couldn't resist laughing at this travesty of orthopedic examination, and Sajiv must have heard it, for that was when he picked up his weapon.

'Maybe you were right,' Burkett says.

'About what?'

'The benefits of non-violent escape.'

He covers his eyes – not from shame, but to protect them from the afternoon sunlight that has just brightened the high window. Light sensitivity, he thinks: *photophobia*. A sign of subarachnoid hemorrhage.

The way Nick describes it, Burkett lifted his hands in surrender, saying, 'Wait, it was an accident', before the butt of Sajiv's rifle slammed into his head. He dropped to an elbow, raising the opposite arm in feeble defense, but that didn't stop Sajiv from striking him again.

'And you were out cold,' Nick says.

'Nothing else? I didn't do anything else?'

Burkett strains to remember, but the memory doesn't exist, and the effort only compounds his headache, as if by trying to remember he were aggravating a splinter in the very depths of his brain. Again sunlight prods him from the small window and when he turns away even the afterimage causes pain.

In the hours that follow he feels a renewed urgency to escape, to carry out their plan as soon as possible now that Akbar is incapacitated. But he can't seem to stay awake. His mind registers the passing time as a series of images: Nick inflating a blood pressure cuff, pulling off his soiled pants. Tarik shining a penlight into his eyes and later hanging an IV bag. Tarik saying, 'We'll have you delivered home in no time. The negotiations are going very well.'

And then the room is crowded with men he doesn't recognize. His eyes drift from one Kalashnikov to the next before settling on what appears to be a scimitar – an ornate weapon with some kind of inscription on the blade. Darkness settles till all he sees is that blade, like a sliver of light in the very shape of the narrow opening between his eyelids.

He has a sense of falling in darkness. His flailing hands discover what he takes for a branch or a vine, but in fact it's a human arm, and he's wrestling with a man, both of them in free fall. He's desperate to take out the knee, but it seems impossible without the ground for traction. And as they wrestle, he realizes his opponent has the exact same goal, both of them using the same techniques toward the same end, but with no result other than fatigue.

He wakes to the sound of voices from upstairs. He remembers the unfamiliar men standing over his bed. A new complement of guards obviously diminishes their odds of escape. Not that he'd get very far with his head injury, the slightest movement causing exquisite agony. He wants nothing more than to lie in complete darkness.

'How's Akbar?' he asks.

'The good doctor gave him a crutch and a splint,' Nick says, 'probably something for pain as well.'

'How long has Tarik been here?'

'A few days.'

Burkett's eyes trace the catheter from the back of his wrist up to the near empty bag hanging from a pole. He reaches between his legs and touches another catheter that emerges from the tip of his penis and drains into a plastic container at the foot of his pallet.

'Where did these medical supplies come from?' he asks.

'They've been making trips to Allaghar.'

Once again playing the part of Burkett's nurse, Nick has kept a written record of his blood pressure every six hours for the last three days, even through the night. He's also disposed of his urine and vomit, changed the IV bags, and swabbed the Foley catheter with alcohol. The lack of sleep is taking its toll. Already gaunt from the sparse diet, Nick with his bleary eyes looks like he too needs IV fluids.

'They're talking about taking us to another house,' Nick says. 'As soon as Tarik's comfortable moving you.'

'Then we have to run,' Burkett says. 'What if the next house has close neighbors? What if its walls are too high to scale?'

He stops at the sound of footfalls on the stairs. Tarik appears in the doorway, wearing his usual khakis and white oxford shirt, yellow stains under the arms. In his hand is an old-fashioned medical bag.

'I hear you're an excellent wrestler,' he says. 'My friend Sharif would like to take you on when you get better.'

'Bring him on,' Burkett says. He imagines working his way through a series of jihadist wrestlers, one knee at a time.

'Was hurting Akbar part of your plan to escape?' Tarik asks. 'That is what Sajiv thinks.'

'It was an accident.'

'I believe you,' he says, 'but my colleagues argue that your present incapacity would prove otherwise. Had it been an accident, they say, Allah would not have allowed you to suffer punishment at the hands of Sajiv.'

This is typical of Tarik, Burkett thinks: a man who plays both sides, an educated skeptic one moment and a fanatic the next.

'How long before we're released?' Nick asks.

'My friend in the capital only days ago received a reply from the woman journalist,' Tarik says. 'Your people have requested proof of life, which we will provide now that Dr Burkett has regained consciousness.'

'What woman journalist?' Burkett asks.

'Miss Véronique Six,' he says. 'She's been surprisingly reasonable in our dealings.'

Véronique. *The women who sleep with you always regret it.* Which of those women told him that? He doesn't know if Véronique had any desire to see him again, but she certainly has reason now to regret knowing him, or at least sharing her phone number. He hopes her negotiations with the Heroes of Jihad will boost her career, perhaps earn her a book deal.

Simply by placing a hand on Burkett's shoulder, Tarik seems to glide into the role of physician. He listens to Burkett's heart and lungs. He tests his eye movements, light response, and his patellar reflexes.

Tarik does him the courtesy of naming each pill or injection – nimodipine, Bactrim, Lasix, metoprolol, and Ativan. Burkett might object to the dank, unsanitary basement environment – and the lack of diagnostic imaging and labs – but these are the drugs he'd likely receive in a typical American hospital.

'I've titrated the Ativan to accommodate your increased resistance,' Tarik says.

'That's awfully considerate,' Burkett says.

'I'd have confirmed your diagnosis with a lumbar puncture,' Tarik says, 'but Mr Lorie wouldn't allow it. Now that you're in a lucid state, perhaps you might reconsider? I could send the fluid to our new hospital in Allaghar. We could have a diagnosis by the end of the week.'

'No thanks,' he says. Tarik's need for permission suggests not courtesy so much as discomfort with the procedure.

'You are my guests,' Tarik says, 'and I want all of your needs to be provided for, including your health. You should receive nothing but the best care during your stay with us.'

'I want to know who killed my brother,' Burkett says.

'Why, the Heroes of Jihad killed him.'

'I want to know which man pulled the trigger.'

'What would you do if I gave you a name? Would you call the police? Would you track down this man and take your revenge? Futility on one hand and certain death on the other. Can't you see that I'm doing you a great favor by sparing you this information?'

'Is the person who killed my brother in this house?'

Tarik laughs. 'Is this a child's game of Question and Answer? What if I told you yes? It would narrow your search but cause you ever more frustration. You would endlessly ponder each candidate, wondering who it was that listened to your brother beg for his life.'

'Why would the Heroes of Jihad kill him rather than hold him for ransom? There could have been a great deal of money at stake.'

Tarik shrugs. 'Why are you pursuing these questions? Don't you see that the more you know, the more likely you are to die? If you knew the name of the one who killed your brother, wouldn't that man and his friends be less inclined to set you free?'

'You were in charge of the ones who killed him,' Burkett says. 'Or was it you who pulled the trigger?'

'You must accept that some questions have no clear answer. Those men who stopped your brother might have intended merely to take him prisoner, but perhaps things didn't go as planned.'

Tarik starts to go up the stairs.

'You're wrong on one count,' Nick says.

Nick's voice comes unexpected, loud enough that Burkett's headache seems to cry out with every word.

'How's that?' Tarik asks, pausing on the stairs.

'He didn't beg for his life,' Nick says.

'How would you know?' Tarik's laugh sounds forced, as if Nick had touched a nerve.

'He had no fear of death,' Nick says.

'Is that so?'

'He was alive in Christ.'

'No fear of death?'

'None,' boasts Nick. 'Unlike your cowardly *fedayeen* who only find courage in the form of drugs.'

Tarik strides back into the room. Nick begins to stand but Tarik kicks him in the chest. He crumples to the floor, choking with pain and struggling to breathe.

'The only drug addict is the man lying beside you,' Tarik says, 'a man whose brother begged and pissed himself before my very eyes.'

The confession lingers in the silence that follows. Burkett sees himself swinging the IV pole with enough force to stave in Tarik's skull. His hand finds one of the castors, then moves higher and grips the pole. He begins pulling himself to his feet. His eyes blur with pain.

'If he wept and begged, you wouldn't have killed him,' Burkett says. He is thinking of the broken bone in his brother's hand.

'You're wrong,' Tarik says. 'The weeping and begging were so shameful that we had no choice but to kill him.'

'Did he disarm one of your men? Were you the one he punched in the face?'

'I have better things to do than babysit drug addicts,' Tarik says, with a look that seems to mock Burkett's efforts to stand.

'You meant to kidnap him, didn't you? But when he punched you in the face you lost control, just like you're losing control now.'

'Your cowardice will be broadcast to the world,' Tarik says. 'Your families will see you renounce your God.'

Nick's eyes flick between Burkett and Tarik. 'A difference between my God and yours,' Nick says, 'is that his grace would follow me even if I renounced it.'

Burkett shuffles toward Tarik, squeezing the IV pole with both hands as he drags it across his mat.

'That is precisely the problem with Christianity,' Tarik says. 'It gives you permission to sin. The result speaks for itself: entire nations overrun by laziness, vanity, and decadence.'

Burkett feels he's heard enough to bludgeon Tarik, but Nick stands, hunched with pain, and places a hand on the pole, as if to use it for support but clearly also to keep Burkett from taking a swing.

Truly the pacifist, Burkett thinks.

'When do you plan on *broadcasting our cowardice*?' Nick asks, making no effort to conceal his sarcasm.

Tarik turns back to the stairs. 'Perhaps tomorrow,' he says with a shrug, his voice sounding calm and arrogant at the same time. 'Perhaps the next day,' he says. 'You'll know as soon as we cut off the first piece.'

21

Electric light seeps dimly into their chamber. Though Nick is most likely still awake, Burkett ever so carefully withdraws the plastic bag – hoping what little noise he makes is masked by the distant grumble of the power generator – and swallows three tablets.

Nick might see death as gain, martyrdom as a path to glory, but it's Burkett who will die first. Nick has the backing of International Medical Outreach, the wife and friends raising untold thousands for his ransom. It is no doubt obvious to Tarik that one prisoner is far more valuable than the other.

The question plaguing Burkett isn't whether or not he will be killed, but how it will be done. Will he have to endure some kind of torture? *Pieces*, Tarik said. He thinks of Abu, whose severed genitals were stuffed in his mouth.

Will they force him to read some statement? Before, he thought he would refuse, but what would be the point? Refusing would serve only to extend the pain. He'll read whatever semiliterate manifesto they set before him.

Or is the better option simply to fight? If he's going to die no matter what, why should he not attack as soon as they try to bind him? They'll assume him to be incapacitated, but no question, he can muster the strength for a last stand. He would have the advantage of surprise – the sudden transformation from dazed invalid to raging killer. He'll snatch the nearest gun and start shooting.

He remembers Tarik's first visit, the morning he thought he was being led to his own death. He'd made that rash prayer: *I'll believe if you let me live.* He went against his word and now the debt is being called in. It will take all his strength not to make that prayer a second time.

'If they kill me,' Burkett says, 'would you do me a favor and make sure my father in Atlanta is taken care of? He might already be dead, in which case you have nothing to worry about.'

'We'll leave here together or not at all,' Nick says. 'It would be ridiculous to keep us alive this long only to kill us.'

A man with a flashlight and pistol comes down the stairs. Burkett winces and raises his arm to block the light which seems to bypass some key optical filter before directly piercing his brain. It is the same man who has been administering his drugs. He kneels over Burkett and clamps and disconnects his IV and detaches the Foley catheter from its receptacle. With the barrel of his gun he waves Nick toward the stairs.

'Where are we going?' Nick asks.

'Wait,' Burkett says as the man takes his elbow.

He opens the plastic bag and draws out the final three tablets. Nick stands watching him, his eyes expressionless.

Burkett climbs the stairs for the first time in days. He glances into the courtyard, where two of Tarik's men stand over a fire and another squats in the opening of a tent.

He follows Nick down the passage, their escort lingering behind them, just out of reach. He has no plan, just the desire to stay alive and a sudden, inexplicable certainty – perhaps drug-induced – that he will.

Tarik waits in the well-lit room at the end of the hall. The pock-marked mural spreads behind him like the backdrop of a cheap play: the same bright blue stream and green meadow, the same man and woman with their gouged faces. A band of mud, left by standing water and splashing rain, skirts the base of the mural. Burkett imagines it climbing higher, eventually covering the meadow and the stream and the human figures as well.

Akbar waits in a chair, a Kalashnikov in his lap. He wears a brace on his straightened knee, a nylon sleeve with metal rods and hinges. Two chairs are propped before a black curtain, close enough to the wall that no one could fit behind them to cut Burkett's throat. Of course they still might kill him, but at least he'll be able to see it happening.

Tarik stands from his campstool and spreads his arms and says, 'Good morning, my friends. Shall we take another picture?'

Burkett and Nick remain silent. Their escort pulls a black mask over his face and hands Nick a copy of yesterday's *International Herald Tribune*. The mask is worrisome, but surely there would be no reason to time-stamp an execution. Burkett notes a side bar on the front page: KHANDAROS TO VOTE ON SECESSION.

Nick displays the newspaper for the camera. Before taking the picture, Tarik asks, 'Do you still think you understand the *Arab mind*?'

'I don't know what you're talking about,' Nick says.

Tarik nods and the man in the mask punches Nick in the face. Blood drips from his nostrils. The newspaper lies on the floor beside him.

'Let me read what you wrote in your blog,' Tarik says, taking a sheet of paper with printed text.

'My blog?'

'There's something in the Arab mind,' Tarik reads, 'something that makes it more susceptible to forces of violence and shame. There is a tendency among them to respond violently to the threat of shame, sexual or otherwise. Similarly, Arab culture sees violence as a way of making amends for shame.' He looks up from the page. 'What exactly do you mean by the *Arab mind*,' he asks, 'or *Arab culture?*'

Nick shakes his head. 'I wrote that more than a decade ago. I was a different person.'

'You were a soldier then,' Tarik says, 'attempting to understand the men you were killing.'

With a nod from Tarik, the man in the mask unleashes a series of punches. When the chair topples, Nick tries to hold himself upright on the floor, but a kick sends him sprawling. When the man in the mask backs away, there are open wounds on his knuckles. Nick sits up, wiping blood from his face. He spits, rights the chair, and resumes his seat.

Nick says, 'I wrote those things before I knew Jesus Christ as my personal Lord and Savior.'

Tarik shakes his head. 'Of those who suppress faith, the Qu'ran says, *Slay them wherever you catch them.*'

'It also says, *To you be your way and to me mine.*'

Tarik doesn't seem impressed. 'What is worse?' he asks. 'That you would defy Allah by elevating his holy messenger to the status of a god? Or that you would set out to convince Muslims of this polytheistic farce?'

The man in the mask steps toward Nick, causing him to flinch, but instead of punching him merely hands him the newspaper, now torn and begrimed and flecked with blood. Tarik snaps a photograph.

When they take away the newspaper, Nick says, 'I hadn't finished reading that.'

It seems fitting that Nick would discover humor only after having his face pummeled by fanatics.

'Is it true,' Tarik asks, ignoring the joke, 'that you were a member of the Navy Seals?'

Nick stares at the ground before him.

'I understand you were a sniper,' Tarik says. 'Which means you killed men, Muslims, from great distances, where they couldn't see you. This seems cowardly to me, no? A courageous man would make himself known to his enemies.'

Nick spits. 'Is it courageous to strike a man who is your prisoner?'

'Did you shoot these men in the head or heart? Personally, I would aim for the chest, a larger target, but perhaps you had other motives. Perhaps this was the source of your interest in the so-called *Arab mind*. Perhaps your primary aim was to traumatize the brains of Arabs.'

'You couldn't be further from the truth. You're talking to a former soldier, a man who did a job and moved on. Some of my closest friends in this world are Arabs.'

'I too happen to be a marksman of sorts,' Tarik says. 'My father recently built a thousand-yard rifle range in Allaghar. You might even have heard about it. Perhaps you and I can go there sometime and place wagers on who is the best shot.'

'No thanks,' he says.

'In the meantime, I would like you to read a statement. My apologies for the crude penmanship.'

He props a scrap of cardboard against the tripod. Capital letters in black ink fill the space between the torn edges:

THERE IS NO GOD BUT ALLAH AND MUHAMMAD IS HIS
PROPHET. CHRISTIANITY IS A BLASPHEMOUS DISTORTION OF
THE TRUTH CONCOCTED BY SATAN TO LEAD MUSLIMS INTO
SIN. I FORMERLY PREACHED CHRISTIANITY BUT I HAVE SEEN
THAT THE TRUTH MUST BE FOUND FIRST IN THE HOLY AND
PERFECT QU'RAN.

The sign falls and the masked man picks it up and tries without success to brush away the dirt.

'When you are ready,' Tarik says, 'I would like you to begin reading the statement.'

He presses a button on the mounted camera and a red light appears. Nick remains silent, his eyes fixed on Tarik.

'I don't think he wants to read it,' Burkett says.

Tarik turns and asks, 'Do you find this amusing?' He doesn't wait for an answer. 'Very shortly he will beg me to let him read it.' As he speaks his eyes fall to the long-handled bolt cutters on the table beside his papers.

Burkett stares at the tool. The stub blades with their silver sheen look brand new, but the grips at the ends of the pipes are worn from use. Tarik spoke of *pieces*. This must be his instrument of choice.

'Read the statement,' Tarik says.

The camera is still recording, but Nick refuses even to look at the words of the statement. Tarik goes to the door and summons Sajiv, who enters with a handful of zip ties. He keeps his eyes to the floor, perhaps ashamed to look upon his former chaupar companions.

The zip ties, the bolt cutters: Burkett can see where this is heading. He looks at Nick and says, 'There's no shame in reading it.'

'Listen to the wise doctor,' Tarik says. 'No one needs to be hurt.'

'I'll read whatever you want,' Burkett says.

'Thank you,' he says, 'but for now it's Mr Lorie whose testimony we seek.'

Akbar sets aside his gun to help the others restrain Nick. They tie his wrists to the flimsy arms of the injection molded chair.

As they approach Burkett, he eyes the Kalashnikov leaning against the wall. The possibilities spring into his mind: Tarik as a hostage, flight into the wilderness, either by car or on foot, but going where? A gunfight when he wouldn't even know where to find the safety catch on the weapon. When he is barefoot and catheterized, weakened by subarachnoid hemorrhage and a probable skull fracture. No, it wouldn't be much of a fight: he wouldn't make it out of the compound alive.

They cinch the plastic bands so tightly, two on each side, that the veins swell and the skin grows pale. At least his legs are free, but what good are they now? How far could he run?

Perhaps he should have gone for one of the Kalashnikovs. How many men would he have to kill? Four in this room, at least three more outside in the courtyard, one of whom, the man with the scimitar, presently appears in the doorway, either as a sentry or spectator – perhaps both.

Tarik holds the cutters upright such that they rest against his shoulder. The man in the mask kneels and begins to pry open Nick's fist. Sajiv has to lock Nick in a bear hug to keep him still. The task of controlling his feet falls to Akbar, who despite his injured knee lowers himself to the floor and sustains a brutal kick to the face.

'We'll start at the proximal interphalangeal joint of your little finger,' Tarik says. 'If you hold perfectly still, perhaps we can avoid cutting bone.'

The one in the mask has Nick's wrist flexed against the arm support, the chosen finger pointed downward. As Tarik opens the blades, the chair twists, its legs scraping against the floor. Nick throws himself against Sajiv, and together they fall in a heap. Akbar, whose nose already gushes blood, loses his hold on Nick's ankles and absorbs yet another kick to the head. Tarik and the man in the mask wait just beyond kicking range while Akbar presses the weight of his body over Nick's legs. Tarik bends down and continues the operation with Nick lying on the floor. The clippers, meant for metal, seem to find little resistance in the skin and bone of Nick's finger.

In the silence that follows, they seem to be waiting for Nick to cry out in pain, and for a brief time, a few seconds perhaps, he resists doing so.

The zip ties have drawn blood in Burkett's wrists. Pain scrapes the backs of his eyeballs when he tries to look away, anywhere but the dripping knuckle and severed finger where Nick lies shivering in the overturned chair.

'The solution is easy enough,' Tarik says. 'You will lose one finger from each hand until you read the statement.'

Nick answers with grunts as the man in the mask rights the chair. Tarik drops the severed digit in a ziplock bag.

'Just nod,' Tarik says, placing the bag on the table, 'and I will give you the statement to read.'

Nick keeps his head bowed, his eyes closed. He seems to have passed out. The stub on his left hand twitches, and blood smears the white plastic beneath it.

With a look from Tarik, the men once again clutch his torso and legs, but Nick seems to put up less fight this time. A hand, the right one now, is pried open, the clippers placed over the little finger. Nick shouts in agony. The chair breaks at the junction of the seat and one of the arms. Nick collapses with an awkward splaying of limbs, his wrists still bound to fragments of the chair.

'I can see you want this to end,' Tarik says. 'All you have to do is read the statement.'

Nick answers with silence. Tarik converses with the others in Arabic. He collects the finger and adds it to the plastic bag.

'These will be sent to International Medical Outreach,' he says, 'to encourage payment.'

With a flip-knife, Sajiv cuts Nick's restraints and kicks away the remains of the chair. Nick offers little resistance as his wrists are bound at his back.

Tarik turns to Burkett. 'Are you ready, Dr Burkett?'

'Ready for what?'

'Did you not realize?' His eyes flash a kind of mock sympathy. 'Everything that happens to Mr Lorie will happen to you also – unless of course he reads the statement.'

Burkett jerks against his restraints. He clenches his fists and tries to stand, but all at once strong hands are gripping him by the shoulders and feet.

'No, please,' he says, as Tarik fits the blades around the little finger of his left hand. 'Please, I'll read whatever you want.'

He can see Nick where he kneels on the floor with his hands bound and head bowed.

'You have the power to stop this,' Burkett says, but Nick doesn't acknowledge him. Two fingers amputated, and he has retreated into his prayers – shut out the world. He'll let them take all of his fingers, and Burkett s as well.

'Listen to me,' Burkett shouts to Nick. 'All you have to do—'

Pain: the so-called best friend no one wants. For years he's studied it, made a career of fighting it. What is a physician's purpose if not to keep it in check? And yet he's never imagined pain like this.

He realizes he is screaming. He always thought he had a clear understanding of the nervous system, how it responded to injury. With only a finite number of sensory fibers, surely there must be a limit to physical pain, a point of divergence beyond which it remains the same no matter how severe the injury?

He understands nothing, knows nothing but pain. It no longer matters to him whether or not this man fired the gun that killed his brother. He'll do anything he asks if it can bring an end to the pain.

Beyond the sound of his own weeping, he hears the voice of Nick.

'I'll read your damn statement,' he says.

22

Burkett wakes to find another man in his bed – unfamiliar limbs nestled beside him. The stranger clings to him. Is this a dream? Perhaps it is another prisoner – a missionary or some government contractor. Could it be that Nick has crawled into bed with him? No, he can hear Nick's agonized breathing from the other side of the room.

If not for the pain in his hand, or this searing headache, he'd shove the intruder out of his bed. The pain seems to be interfering with his ability to think. Is it also keeping him from locating the intruder's exact position? Someone is sharing his bed, no question, but *where*? When he reaches his uninjured hand across his body, the only skin he encounters is his own.

He falls in and out of consciousness, and each time he wakes the stranger remains. What he needs is something to help him stay asleep. In titrating the Ativan, Tarik didn't account for the added discomfort of sharing a bed – which would certainly be grounds for a higher dose. He lifts his hand to the crack in the wall, even though he knows it is empty, the pills gone. He finds only stone and mortar.

His fingers are wet when he withdraws them from the crevice. His whole body, in fact, is soaked to the skin. The moisture seems to be coming from tears, for a giant eyeball has replaced the ceiling. Repeatedly he is grazed by the long lashes as they sweep across the floor. He finds it disgusting and irritating. The only way to find peace is to destroy the eye, so he stands up and jabs and claws at the cornea, causing the eyelids to clamp down. With his fingernails he rips through the fibrous scleral layers, causing a gush of ocular fluid. The water level rises to his chest, his neck, and finally covers his face. He holds his breath, feeling calm despite the knowledge of drowning. He floats against the increasingly flimsy surface of the eyeball.

An idea comes to him. He finds the small rent, the source of the flood, and pries it wider, tearing the edges till the opening is large enough for his body. He swims upward and breaks the surface and finds himself in the cavernous interior of the eyeball. The viscosity of the fluid, almost like syrup, makes it easy to float on his back. He could almost sleep like this.

But he is no longer asleep. In the faint light, he can tell that Nick too is awake. Nick lies on his back with his elbows bent and his wounded hands before him as if waiting to catch something from above. Now he too has an IV line and a urinary catheter.

'Probably better not to elevate your hands,' Burkett says, though he isn't sure it matters. 'For healing, keep them on a level with your heart.'

Nick's hands fall against his abdomen.

'How do they feel?' he asks, but Nick remains silent.

Sajiv lumbers down the stairs carrying a plastic cooler identical to one that Burkett, in another life, used for transporting beer at picnics and football games. He speaks in Arabic, but there is no reply. He wears blue latex gloves to remove the tape and gauze from Nick's hands. Sajiv dabs iodinated ointment to the stubs and applies fresh bandages, while Nick groans at each touch. Sajiv puts on a fresh pair of gloves before peeling away Burkett's bandage. Burkett sits up for a look at the stump, the skin bright red, the edges still flared, and the cap specked with fibers of gauze and glistening with blood and ointment.

Bloodstained bandages lie in a heap at the base of the single IV pole. Sajiv hangs new bags of cefuroxime and lactated ringers. Ativan for Burkett. He injects medications into Burkett's IV line – probably Lasix and nimodipine, but Burkett doesn't ask. They are given oral medicines as well. He recognizes the green, oval tablets as Percocet. Sajiv runs their plump bags of urine outside and brings them back empty.

Burkett waits for the narcotic to take hold. Only by keeping his hand perfectly still can he tolerate the pain. The headache and nausea, either of which would be incapacitating, seem trivial compared to his hand.

He imagines their fingers shrink-wrapped and boxed, traveling across continents and oceans to the IMO offices. What horror for the poor assistant who opens the package. Two parts Nick and one part Burkett, perhaps a reflection of their relative worth in ransom. If nothing else, he suspects their amputated digits will invigorate someone's efforts to come up with the money. Perhaps their fingers represent the cost of their freedom. Better their fingers than their lives.

Of course he'd still be whole if Nick had read that asinine statement sooner. All he had to do was utter a series of words that no one would possibly mistake for his own. There was no requirement of sincerity, only a monotone recitation – no risk of actual apostasy. What did Nick's resistance accomplish beyond the additional amputations?

Burkett wonders how many fingers Nick could have withstood losing. Did the pacifist expect Navy Seals to rescue them at the final moment? Did he expect angels to knock down the walls and carry them to safety?

Nick's silence suggests guilt, the mental flagellation of a Christian forced to recant. Perhaps he sees the wounds to his hands as punishment earned. But the silence also carries an element of anger – anger directed not just at Tarik and the others but also, it seems, at Burkett. As if Burkett hadn't also suffered. As if bolts of pain even now weren't radiating from his hand into the bones of his spine and skull. As if he could be blamed for Nick's apostasy. Or pseudo-apostasy – for how can there even be such a thing as apostasy under torture?

It is perhaps five minutes after Sajiv's departure that Burkett becomes aware of commotion above, shouts from the courtyard. He imagines a brawl among the jihadists and even smiles at the thought of their coming to blows over some fine point of theology. But quickly he realizes that what he's hearing are the sounds of men in panic. Men shouting in fear, gathering their valuables.

He sits up and looks at Nick, whose eyes bulge with the same sudden awareness of danger.

A pulse of heat, a deafening thunderclap, and the earth itself jolts with life. For a moment he seems to float in a void, neither falling nor rising. Then he slams against the stone wall.

He finds himself curled on his side, lying on the bare earthen floor, pain screaming from his hand.

Dust coats his tongue and abrades his throat. It seems to fill his lungs, as if he were breathing not oxygen but some compound of dirt and darkness. He breaks into a fit of coughing but can't hear himself over the shrill tinnitus.

There is a tug in his groin as he rises to his knees. The Foley catheter, still anchored in his bladder. He follows the catheter to where it connects to the receptacle. He gathers the wherewithal not just to break the connection but to pinch shut the clip that blocks the flow of urine.

He is gasping for air. With his good hand, he gropes blindly toward Nick's side of the chamber, where a small window sits high in the wall. He can sense the window by the taste of cleaner air and a faint glow from outside, presumably fire. The window is a light that fails to illuminate the darkness around it.

His foot bumps against the unconscious form of Nick. Burkett finds his pulse, feels the rise and fall of his chest. The breaths are short and shallow. He runs his hands over Nick's limbs. All that remains of the IV line is a bit of tape on his arm. The urinary catheter has been ripped out of him, the balloon still inflated.

He feels moisture on Nick's face, in his hair. Warm blood oozes from a gash in the scalp – a deep laceration, maybe three inches in length. It's not the blood that worries him: scalp wounds tend to be particularly bloody. It is the possibility of a skull fracture or brain injury. He walks his fingers through the tangle of hair, over the normal bumps and ridges, but he finds no abrupt depression, no yielding fragment. What was the mechanism of injury? Was his body thrown against the wall? More likely, he was struck by some falling piece of rubble.

He holds pressure on the wound till the bleeding abates. Then he palpates Nick's ribs and pelvic bones. He runs his hands again down his shoulders and arms, the bandages at the ends. There is no sign of additional trauma. Of course, Nick could have suffered any number of injuries. Spinal fracture, pneumothorax, aortic tear, splenic laceration – the possibilities are endless.

He stands up to reach the better air from the small window. Nick probably needs it as well but he fears lifting him without knowing the condition of his spine.

All at once Nick lurches awake, rolling to his elbows and knees before Burkett can restrain him.

'Be still,' Burkett says, his own voice muffled and distant. He is shouting but can't tell if Nick even hears. He feels a splash against his bare feet and legs, and after a moment recognizes the stench of vomit. Nick trembles as Burkett helps him to his feet.

The dust and smoke have begun to clear – or so it seems from his easier breathing, his greater sense of the firelight in the window.

He needs to get rid of his Foley catheter. He resists an urge to yank it out: he'd do himself serious injury by dragging the inflated balloon through his penis. Nick's catheter, which came out in the explosion, has almost certainly caused urethral injury, tears that could block with the flow of urine or later form constricting scars. To decompress the balloon Burkett will need scissors or some kind of knife. Until then, since he's nude under his tunic, all he can do is let it dangle between his legs. Fortunately it isn't long enough to step on.

He runs his hands over his own face, through his hair, finding no evidence of bleeding. He begins making his way toward the stairwell. He shuffles his bare feet, careful amid the debris. When he falls, striking concrete edges, his body roars with pain even though he manages to keep his injured hand clutched to his chest.

On he crawls with a hesitant probing of hands, dragging his catheter like a flaccid tail. He moves in the direction of the stairwell, where he remembers it, but he is blind this far from the window. A layer of rubble now separates him from the floor, and the craggy edges stab his knees and palms, hurting no matter how carefully he lowers his weight.

A beam of light combs over the piled stone filling the stairwell. Nick seems to have discovered an intact flashlight. The beam turns sideways when he begins crawling toward Burkett. Their chamber seems smaller by at least a third: a pocket of air somehow preserved in the collapse.

More likely than not their captors are dead. Tarik, Akbar, Sajiv, and the others. What was the explosion if not a drone attack? Akbar's greatest fear made real, perhaps a consequence of Tarik's visit – Tarik or one of the others, the odds of a drone attack no doubt rising in proportion to the number of jihadists gathered in a single place.

The flashlight catches a swatch of fabric – a threadbare shirt caught in the rubble from upstairs. Burkett reaches and tears off a strip to cover his nose and mouth, another to secure the urinary catheter to his thigh.

With each fit of coughing his headache surges as if the violent clench-ing in his chest were forcing geysers of blood into his brain. Awkwardly with their damaged hands they pry loose splintered wood and slabs of mortar, shifting the lighter pieces from the stairwell into the chamber. Nick crawls out first, dragging himself through a passage barely wide enough for his wasted body. Jagged stone scrapes Burkett's skin and tears the gossamer fabric of his tunic.

In the morning sunlight Burkett is struck by the emaciated figure before him, Nick's hair a dark plaster of blood and soot, the wound in his scalp gaping and moist. What looks at first like a gel stiffened wedge of hair is in fact an upturned flap of skin. Burkett takes the flashlight and beneath the flap finds a congealed mat of gore embedded with gravelly debris and ropes of hair. The wound needs cleaning and dressing, but for now he resists plucking out that largest tangle of hair lest it cause further bleeding.

Burkett looks down at himself, bare-legged and barefoot. Like Nick, his skin and clothes have collected a uniform layer of fine dust – either in the explosion or the work of upward digging. Standing in what was once the courtyard, they look like shabby clay figures molded from the surrounding wreckage. Burkett rotates his frayed bandage with its coat of dirt. Their hands, Nick's scalp: how long before the onset of infection?

They find the probable site of impact, a charred pit. Of the wall, little but shards remain, the highest just a few feet. Chunks of mortar and stone lie strewn across the clearing. A large oak tree stands blackened on the side facing the crater, with most of its leaves blown off and replaced by shreds of fabric.

Thirst drives them down to the creek, where they kneel in the bul-rushes. Burkett with his good hand cups water into his mouth. Nick lies flat, drinking directly from the stream and soaking his outstretched hands. Burkett slips off his tunic and lies naked in the shallow water.

'We need clothes and shoes,' Nick says. 'We have a long walk ahead of us.'

Nick stands and tries to urinate but only blood trickles into the water. Burkett pretends not to notice. Nick has enough medical training to appreciate the dire seriousness of a urinary obstruction. This will require surgical intervention, and soon: the obstruction could kill him faster than any wound infection.

'There was a car,' Burkett says as he puts the tunic back on.

As they make their way back up the hill, Akbar's knee brace glints in the underbrush – the sun on its metal hinge and its sleeve still tight on the severed limb.

A Toyota SUV lies on its side. It bothers Burkett that there is only a single car. One vehicle with room for five including the driver. He remembers the men at the compound, Tarik and the other jihadists: a total of eight at least – six without Akbar and Sajiv. Would Tarik and the other five share a single vehicle? No, Burkett thinks: there must have been another car.

The guard with the scimitar is clamped dead in the driver's side door. Nick climbs through the back window, leaving traces of blood where he grips the bumper for balance. He tears open a box of bottled water and tosses one to Burkett but allows himself only a sip. To refrain is to delay the accumulation of urine, the inevitable renal failure. He steps around an AK-47 that leans against the roof. He treads over broken glass, holding the sideways headrests for balance. He leans between the front seats and pats the front of the man's pants and hooks a set of keys from one of the pockets. He removes the man's shoes but can see they're too small before even trying them on. Nor do they fit Burkett, whose feet and ankles bear new lacerations from climbing out of the rubble.

In the footwell Nick finds a shoulder satchel with a laptop inside. The laptop still works despite cracks in the screen, but of course it's password protected.

'Will you hand me that sword?' Burkett asks.

The scimitar is sunk so deep in the man's thigh that Nick has to use both of his bandaged hands to pull it free of the bone. Burkett tries to clean the blade by wiping it against the dead man's shirt, but the blood clings like paint. He finds a bare patch of ground and sits down. With the sword he cuts the side branch of the catheter and then carefully slides it from his penis.

The one who wore the mask lies on his back as if sleeping, but coils of intestine protrude from a bloodless wound in his abdomen. Burkett feels the neck for a pulse. He thumbs open one of the man's eyes. The pupil is dilated, the cornea not yet clouded. They take his shoes, a closer fit for Nick. Glued to the fabric in one of his pockets they find the melted remains of a cell phone. Another body lies bent against the base of a tree trunk, as if thrown against it by the explosion. Burkett takes the man's sandals and *salwar* pants.

There is movement uphill from the bombsite. They duck behind the SUV. Burkett grips the AK-47. Nick looks at him, then reaches over and snicks the safety catch. Either on or off, Burkett can't tell.

Asadullah, the teenager from the neighboring compound, works his way over the scree.

'Maybe he'll help us get out of here,' Burkett says.

'I wouldn't count on it,' Nick says.

'He could at least point us in the right direction.'

All they know of their location is that they're maybe twenty miles from Allaghar. The boy might know about military bases or nearby villages.

'Now that he's seen us,' Nick says, 'who's he going to tell?'

The boy kicks the still smoking debris. He squats down to pick something up and then tosses it aside. Burkett and Nick wait for some acknowledgment but receive none.

'Hey there,' Burkett says.

The boy mutters in Arabic, hardly looking up from where he squats.

'He says he can get us a cell phone,' Nick says.

'In exchange for what?'

The boy answers before Nick can interpret the question.

'He wants the rifle,' Nick says, nodding toward the AK-47 still in Burkett's hands.

The boy blows the ash from one of the chaupar game pieces, intact but for an amputated fin. He stands, pocketing the draftsman. He points at the rifle and says, 'Kalashnikov.'

'Phone,' Burkett says, forming one with his thumb and remaining little finger.

The boy speaks, a sort of conspiratorial excitement in his voice.

'It's a satellite phone,' Nick says. 'At his family's compound. His brother-in-law uses it to talk to the fighters.'

'The fighters being the Heroes of Jihad,' Burkett says, his head throbbing all of a sudden. 'If they have a phone, why didn't they use it to call for help when their baby was sick?'

Nick asks the boy. 'Apparently they did,' he says. The boy is speaking volubly now, apparently telling a story. 'They were advised to come to you.'

They follow the boy along the path toward his family's compound. Nick takes the rifle from Burkett, removes the clip, checks the breech and passes it back to him. They won't give it to the boy till they have the phone.

When they reach the compound, they wait in the eaves while the boy goes inside. He could easily betray them, but they still have the gun, and

Burkett can't imagine him giving it up for the glowering jihadist married to his sister.

A woman in a burqa emerges from the compound. She stands outside the closed door, perhaps scanning the tree line from behind her mask, perhaps staring directly at them where they hide. It can only be the boy's sister, the mother of the baby, and as she and the boy approach, Burkett sees that she is the one carrying the phone. They slide deeper into the woods, out of view of the compound.

The woman has hardly begun to speak when she stops short. They can't see her face, but no doubt she's registering their bandages, the shortened digits, the gaping wound in Nick's scalp. A moment passes and her voice comes whispering from the burqa.

'Her husband is in Allaghar,' Nick says. 'She'll wait while we use the phone.'

'I thought we were keeping the phone,' Burkett says. 'Tell her we need to take it with us.'

'Her husband will kill her if we take it,' Nick says, already dialing.

His first call is to Beth's cell phone, which sends him directly to voicemail, and Burkett steps away and turns his back during Nick's professions of love and assurance of safety. After hanging up Nick dials an operator and reaches the US embassy in the capital. The embassy transfers him to an official who seems irritated when they can't give their address, even though the compound doesn't have one, and even though Asadullah provides the exact distances from Allaghar and the southern pass. It would seem to be enough, since they were the target of a drone attack just last night, but the process of locating them, much less extracting them, seems beyond the capability of anyone in the embassy. After burning twenty minutes of battery power – much of that time on hold – Nick is told to hang up and wait for a call from someone named Anders.

While they wait, Burkett learns from the woman that her baby has begun to crawl. He feels a twinge of pride at the thought of that makeshift enema.

All at once a powerful nausea takes hold of him. He walks away from the others and grips a tree branch and vomits against the bark.

Nick and the boy watch him with blank expressions. The woman turns away and, lifting the hem of her burqa over a pair of tattered military boots, she steps up a small embankment to distance herself from Burkett, either from courtesy or disgust or some combination.

Through a break in the foliage, they have a view of the compound. Burkett suggests she silence the phone, so no one from the house can hear it, but she already has. How often does her husband use the phone? What are the odds of his arriving home and discovering its absence?

The phone buzzes and she passes it to Nick. Burkett leans close enough to hear the man on the line, Anders, who asks for their birthdates and social security numbers. He proposes a rendezvous three hours from now in a valley about four miles away. He gives the co-ordinates, no doubt assuming they can use the GPS in the phone.

'It doesn't have GPS,' Burkett says into the phone. 'We're going to leave it with its owner.'

It would be better not to draw Anders' attention to the family, the jihadist brother-in-law: no reason to add the possibility of a drone attack to the threat of domestic violence. Burkett sees that Nick understands.

'We have a guide,' Nick says into the phone. 'A boy who knows the valley and can take us there.'

Anders seems to accept this. 'How long will it take you?' he asks.

Nick converses with the boy and then says, 'An hour.'

The woman stays behind with the phone, and Asadullah leads them back to the bombsite. They keep to the trees, knowing the explosion could have attracted others. At the stream Burkett kneels to fill his water bottle. He starts at the sound of a voice, a groan of pain from the weeds nearby.

Despite obviously broken legs, one of the jihadists has managed to pull himself down the embankment toward the stream. From the trail of blood and matted grass it seems he's crawled at least fifty yards. Burkett doesn't immediately recognize Sajiv's face behind the mask of blood.

'Careful,' Nick calls from downstream.

Sajiv stops crawling. He clutches what must be a wound in his abdomen. Burkett rolls him onto his back, expecting the worst, perhaps an eviscerating laceration, but there is nothing of the sort. Burkett doesn't notice the grenade till he takes Sajiv's wrist to check his pulse. Metal clanks in the dirt. Burkett runs, shouting for Nick and Asadullah to do the same. He feels the explosion against his back without ever hearing it.

23

Nick has him in a fireman's carry. He stares at the backs of Nick's legs and the ground moving below. He glimpses Asadullah in the lead, strapped with the Kalashnikov half his height. Faced with the need to carry Burkett, Nick must have decided it was easier to trust the boy than deal with the added burden of the gun.

Burkett might have remained unconscious if not for the pain. His hand, his throbbing headache, the deep lacerations in his back and thighs: pain from everywhere seems to pulse not with his heart but with Nick's footsteps. Even his nausea seems to rise and fall as he bounces against Nick's shoulder.

Fireman's carry. It's the name of a popular wrestling move, one of the very first he and his brother ever learned.

He explores the wounds he can reach with his good hand. He feels coagulated blood on the makeshift bandages and wonders how long it took Nick to get the bleeding under control.

These lacerations will need irrigation and debridement. If the shrapnel carried fragments of cloth or dirt through his skin, he'll likely develop an abscess.

His groans prompt Nick to stop and lower him to the ground. After less than a minute he lifts him again, now on the opposite shoulder, but Burkett cries out, begging to be put down. This side hurts so much worse than the other (the shrapnel must have fractured his femur) that he can't hold back his screams and finally Nick obliges him by changing shoulders.

It seems to Burkett that they've walked much farther than the four miles mentioned by the man on the phone. But the pain no doubt magnifies his sense of time, and it is difficult to contemplate distance when his view is limited to the ground at Nick's feet.

Burkett is slowing them down. The pain of his fractured femur is unbearable. He asks to be left behind but Nick doesn't acknowledge the question. He's speaking to the boy about the Kalashnikov. A gun is a curse rather than a blessing, he says, or something like it. Burkett catches only fragments of the Arabic: a tool of sin. In the *Ingil, Isa al-Mesih, Jesus the Messiah*, taught his followers to love their enemies.

They stop on reaching a well trodden path, and Asadullah points them downhill. Nick lowers Burkett to the ground while listening to the boy.

'He says to turn right at the bottom of the hill and follow the stream to the clearing.'

'Easy enough,' Burkett says.

'He says he thinks Allah will bless him for helping us.'

'I hope he's right.'

Nick has his back to Burkett. He faces uphill, his feet staggered. He shakes the boy's hand and thanks him.

The back of Nick's shirt bells. He jerks backward and comes off the ground as if yanked by a rope. The crack of a gunshot echoes past them.

It takes all of Burkett's strength to prop himself on his good knee and turn Nick onto his back. Nick's mouth guppers in a froth of blood. Burkett places his finger on his neck and catches the final throbs of an irregular pulse. He tears off Nick's shirt to reveal the wound, a small hole with little blood. Burkett stacks his palms against the sternum and begins a rapid sequence of thrusts.

The boy squats in the greenery and points his Kalashnikov into the distance. Burkett thinks with the boy's help he might be able to drag Nick to the rendezvous. He feels ribs crack under his weight. With each thrust warm blood spurts from the wound. The bullet must have ripped open the heart or aorta.

There is another gunshot. It follows by only an instant the splintering of bark to the right of the boy.

Asadullah shoulders his rifle and grips Burkett by the wrist and begins dragging him down the hill, pulling with both hands. The narrow path forms switchbacks, which the boy attempts to bypass by scrambling straight down the incline, and when its steepness becomes too much for him he loses his hold, and Burkett tumbles in jolts of agony over the stones and roots. The boy follows, sliding on his backside and holding the Kalashnikov in his lap.

Burkett knows the boy will have trouble dragging him on the flat terrain. He manages to stand on his good leg, using the boy for balance. Together they hobble toward a copse of trees. He tries to keep his right foot from touching the ground, but the effort of lifting it – the shredded muscles pulling against fragments of bone – seems just as painful as letting it jostle against the ground.

Just beyond the treeline they come upon a high banked creek. The boy tries to ease Burkett over the edge, but Burkett falls on his injured thigh. He shouts despite the boy's urging for silence. He lies in the mud hoping to wait out the pain. The boy gestures toward a mangrove leaning over a bend in the creek.

'Let me have the gun,' Burkett whispers. The boy has no English, but it's clear from his eyes he understands. If Burkett has to lie here and wait for the sniper he might as well have a way of defending himself. But the boy turns away, taking the gun with him.

Burkett crawls the short distance on his elbows. The mangrove roots splay over a depression in the bank. He pulls himself through a gap in the roots just wide enough for his emaciated body. It is a kind of damp grotto and between the roots he can see the trickling stream and the opposite bank.

In the distance, perhaps a hundred yards away, a man in a white shirt appears in the creek bed. It is Tarik. He stalks downstream over the smooth stones, his khakis wet to the knees, and his rifle at his shoulder. He pauses and seems to stare directly at Burkett.

The mangrove is an obvious place to hide, the first place Tarik would check. If only the boy had left him the Kalashnikov. He'd have a momentary advantage shooting at Tarik from behind the thick roots. Nothing would give him more pleasure than to shoot Tarik, the man who cut off his finger and killed Nick and probably Owen as well.

The clearing, the site of the rendezvous, is downstream, and Burkett wonders if he should try to make a run for it. Can he hope to reach the clearing in time? Probably not – and even if he could he has no way of knowing when or if the helicopter will even arrive.

Tarik crouches at a burst of automatic fire, waits a beat before starting upstream away from Burkett.

Is the boy just eager to shoot his new gun? Or is he trying to draw out Tarik? He should have just returned home. Whatever he felt he owed Burkett, he more than paid it by bringing him this far. Why must he put himself in more danger?

Burkett pulls himself from the cavity under the tree. He crawls on his forearms over the stones and trickling water. He starts at the report of another gunshot, a single pop from the sniper rifle. From much farther away comes a sputter of automatic fire.

The creek merges with a larger stream, perhaps the very stream that ran past their compound. Burkett makes his way to the center, where the current helps carry him over the stony bed. It isn't long before he reaches the clearing, gentle slopes rising on either side of the stream. He drags himself into the field of mud.

A puddle holds his reflection: a bearded, gaunt face he hardly recognizes. If not for the blinking eyes it might be the face of a cadaver staring up from an unfinished grave. He hears the helicopter before he sees it: a sperm-shaped silhouette in the nimbus of its propeller. He turns back to the water just as his reflection vanishes in the downdraft.

24

At an outdoor table Burkett and five other physicians are drawing self-portraits. It's the sort of infantile situation he's come to expect at Sapphire Meadow, the Appalachian facility where he's lived these last five weeks. Only three more before he graduates – assuming he passes his drug screens and shows up for therapy and lectures.

Burkett has drawn a figure in repose, the head turned to the side. It's the setting that gives him pause. Is he lying in that basement cell, or his bed at the army hospital? He's drawn himself on the left side of the page, the perspective from directly above. A subconscious decision, leaving so much blank space on the right: a place for a roommate.

He is tempted to draw an identical figure in the same bed – that strange presence he felt the night of the explosion. The neurologist ascribed that experience not to some spiritual or sexual visitation, but instead to the rare phenomenon of *hemineglect* – an injury to the right frontal lobe that prevented him from recognizing the left half of his body. Scans of his brain showed subarachnoid blood over the right hemisphere and, sure enough, a tiny infarction in the frontal lobe. Presumably the blood products caused vasospasm, abnormal clamping of the arteries. He considers himself fortunate: a larger stroke might have left him with the permanent problem of having to share his body with a stranger.

Or perhaps the figure he's drawn isn't lying in a bed at all, but on the floor of that helicopter, shoulder to shoulder with Nick. The team of Navy Seals might not have gone to the trouble of retrieving the body, but Burkett told them Nick had been one of their own. And they wouldn't have even found the body if not for Asadullah, who came upon them waving a white flag and boasting that he'd singlehandedly fought off a sniper.

Burkett glances at the self-portrait to his right, a work undeniably superior to his own. Rory Bird, an anesthesiologist, shades orange the flames engulfing a figure near the center of the page. Bird is no artist, but the fiery detail suggests he could do better than dots for eyes. Or maybe that is the point: maybe he's trying to say something about how addiction destroys personality.

'Have you applied yet for your Tennessee license?' Rory asks without looking up from his drawing.

'Finished it this morning,' Burkett says.

Of the six physicians spending the months of March and April at Sapphire Meadow, Rory Bird, at thirty, is the only one younger than Burkett. He's been trying to persuade Burkett to move to Nashville. He says there's no place like it for a single man. If he could measure a city's concentration of female beauty, Nashville would rank higher than any other. Rory's medical training has taken him to New York, Chicago, and Los Angeles, but none compares to Nashville in what he calls 'per capita pulchritude'. Another selling point is Rory's father, a physician-entrepreneur who owns a chain of imaging facilities. He's offered to hire Burkett in a full-time role supervising the patients during their scans.

Their therapist, a slim woman in her thirties, strolls around the table appraising their self-portraits. She mumbles her admiration of Rory's personal inferno. She pauses behind Burkett and says, 'Dark,' as though it were a compliment.

'I haven't filled in the colors,' he says, though he doubts he'll bother finishing it. Even if he weren't expecting Beth Lorie any minute, the self-portrait has begun to seem like a lost cause. He started with the idea of keeping it simple: lines and curves, a man lying still. But lying where? The problem, if he were forced to label it, might not be the setting so much as the man's perception of it. How with pencil and paper can he convey this nagging idea that the world around him is artificial, the objects and people like projections on a screen? Or his fear that if he looks too closely the illusion will fall away and he'll see the screen itself?

Why does a portrait have to have a background at all?

Last night he woke thinking he was still in that basement keep with Nick. The impression was so powerful that even after he recognized the bedside lamp and glowing clock, he wondered if the last six months had passed in a dream. All the therapist here can tell him is that he's experiencing mild anxiety related to PTSD and alcohol withdrawal. She means well, and she might even be right about one thing: if he were drunk, he would probably be more at ease with the world around him.

The *world*. He keeps coming back to that word but can't say exactly what he means by it. Perhaps he should take a cue from Rory and surround himself with flames and title his picture *Drone Attack*.

After six months in a blighted pit, how could he be expected to pick up where he left off? He finds himself missing Nick, even Akbar and Sajiv at times. To think of them dead almost saddens him, even as he feels the stub of his finger, even as those bolt cutters flash before him yet again. He keeps going back to that cliché: he left behind a part of himself. Not a literal part – Tarik made good on his word and sent their severed fingers to the headquarters of International Medical Outreach. Or so he heard on returning to Atlanta. Perhaps he should have given IMO an address for delivery. His finger might have served as a grim keepsake, a desk ornament in a jar of formaldehyde. Perhaps their therapist – who often seemed to be quoting from a pamphlet on PTSD – would have pointed out the 'therapeutic value' of reclaiming the lost part.

But at the time of his return he was preoccupied by the death of his father and all the paperwork and mail at the care facility and funeral home, not to mention the storage unit holding all of his father's useless possessions, over a thousand cubic feet of dust and garbage interspersed with the occasional item of sentimental value. He has yet to sort through it all, but in one of the boxes he discovered a cloth sack with a drawstring, and inside it the military-issue pistol that had once belonged to his grandfather – the very pistol he and Owen used for shooting cans on their uncle's farm in rural Pennsylvania.

An unexpected challenge of re-entry was finding a place to live. He'd been evicted in absentia, having gone months without paying his rent or responding to the notices passed under the door. His belongings had been left outside in what sounded like a free-for-all yard sale. The insurance company requested a list of what was lost. The value of the furniture, appliances, and electronics totaled more than five thousand dollars, the most his renter's policy allowed, so there was no need to include the particular items he actually cared about. He didn't mention the tattered pair of wrestling shoes he'd worn during his five years at Penn State. Nor did he mention the brown bag under the sink, his cache of Xanax and Valium. Perhaps a member of the grounds crew, recruited to carry furniture, discovered it and kept it for himself.

His Honda still sat in the parking lot of the apartment complex – not that he could drive with a cast reaching from hip to ankle. Shrapnel had fractured his femur and torn his femoral artery. The damaged vessel swelled to the size of a man's fist and almost certainly would have ruptured and killed him if surgeons in Germany hadn't operated in time.

That first night back in Atlanta, after retrieving his father's ashes from the funeral home, he took the train downtown to Grady Hospital where, to his pleasant surprise, his ID badge still gave him free food in the cafeteria as well as access to the residents' call room. After eating he tried to sleep in one of the free bunks, but the intern's pager went off every five minutes. The intern, who had heard about Burkett and his kidnapping, pressed him for details when not fielding calls. He even offered a prescription for Lortab, which Burkett declined even though it might have helped the chronic itching inside his cast.

Far more tempting was an anesthesia cart in the hallway. A drawer protruded just enough that he could tell it was unlocked. He stood before it, leaning on his crutches. He wondered how many other drawers were unlocked, perhaps all of them. The Librium or Versed he would have to inject, but everything he needed was there in the cart: needle, syringe, swabs, and tourniquet. A minute passed, maybe two, before a tech emerged from the bathroom to claim the cart. When it bumped over a threshold, Burkett could hear the jangle of glass vials.

He wished someone could offer a prescription for his finances. Even if the surgical practice hadn't requested that he pay back the signing bonus, a portion of which remained in his checking account, it wouldn't have been enough to cover his med school debt, back taxes, or unpaid rent. Or his credit cards, which had drawn the attention of collection agencies.

He was eating his meals in the hospital cafeteria and sleeping at the Wayfarer, a nearby motel, when Véronique Six came to interview him for a book she was writing. She put him up at the Marriot, though not in a shared room: it was clear from the start they wouldn't be having sex. She referred to their past intimacy, if at all, in only the most oblique terms. He might have tried to coax her away from her journalistic scruples (and the fiancé back home) but restrained himself on account of either some scruple of his own or the physical limitations of a fully casted lower extremity.

Over his months of captivity, Véronique received several calls from someone named Sunir, who demanded twenty million dollars in ransom. It's unclear how much effort she expended in producing those funds, but she prolonged the negotiations as long as possible, in part by referring to Burkett as her fiancé. She even traveled to Khandaros for a meeting with an intermediary. After the intermediary failed to appear, her magazine published a piece on a 'hostage crisis involving an American surgeon'.

In the interest of exclusivity, she hadn't discussed her phone conversations with anyone outside her magazine, so the article and subsequent cascade of TV reports came as a shock to Beth and those on the American side who had taken pains to keep her husband's predicament from the press. They feared the slightest media attention could tip the scales in favor of public execution. But as it happened, the stir of publicity served only to bring the two captives closer to release.

Around the same time, Beth received a demand more realistic than the twenty million the FBI had managed over those many months to negotiate down to ten. The latest number – three million for the release of both prisoners – suggested a renewed desire on the part of the jihadists, finally, to free rather than kill Burkett and Nick. Of course she had no way of knowing that their severed fingers, perhaps that very day, were traveling by parcel post to the IMO offices in Miami. IMO tapped into their formidable network of donors and raised nearly two million dollars, with further pledges covering the difference. IMO's president was ready to transfer funds to an anonymous Swiss account, but negotiations stalled when the kidnappers, having been bombed by a drone, failed to supply proof of life.

*

At the sound of tires on gravel, Burkett folds his meager self-portrait and limps toward the house. After weeks of physical therapy, he's now able to walk without a crutch. Having progressed from bed to wheelchair to walker to crutches, he's proud to be free finally of artificial support – not counting the metal rod in his femur or the stent in his femoral artery.

In the living room, Beth rocks her sleeping baby in a detachable carseat. His first thought, to his shame, is relief that he failed in his preposterous attempt to sleep with her – relief that there is no question as to the child's paternity. He hasn't seen her in the months since his return, except in the occasional magazine or talk show. She has been lionized in the media for her efforts to free her husband, traveling in the third trimester of pregnancy between Khandaros and Washington and managing to gain support from even the most jaded and elusive politicians.

'Hey, stranger,' she says as they embrace.

It was on YouTube that Burkett saw her speech at Nick's memorial service. 'The brevity of this painful life is one of its many consolations,' she said at the lectern. Burkett's injuries prevented him from making the trip, and perhaps it was better that way, since everyone there, Beth included, would have questioned the justice of his surviving instead.

The baby grizzles, so she releases it from the harness of the carseat and lifts it into her arms.

'He looks like you,' Burkett says, although in truth he can't tell. 'What's his name?'

'Owen,' she says.

'I like it.' He hesitates and says, 'I guess I'm surprised you didn't call him Nick.'

'We'd used that one already,' she says.

Burkett gives her a puzzled look, so she adds, 'We had a stillborn son almost five years ago.'

'I'm sorry to hear it,' he says.

How did Nick never mention that in all the time they spent together? Of course the fault is partly Burkett's own. Did he ever seek to know the man? Only after his rescue, during the seemingly endless hospital debriefings, did he learn that Nick had been awarded the Congressional Medal of Honor many years earlier.

On the coffee table he recognizes the canister of his brother's remains. Someone has secured the cap with duct tape.

'You could have sprinkled the ashes in Mejidi-al-Alam,' he says.

'If that's what you'd wanted you'd have done it yourself,' she says.

It is what he wanted – or at least he can't think of anything better. But he'll never visit that place again, even if things have been relatively stable since the secession – since the formation of that caliphate in the south, the Islamic Republic of South Khandaros, known to the world as South Khandaros. So strong was public support for a separate nation that after the death of President Djohar, the staunchest of unionists, many of his allies turned sides in favor of the referendum. And it wasn't long after Burkett's escape that an overwhelming majority of Khandarians from the north and south alike voted in favor of secession.

'What about you?' he asks. 'Will you go back? Will you resume your post at our clinic?'

She shakes her head. 'I'm taking Owen to Mozambique. There's an IMO clinic in a village there with a tremendous need.'

'I imagine the political situation is more stable.'

'Even if I had a strong desire to go back to Khandaros – which I don't – IMO wouldn't have it, not after all that's happened.'

'You'd think the fence would change their minds,' Burkett says. A modern version of the Khandarian Wall, an electric fence, so far covers thirty percent of the border.

'The fence is ridiculous,' says Beth. 'A decade from now, people are going to look at the hideous thing and ask, "How did anyone ever think this was a good idea?"'

'Have the bombings stopped now that the extremists have their own country?'

'I wouldn't say stopped – more like slowed down. The upper level Heroes have gone from being guerilla warriors to parliamentarians.'

'A place on earth for those who prefer the dark ages.' He thinks of Asadullah and his sister. 'Pity not everyone lives there by choice.'

'Before the official sealing of the border, there was a three-month period when residents of the south were supposed to be able to leave.'

'How many came?'

'Fewer than expected,' she says. 'Supposedly there were intimidation tactics. A lot of northerners have relatives in the south who weren't able to get out for one reason or another – an imprisoned family member, confiscated property, so-called emigration taxes, whatever. A good reason to maintain the clinic in Mejidi-al-Alam is to offer shelter and work for those who escape from the south.'

'So you've kept in touch with friends from the clinic?'

She nods. 'Hassad and some of the others.'

'How is he?' Burkett asks.

'He's the one in charge now that Nick's gone.'

'I'm glad to hear it's in capable hands.'

Beth fits the baby's carseat into the frame of a stroller. Outside they follow a path toward the white fence surrounding the property. The other residents, having just finished their therapy session, file past them toward the house.

'If you're ever interested,' she says, 'I could use a surgeon in Mozambique.'

'I'll keep that in mind.'

'I hope we can count on your support either way.'

'These days I'm a little short on cash.'

'No,' she says. 'What we need is prayer.'

'I might be a little short on that, too.'

She offers a brief smile, but all he sees in it is pity.

After a moment of silence, he says, 'I'll do my best.'

Words from his brother's notepad come back to him: *Grant me the words to pray as You'd have me pray.* What strikes him as odd, remembering it now, is the capital Y. It brings to mind the bloodless incision spanning his brother's torso.

25

His job at the imaging center in Nashville is to manage adverse reactions to gadolinium, the substance administered during scans. As it happens, such reactions are rare enough to be virtually non-existent, so once he's comfortable with the protocols and resuscitation equipment, he has nothing to do beyond reading novels and surfing the web. He never expected an immediate return to the operating room, but he'd prefer the kind of job that would at least require him to stay awake.

Other opportunities arise, through Rory Bird as well as IMO – idylls of low-intensity doctoring on the periphery of healthcare: physical exams for an insurance company, medical emergencies at a psychiatric hospital, chart review for a malpractice defense attorney, and the occasional trip on a private jet designed for patient transport, a kind of airborne intensive care unit in which he faces the sometimes difficult task of keeping a patient stable between runways.

A year after his move to Nashville, he takes a job in the emergency room of a small hospital in the suburbs. Rumors of his drug history somehow reach the nursing staff, or so he imagines from a particular manager's obsessive documentation of his patients' reports of pain. But there are no discrepancies, and by the second month that manager has begun to regard him with the same attitude of weariness and affection that has earned her the nickname 'Mom' among the other physicians.

An elderly general surgeon, impressed by Burkett's handling one night of a ruptured gallbladder, offers him part time work as a surgical assistant. Burkett scales back his shifts in the ER, even if it means a loss in income. He'd far prefer the steady intensity of surgery to the emergency room, where long periods of monotony are punctuated by spasms of uncertainty.

The surgeon, whose name is Waverly, has the versatility of an old generalist, probably as comfortable with a c-section as a thyroidectomy – not that he does much of either in these days of subspecialization – but he's developed arthritis and therefore needs a young pair of hands to tie off the leaking ducts and spouting arteries. (Burkett's shortened finger leads to minor awkwardness with gloves but seems to have little impact on his technique.) The work is steady and eventually even lucrative – he's able to quit the ER altogether – and it serves as a kind of apprenticeship, a second residency to regain those skills he lost during his two-year hiatus.

It isn't long before Waverly grants him the status of 'junior partner', paying him extra to answer pages at night and manage the scutwork of admitting and discharging patients. Waverly, who boasts of having worked thirty years without a vacation, proves his confidence in Burkett by taking his family to Hawaii for ten days. When the old surgeon finally retires, Burkett slides easily into his role, the only general surgeon in that small hospital.

The women Burkett dates tend to be nurses in their late twenties or early thirties. He would prefer a non-medical type, but his avoidance of bars limits his options. Sex was one of the problems of life that drunkenness made easier. This sober version of himself manages two sustained relationships, both with nurses, and both following the same basic trajectory: an initial attraction followed by growing irritation and finally the pain of extricating himself.

Another obstacle to sex is that women no longer seem to find him physically attractive. They used to respond to his gaze – a look alone would draw an inviting glance or even a smile. But that power eludes him now. Perhaps it is the truncated digit, the residual limp, or the hair that grew back brittle and gray after being shaved for lice. Perhaps they detect his baseline anxiety, the subtle tremor. Not even forty, but he feels like an old man.

He's lived in Nashville almost three years before he sees Amanda Grey in a shopping mall. He is riding up an escalator when he spots her in the window of a descending elevator. She doesn't appear to see him. Perhaps she senses a man staring and avoids looking for that reason. The elevator descends into the thicket of an indoor garden, and moments later she emerges with a stroller. He tries not to look at her again, but when his resolve crumbles she is already gone. He imagines her making a quick retreat, ducking into the nearest store. He'd heard about her second marriage, so the baby shouldn't come as a surprise, but that night the benzo ache is bad enough that Rory Bird has to come over and sleep on his couch.

In those first months after Sapphire Meadow, he'd known no one in Nashville other than Rory, so it didn't take long for the AA meetings to become the most interesting two hours of his week. There was even an attractive woman, a flight attendant named Elizabeth, but despite his best efforts she took up with Rory instead, which was just as well. The meetings needed to remain free of the problems that seem inevitably to follow his sex life. When Rory and Elizabeth got married, Burkett served as a groomsman – his first time, surprisingly enough. He'd had plenty of close friends, but no one had ever requested his presence at the altar. It was a role better suited to his brother, a groomsman at least four times during their twenties.

He's lucky these days to make it to more than one meeting a month. While he recognizes the benefits of the twelve steps, he isn't sure he'd even be capable of making a list of those he's harmed. It would have to include his brother, and perhaps his father as well. Perhaps Nick too, though he isn't sure Nick himself would have agreed. Of those living, should he apologize to Beth for that fleeting attempt at seduction? For the drugs he stole from her pharmacy? And what of all the women during medical school and residency – those he slept with and subsequently ignored, or those who assumed commitment only to discover that he'd been sleeping with others as well? Surely such cruelties are common enough to rank low in the hierarchy of sins. And is it not presumptuous to think those ten or twenty women did anything other than forget him in short order and move on with their lives?

But of course Amanda Grey is a different matter altogether. In four years, more than three living together, he never managed to stay faithful for more than a few months. The problem, it seems to him now, was that their relationship began as an unforgivable betrayal. Would faithfulness to her not have been the equivalent of consecrating that original offense? Or is he compounding his betrayal by making it the basis for a litany of others? Whatever the case, he's beginning to think he could redeem years of harm simply by making amends with Amanda. If she were willing, he could start with a clean slate – they could establish a friendship of sorts. He could befriend her husband and come to know her child as well. Her husband of course might not approve – he might see Burkett as a threat – and Burkett couldn't blame him for that.

He composes an email. He saves it as a draft and over the course of a week makes small changes to the wording.

Hi Amanda,

I thought I saw you other day at the Green Hills Mall, but didn't get a chance to say hello.

You might not be aware that I live in Nashville now and practice general surgery. The plastics fellowship didn't work out.

I'm sure you heard the bad news about Owen. I had an ordeal of my own, which you can read about <u>here</u> and <u>here</u>.

Anyway, it would be great to catch up. We could grab a cup of coffee sometime. Just let me know what would work for you.

Best,
Ryan

That very day she responds:

Great to hear from you, would love to catch up. Any interest in stopping by the office?

He sees in this the challenge of a married woman with a sexual history. If he put her in an awkward position, she at least found a reasonable compromise in the idea of meeting at the office she shares with her husband, a morgue in fact, and perhaps there is nothing like the proximity of death to trivialize romantic tension.

In the atrium, visitors are greeted by an engraved motto:

Let conversation cease. Let laughter flee. This is the place where death delights to succor life.

He gives the receptionist his name. He's ten minutes early, so he takes a seat amid the fake plants and occupies himself with the out-of-date magazines.

Through the plate glass he watches a hearse cross the parking lot – perhaps carrying the body of one of Amanda's patients. Are the bodies she examines called patients? Perhaps the more accurate term would be *subjects*.

The receptionist conducts him down a brightly lit hallway to the only open door. Amanda walks around her desk to meet him. On the pants of her blue scrubs he notices a dark stain – a spilt drink, he hopes, rather than seepage from an autopsy.

'Good to see you,' she says when they are alone.

There is a moment of hesitation before they embrace. Of the two chairs for visitors, one is occupied by a pile of laundry. The other she must have cleared in the moments before his arrival. He sinks into the cushions, surprisingly deep. His view of her is partially blocked by the papers and journals heaped on her desk, and he has the sense that with the slightest nudge she could bury him in an avalanche of medical literature. He wonders if this is intentional, the low-slung chair a means of demeaning visitors. More likely a result of poor planning: she was always disorganized, most comfortable amid clutter.

'I was so sorry to hear about Owen,' she says.

'I had to travel there to claim the body,' he says, hoping to appeal to her forensic sympathies.

She gives him a look of pity that borders on mockery, and he girds himself for the inevitable *Poor baby*.

Instead she says, 'The worst was yet to come.'

With a smirk he holds up his left hand, displaying the amputation stump.

'It is what it is,' he says, though he's not sure if this is the right cliché. He was trying for a kind of humorous fatalism but he somehow missed the mark. She is looking away, out the window toward the distant Nashville skyline.

'Did they ever catch the people who killed him?'

'Our kidnappers were the same ones who killed him.'

'The Heroes of Jihad,' she says with a frown. 'Did you find out what happened, who did it?'

He offers an account that for him has nearly hardened into truth: how Owen was baited by a stranded motorist, and shot when he resisted being taken. Burkett envisions three gunmen, Tarik as the leader. This time, but not always, the other two are Akbar and Sajiv. From day to day he sees variations in Owen's fight – perhaps he disarmed one of them, perhaps there was some kind of standoff – but it is always Tarik he punches in the face, and always Tarik in the end who shoots him.

'So this fellow Tarik,' she says, 'did they ever catch him?'

'Not that I know of.'

'That's disappointing.'

Silence fills the office. He notices a human skull serving as a bookend. Small numbers are written on its dome, perhaps a vestige of some anatomy class.

'So Ryan,' she says, turning back to him, 'what can I do for you?'

It is abrupt, a bit off-putting, but he tries to see this from her perspective. She probably has bodies waiting for autopsies – preferable company, no doubt, to the ex-boyfriend wanting to dissect the past. He has yet to give her any indication as to why he's come.

He clears his throat, a sound to punctuate the silence. 'For years I had a problem with substance abuse,' he says. 'You saw the worst of it. I'm just here, you know…' He shrugs, trying to give an impression of spontaneity. 'I just want to say I'm sorry.'

How artificial it sounds: a canned apology, the sort of thing he might have come across in a pamphlet.

'All right,' she says, her voice freighted with doubt.

'I'm serious,' he says. 'I've been going to AA meetings, haven't had a drink or pill in over three years.'

'Good for you,' she says, obliging him with a remote smile. 'Congratulations.'

The coldness strikes him as rather juvenile. He'd almost prefer that she lash out, berate him for all the lies and betrayals to which he subjected her more than a decade ago. All the crimes she should have expected from a man who would steal his twin brother's girlfriend.

'I hate to break it you,' she says, 'but I don't sit around brooding about the time I spent with the Burkett twins.'

He shrugs to conceal his irritation. 'I just wanted to make things right. If it's meaningless to you—'

'What my past experiences may or may not mean to me – frankly, it's none of your business.'

In silence she leads him to the foyer, where they shake hands, and all at once her expression softens. Saying nothing, she leans close and kisses his cheek. He detects a faint odor of putrefaction – from a body nearby, or more likely from Amanda herself, from her hair and clothes. It draws him back to the basement morgue in Khandaros, to the body of his brother. This modern facility stands in sharp contrast to that cramped space of linoleum and tile, and yet the common smell gives him a sense of repetition, a segment of time between then and now like a rope held in tension by two different versions of himself.

She calls to him in the parking lot, 'Wait,' and he turns and walks back to where she stands at the curb.

He resists an urge to apologize all over again. He already feels it was a mistake to come here. What more could she want from him?

'Did you ever wonder why your brother went abroad?'

'It's what he felt called to do.'

'I can't help but feel partly responsible for his decision to leave.'

'That's ridiculous,' he says as a dead leaf wavers in the air between them and clings to the tie at the waist of her scrubs.

'Do you remember the time he came to Atlanta?'

'Which time?'

'You were in your final year of surgery,' she says. 'The resident on call had a funeral at the last minute, which meant you had to cover the entire weekend.'

He nods, remembering. 'I hated having to work during one of his few visits.'

'He called that Saturday,' she says. 'We met for a drink.'

'Really,' he says with a pointless twitch of jealousy.

'We went to Neighbors.'

Neighbors. An unwelcome memory comes to him: the moment they locked eyes in the mirror behind the bar, when he realized she'd seen him with another woman. Why so many years later would she choose that particular bar to meet Owen? Was it coincidence? Did she use his twin for some masochistic revision of the earlier scene? Or perhaps they met somewhere else entirely: perhaps she has brought up Neighbors only out of spite – to spurn his all too vague apology by reminding him of a specific reason for it.

'So what happened?' he asks.

'Things got – strange.'

'You slept together?'

'Not that kind of strange,' she says. 'Come on, this is Owen we're talking about. We had a bottle of wine – or I did – and we sat there talking. We spent hours talking. It took me back to my sophomore year at Penn State.'

He waits for her to continue but almost wishes she hadn't brought it up at all. If Owen had kept a secret from his brother, would he have wanted it unsealed now?

'I'd just gone through a divorce,' she says, 'which was likely part of the problem. Being with Owen that night I had this overwhelming sense that we'd been meant for each other all along. Next thing I knew I was crying and telling him I'd always loved him.'

'That's what you get for sharing a bottle with a teetotaler.'

She gives a hint of a smile and goes on: 'In the weeks afterward we talked just about every day. But of course something was wrong. It felt like I'd stumbled into someone else's relationship.'

'He wanted you to be someone you weren't.'

Burkett wonders what bothers him more – that Owen's history with her went beyond his own, or that he knew nothing of it.

'He came down to Atlanta the next time we both had a free weekend,' she says. 'I told him we needed to call it off.'

'And that was around the time he decided to become a missionary.'

She lowers her eyes. 'It was only a few weeks later that he sent out the mass email asking for donations.'

He can see how she would make the connection, but it strikes him as rather egocentric on her part to take responsibility for an outcome so far beyond her control. Does she actually think she could have saved Owen's life by loving him? By pretending to love him? He knows what she wants to hear – that it wouldn't have made any difference, that Owen would have gone to Khandaros no matter what. But he remains silent. He can give her no such comfort, not if it means yet again belittling her role in his brother's life.

26

A package waits on his doorstep. A book, he can tell, though he doesn't recall placing an order. It is late, past midnight, and he has to be back in the operating room at seven. He rips off the tape and pulls back the flaps. *Gods of the Rock,* by Véronique Six.

It's been almost four years since her visit to Atlanta. He has tried to follow her career, the meteoric rise after her coverage of the Khandarian secession. Now a foreign correspondent for CNN, she reports from Middle Eastern 'trouble spots' so dangerous that she rarely appears on camera without a helmet and Kevlar vest.

He lies in bed with the book. Although they've exchanged emails, he has no idea how she might have portrayed him, but if it covers two decades of jihad in El-Khandar, as the jacket claims, he can't imagine his own experience warranting more than a sentence or two. The cover shows a woman in a burqa against a background of ocean and palm trees. He flips to the glossy pages at the center of the book and scans the black-and-white photographs. There are politicians shaking hands: white men in suits, Arabs in thobes. Jihadists posing with guns. The Aljannah Hotel in its prime and then as a smoldering ruin.

He catches his breath at the picture of himself and Owen. It is that same photograph from their wrestling days – the night Owen won the national championship. A moment passes before he realizes that the image is reversed – like a reflection of the original – such that Owen's injury, the broken clavicle, is on the right rather than the left. The caption reads: 'Brothers Ryan, left, and Owen Burkett.' He finds no picture of Nick.

His eye drifts to a face at the top of the next page. Five men in suits, all of them Arabs, but it is the youngest at whom he is staring. The face was bearded when he last saw it, but there is no mistaking the smug expression, the eyes behind those wire-rimmed glasses. It is Tarik.

The caption reads: *Yousef Al Bihani, the minister of health, with advisors.* The minister is undoubtedly the white-haired figure at the center. Tarik, one of four others, stands at the edge of the picture to the minister's right.

The index lists no one by the name of Tarik, but he finds several references to the minister of health, this Yousef Al Bihani. A physician trained in the United States, he served on Quadri's counsel before becoming minister of health under President Djohar. He was responsible for negotiating a brief but well publicized ceasefire with the Heroes of Jihad, a ceasefire that came to an end when the president was killed by a suicide bomber. Burkett remembers the shaky footage from Tarik's laptop, the suicide bomber strolling up to the line of traffic. Al Bihani now serves on the cabinet of the new Islamic Republic of South Khandaros, which in retrospect might cast doubt on his allegiance to Djohar. He was one of several conservative members of that regime to defect to the south in the wake of the secession.

Véronique's number is still in Burkett's phone.

'The book looks great,' he tells her.

'Sorry not to include more of your experience,' she says.

He hasn't bothered yet to read the parts about himself. He drops out of bed and pads into the bathroom.

'Do you remember the man I told you about?' he asks. 'The bolt cutters.'

'The good Dr Tarik,' she says. 'We never figured out his real name.'

Absently he opens the medicine cabinet. He checks under the sink. There are no vials of pills, not that he expected any – not that he's ever had a stash of pills here at his new house – but the habit of checking drawers and cabinets somehow puts him at ease.

'You have a picture of him in your book,' he says. 'Page 190.'

'Which picture?' she asks, clearly surprised.

'The minister of health with his advisors.'

'Djohar's inaugural gala.'

'Tarik is the one on the far left.'

'Hold on, let me get the book,' she says. He hears her turning pages. After a pause she says, 'That is Hussein, Yousef's son. He *was* a physician if I remember correctly.'

'It fits,' he says. 'Tarik was educated, connected.'

'Perhaps,' she says. 'A lot of people are educated and connected.'

'Weren't we assuming all along that Tarik was a nom de guerre?'

'It seems rather far-fetched, but let me look into it and see what comes up.'

He lies in bed but hardly sleeps. Four hours later, when he rises for work, he finds an email from Véronique: Hussein Al Bihani is still alive. Having obtained a work visa and medical license, he is currently in the second year of an endocrinology fellowship at the University of Louisville.

How does a terrorist obtain a visa, much less a Kentucky medical license? Is he planning some kind of attack? Or perhaps he was serious about the swords and plowshares.

The internet doesn't turn up anything useful. There is a photo from his medical school yearbook, but it is ten years old, and the face bears only a slight resemblance to the Tarik Burkett remembers. On the University of Louisville's website, Hussein is listed as a fellow in endocrinology, no picture included, but it seems he's taking the year to pursue research on

251

diabetes. The lab where he works has a separate website of its own, but the staff photos haven't been updated in years.

Hussein recently co-authored a paper in the journal *Psychoneuro-endocrinology*: 'Counterregulation of cortisol levels during extreme hypoglycemia'. Burkett scrolls through the text and charts, not sure what he's looking for. Does he hope to recognize Tarik's voice in the scientific language? The odds are slim that Tarik contributed to the actual writing of the paper. More likely he earned his place among the ten or so authors by drawing blood from rats or managing a centrifuge.

Another message from Véronique: during the period of Burkett's captivity, Hussein Al Bihani held a position as a hospitalist in Saudi Arabia. Could he have traveled back and forth, managing his revolutionary activities on top of a medical practice?

Véronique sends the contact information for someone she knows in the FBI. 'He's an old friend,' she writes, which makes Burkett think she probably slept with him. She also suggests that he 'talk with someone, perhaps a counselor'. Maybe this is her way of asking if he's started drinking again. He could tell her he's been sober now for almost four years. And perhaps that is the problem: if he were drunk, would he see the truth of that picture? Is his deep-seated anxiety now expressing itself in the form of paranoia? Has he become the sort of man who finds connections where none exist?

Late that evening, Burkett sits on his couch, the television muted. He's just eaten a packet of tacos, and the wrappers lie before him on the coffee table.

He's wondering if that tiny stroke could have distorted his perception and recognition of human faces. Perhaps the scarring, however small, has caused some network to be rerouted. Perhaps there is a disruption of the subcortical fibers that link facial memory to whatever nucleus is responsible for generating an appropriate emotional response.

Again he opens Véronique's book to the picture of Tarik. It causes involuntary changes in his breathing and heart rate – his sympathetic nervous system responding to an enemy. A phrase from medical school comes to mind: *fight or flight*. And yet he can't be sure, not if this man was working in Saudi Arabia at the time.

In the index he finds his name paired with his brother's. He turns to a passage describing him and Nick as health workers, victims of 'one of the more brazen kidnappings'.

> The men were accused of evangelizing Christianity, which may have
> been true in Lorie's case, but Burkett, a surgeon, describes himself
> as 'agnostic'.

She goes on to discuss International Medical Outreach and their misleading denials of religious affiliation. She quotes an anonymous source:

> 'We have to balance safety concerns with our goal of sharing Jesus –
> not that our brothers and sisters act out of fear.'

It takes a few pages for her to return to Burkett and Nick. He'd expected an exaggerated account of brutality and ultimate escape, but she avoids sensationalism altogether.

> The men suffered torture at the hands of a young jihadist commander
> known as Tarik, who was also likely involved in murdering the surgeon
> Owen Burkett, brother of Ryan. Lorie, under duress, read a statement
> condemning the Christian church as 'a tool of Satan' and proclaiming
> Muhammad 'God's highest prophet'.

Under duress? It doesn't do justice to what Nick endured – or what more he could have endured had Tarik not started in on Burkett, if Burkett hadn't been there to suffer in his place. How much longer could Nick have held out? If he'd read the statement at the outset – if he'd been practical about torture – Burkett would still have a full complement of fingers.

He wonders if Véronique saw the video of Nick's renunciation. Perhaps she discovered it on some jihadist website. A memory comes to him: the men and boys at that madrassa gathered around a laptop, cheering the videos of suicide bombs. He wonders if Nick's apostasy has provided similar entertainment.

Why does he remember – or believe he remembers – the face of Tarik so much more clearly than those of past friends and girlfriends?

He tries to picture his brother, but the face that comes to him is his own. Though genetically identical there were always subtle differences of appearance. In high school and college it was never a problem for the close friends they shared, their wrestling coaches and teammates, to tell them apart. It was never a problem for Amanda Grey. She and those others saw differences in the Burkett twins that went beyond their hair-cuts and clothes, differences perhaps in the way they stood still, the way their faces relaxed between expressions. Those differences, whatever they might have been, seem to have slipped away from Burkett's memory, if he ever understood them at all.

He goes to the closet and opens a shoebox of old pictures, mostly from their days of wrestling. He takes a stack at random. Shuffling through them, he's relieved at how easily he can distinguish himself from his brother, but it doesn't take him long to realize his need for contextual clues, like Owen's ring or perennially mismatched socks.

But the face of Tarik he sees with clarity. As he closes the shoebox his eye drifts to the gun safe in the back corner. *Fight or flight.* He dials the combination and opens the lid and stares at the gun on its bed of rippled foam – the .45-caliber pistol that his grandfather had with him when he died in the Battle of the Bulge. It is one of the few items from his father's storage unit that he decided to keep.

He sits on the couch with the gun. As his father taught him he pulls back the slide to make sure the chamber is empty. After years the method of disassembly comes back to him. He lays the parts on the coffee table, wipes each with a moist cloth: the spring, the firing pin, the ejector. The simple machinery of killing.

27

The laboratory occupies a five-story building in downtown Louisville, near the campus of the medical school. Burkett takes the elevator to the top floor and follows the corridor to room 506, where he gazes through the window in the door at the polished counters and faucets, mouse cages, and cluttered desks and computers.

'Can I help you?' A woman stands behind him, waiting to enter. She is young, probably a graduate student.

'Just looking for a friend of mine,' he says, thinking he might have worn his white coat and scrubs just to give an impression of belonging.

'Hussein,' he says.

'Oh.' The name makes her smirk. Perhaps Tarik has shared his feelings on female scientists in tank tops.

'He's at lunch,' she says, glancing at her watch. 'You're welcome to wait.'

'No,' he says, 'I'll come by later.'

At the end of the hallway he finds an alcove with vending machines and a table and chairs. The window offers a view of the courtyard and main entrance. There are other ways to enter the building, but from where he sits he can hear the elevator well enough to keep track of its coming and going.

Less than half an hour passes before he spots Tarik crossing the courtyard. He carries a briefcase by a shoulder strap and wears a plaid oxford shirt buttoned to the throat. He shaved the beard, but the same wire-rimmed glasses sit crookedly on his face. The tattered khakis look familiar as well. An image of Tarik's face flashes before him: a look of surgical concentration as he works the clippers.

A ding signals the arrival of the elevator. Instead of going straight to the lab, Tarik makes a stop at the bathroom. Burkett waits before following him inside. Tarik stands at a urinal, keeping his eyes fixed on the tiles as Burkett passes behind him to the farthest sink. Burkett holds his hands under the warm water, and before long Tarik approaches the counter and bends over the second sink down. Their eyes meet ever so briefly in the mirror. Burkett is certain it's Tarik, even if Tarik shows no sign of recognition.

A nametag hangs by a Louisville Cardinal lanyard:

HUSSEIN AL BIHANI, M.D.

Fellow, Endocrinology

If Burkett were holding a gun, he could kill him without remorse. There would be justice in it, a life for a life. He imagines doing the job with his bare fists: blunt, repeated trauma. He feels an ache, a pressure building in his chest that can only be relieved by the crack of bone under a cushion of flesh. Tarik's brittle facial bones and hollow sinuses seem to have been designed for the sole purpose of being ground to bits by Burkett's knuckles. He thinks of Owen's broken metacarpal, the boxer's fracture he might well have sustained against this very face. The desire to do harm feels deeper than any idea of hatred or vengeance, and it takes all his strength to keep his balled fists from the course laid out in his mind.

Tarik dries his hands at the towel dispenser and exits the bathroom. Burkett studies himself in the mirror. What drove him just now to risk being recognized by Tarik? Burkett hardly bears any resemblance to that bearded, emaciated prisoner back in Khandaros, but if he had to follow

Tarik into the bathroom, why couldn't he simply observe him from inside one of the stalls? Is there a part of Burkett that wants to be recognized? He's come here ostensibly to confirm Tarik's identity, but on a deeper level it's clear that he yearns for some kind of physical confrontation. And how close they came to it: if Tarik, standing at the sink, had only taken a second look – if he'd uttered some word of recognition – perhaps Burkett would have tried to beat him to death.

Passing the laboratory, Burkett pauses again at the window in the door. The woman is seated at a desktop computer. Tarik dips his hand into a cage and lifts a squirming mouse by its tail.

The official reason for Burkett's visit to Louisville is a conference on bariatric surgery, a subject that holds little interest for him, but he needed an excuse to make the trip. He returns to his hotel and changes into his suit for a cocktail party with the other surgeons from the conference. Wearing his name tag he glides among the guests, his eyes seeking out the one or two youngish female surgeons, but instead finds himself in tedious conversation with some gray eminence from Mass General who sips an old fashioned. More than once a waiter comes by with a tray of drinks, but Burkett declines.

The following afternoon he sits in his car watching the entrance to the research facility where Tarik works. When a policeman chastises him for blocking the fire lane, he circles the block and pulls into a Taco Bell. He buys his usual four tacos and forty-ounce Coke and takes a table with a view of the research building.

Not till dusk does Tarik emerge in the courtyard. He makes his way down the sidewalk. Burkett eases his car to the curb across from a parking structure. He shifts into park and turns on his hazards. A disheveled vagrant, obviously schizophrenic, paces the sidewalk and shouts at some imagined foe. Burkett risks provocation by clicking his automatic locks, but when the man turns the confusion and anger seem to fall from his grimy face.

He almost misses the Red Honda Accord. On the highway Burkett holds back two to four car lengths, vaguely irritated by Tarik's strict adherence to the speed limit, his formal use of blinkers. He lives in a nondescript, two-story house. Tarik parks and climbs his front stoop and fumbles with his keys. Burkett watches him in the rearview mirror while NPR plays at a low volume. Tarik stands for a moment in the open doorway, shuffling through his mail, before he disappears inside.

Véronique's friend in the FBI, Peter Gorman, shares with Burkett the privilege of being a minor character in her book. Having been stationed in Khandaros at the time of Owen's murder, Gorman served as a liaison during the investigation. He still regrets the lack of progress in that case, which to Burkett's mind makes him the perfect man to bring justice to Tarik.

Burkett tells him about the picture in the book, how Tarik is practicing medicine in Louisville. If Gorman, during their conversation on the phone, doesn't respond with quite the outrage Burkett might have expected, he makes up for it with swiftness of action, sending a text message in less than twenty-four hours. *Subject in police custody.* The courtesy of a text likely owes something to Véronique, but Burkett sees too an abiding commitment on Gorman's part to tracking down Owen's killer.

And now that Tarik is in custody, all Burkett has to do is wait for the inevitable. He imagines Tarik in an interrogation room with two-way mirrors while forensic experts overturn the contents of that house, uncovering maps of so-called soft targets, blueprints of some stadium or shopping mall. It is only a matter of time.

His next contact with the FBI comes not from Gorman but from a woman in her forties with short, gray-streaked hair. She sits facing his desk in a business suit while he studies a recent mug shot of Tarik. He assures her that they have the right man, the very same sociopath he knew in Khandaros, a doctor by training who took time off to pursue side interests in kidnapping and terrorism.

'Why would a physician become a terrorist?' she asks in a disingenuous tone that all at once makes Burkett feel like he's the one under suspicion.

'Aside from being a religious fanatic? The question you should be asking is how a terrorist could obtain a license to practice medicine in the United States.'

'Please,' she says with a conciliatory smile. 'I know this is a sensitive subject, I know you've been through quite a bit. But if we could just sort out the facts?'

Sound travels all too easily through the walls and doors of his clinic, so he's almost whispering when he says, 'What did you find when you searched his home?'

'I'm sorry but I can't comment on that.'

'Will he be deported or tried here in the States?'

'I couldn't say.'

'Is he even still in custody?'

'We're following every lead,' she says, as if this were an answer to his question. 'You might be aware that his father is a prominent figure in the newly formed government of South Khandaros.'

'And no doubt their family got rich through the secession. Have you looked into their bank accounts, their investments?'

'We're exploring every angle,' she says. From her briefcase she draws a sheaf of stapled pages. 'This is the text of the statement you gave four years ago. You describe Tarik as having brown eyes and a beard, but no distinguishing marks on the face.'

He shrugs. 'That's true.'

'Hussein al Bihani, as you might know, has a prominent mole on his left cheek.'

'It was covered by the beard!' Burkett says, exasperated. 'Surely you wouldn't see that as an inconsistency.' He jabs his finger against the mug shot on his desk. 'This is the guy, no question.'

'In a case like this,' she says, 'we can't leave any stone unturned.'

A week passes before he hears from Gorman. From the voicemail he can tell things aren't going as planned. It is not anything Gorman says, just the tone of voice, hints of vexation and apology. He returns the call that same afternoon, as soon as he has a break between appendectomies.

'This guy's clean,' Gorman says.

'You have to search his house,' Burkett says. 'Sit him down for an interrogation. Turn up the heat.'

A ridiculous cinematic cliché: he imagines the faint static on the line as the sound of Gorman's eyes rolling.

'Just so you know,' Gorman says, 'we have searched his house, we've interviewed his contacts abroad. There is documentation of his work in Saudi Arabia during the time of your captivity.'

'He has to be in the United States for a reason.'

'Apparently he's interested in doing a fellowship in endocrinology,' Gorman says, as though pointing out the obvious.

'How noble,' Burkett says.

'It's not at all uncommon for foreign physicians to study here. He says he plans to open a diabetes clinic at the new children's hospital under construction in South Khandaros.'

'I should go up there and talk to him,' Burkett says. 'I could wear a wire.'

'That's the last thing you want to do. He's got the best lawyer money can buy.'

'I wouldn't mind going to court,' Burkett says.

Burkett's pager goes off: his last patient, a routine appendectomy, is complaining of chest pain. He logs into the medical record and checks the latest vitals and labs.

'Will you continue investigating him?'

'We'll keep an eye on him, sure.'

'Do you still even believe me? Do you believe me when I say this guy's a terrorist?'

'It doesn't matter what I believe,' Gorman says. 'It matters what I can prove.'

Burkett sighs. His pager goes off yet again – the same patient, now short of breath.

'You've been through a lot,' Gorman is saying. 'You should think about getting some help.'

Some help. When he goes upstairs to see his patient, the phrase echoes in his mind, adopting the rhythm of the heartbeat in his stethoscope. The psychiatric euphemism might be annoying, but he has to wonder if he could be wrong about Hussein, if his history of drug abuse and head trauma have made him susceptible to delusions. Perhaps it isn't unusual for crime victims to see their assailants in the faces of strangers.

But the man in the bathroom was Tarik, no question. Gorman and probably Véronique both seem to suspect him of being delusional. He lost his brother, suffered trauma, witnessed the murder of his friend. No surprise that he should imagine his chief tormentor living just a few hours away. An individual who can become the focus of all blame, a fitting target for revenge.

He recalls that his brother had a brush with mental health during their first year of medical school. The dean and several of Owen's classmates had expressed concern over what they called 'excessive religiosity'. It was a fleeting controversy – Owen was given a clean bill of health – but Burkett had always been embarrassed for his brother, that he would jeopardize his reputation among the faculty and students.

28

Tarik's house stands out for its lack of Halloween decoration. Through a lighted window Burkett can see him in a reflector vest lifting his arms overhead in what looks at first like some prayer ritual but in fact represents an exercise routine. He's preparing for a jog, which is convenient for Burkett: it will give him a chance to reconnoiter the house.

It is almost eight p.m. and nearly dark. Burkett worked all day in Nashville. He has to be back in the operating room at seven a.m. to take down a colostomy. He is wearing jeans and a hooded sweatshirt. He left his phone in Nashville should someone later pull the record of its location. He has a disposable in the console but doesn't expect he'll need it.

The yards on either side of Tarik's display all manner of gore and dismemberment. A boy of about ten brandishes a severed arm while a man, presumably his father, hoists some kind of bloodstained corpse or zombie into a tree.

Tarik emerges in sleek running tights, his arms and legs sheathed in Lycra. It is the look of a serious runner, a marathoner perhaps. He never imagined Tarik as a runner. Even if he has no intention of challenging Tarik to a foot race, it bothers him how little he knows of his personal life, this physician and jihadist who runs with brisk, loping strides.

A motion sensor illuminates Tarik's front yard and driveway. This could be a problem for Burkett. To avoid it, he'll need to approach from the other side of the house, the side closest to the father and son, and even then, he can't be sure there isn't a second light.

He waits for the father and son to go inside before he emerges from his car. Hands in his pockets, head down, Burkett climbs across their macabre display, circling the foam graveyard and brushing past the noosed effigy. He pushes through the branches of hyssop that seem to mark the border of Tarik's property.

Light emanates from a shuttered window. Through the tilted louvers he can make out a tiled floor and part of a toilet. A chain link fence forms a perimeter around Tarik's back yard. Burkett kneels and opens his backpack and finds what he expects – the pistol, flashlight, and box of latex gloves. He snaps on a pair of gloves and uses a rubber band to tie down the loose finger.

Sliding doors lead into the back of the house. Through the glass he can see a small kitchen that opens onto a living room. The only light comes from the front of the house, but he can make out the couch and coffee table, the shape of a flat screen television. On the wall the new flag of South Khandaros is cast in shadow – the inscribed *Shahadah* barely visible against the background of purple and green. A free standing sculpture catches the light – a shark carved from driftwood in the tradition of Khandarian folk art. He pulls the handle but the door is locked.

At the bottom of a concrete staircase is a door with a window. He shines his light into an unfinished basement with puddles on the floor, a crawl space beyond.

A thumb twist lies within easy reach of the nearest pane. He reverses his grip on the flashlight, holding it close to the lamp to keep from cutting himself. He hesitates ever so briefly (the moment I become a criminal, he thinks) before knocking the flashlight against the pane. He clears the tinkling shards from the sashes and reaches inside and unlocks the bolt.

The basement is partitioned into three rooms, all empty but for the washer and dryer and utilities. The door at the top of the stairs is latched on the other side with what feels like a hook and eyelet. He wishes he'd brought a knife, but the door opens easily enough when he slams his shoulder against it.

He stands in a kind of pantry, a vestibule off the kitchen. The shelves hold an array of spices and condiments. A stained apron hangs from a hook, embroidered with the word *Chef*. Could someone else live here? He can imagine killing Tarik, but not the hapless roommate or wife who happens to come home at the wrong moment.

He pads down a short hallway and checks each door. The layout is simple: in front a bedroom, bathroom, small foyer, and office – and in back the kitchen and living room. There is no further sign of a roommate, no sign of anyone living here but a single man.

Back in the kitchen he checks the refrigerator, drawers, and cabinets. On the glistening marble counter, a set of steak knives is sheathed in a wooden block. A checkered towel hangs from the stove handle. In the bedroom he finds the carpet vacuumed, the bed made, and clothes folded neatly in each drawer.

It is almost a cliché, he thinks: the torturer who is finical in his personal life – who relishes the sight of men bleeding and fouling themselves, but at home finds the slightest stain intolerable.

He looks under the bed and in the closets. He finds a set of empty suitcases with tags bearing the name Hussein Al Bihani.

In the office, he sits in the cushioned chair at the desk. A Qu'ran lies on a square piece of felt. Burkett picks it up and flips through the pages and thinks how Akbar would approve of his wearing gloves. He wakes the laptop but finds it locked. On the desk is an old family photograph: a *hijab* covering the mother's hair, and the father in a black suit that seems to match the gloom in both of their faces. There are two children – a baby girl in the arms of her mother, and a boy around three or four. The son must be Tarik.

A photo album in one of the desk drawers memorializes Tarik's stint at an English university. He lived in a dorm, he rowed crew. An attractive blonde appears in enough of the photographs to qualify as a girlfriend. The young version of Tarik had the same look of natural arrogance, but he must have held more liberal views, enough at least to tolerate pubs and short skirts, his girlfriend in a bikini. Perhaps he broke things off when their cultural differences became too much to bear – the pressure from his parents to marry a Muslim – and perhaps he later came to realize his mistake, but only when it was too late, only after she'd taken up with another man. If he had married this woman would he still have adopted jihad as the sixth pillar of Islam? Would he have taken leave from medicine to champion the secessionist cause of South Khandaros? Perhaps Owen, Abu, Nick, and untold others would be alive. Burkett would still have his finger.

Light comes through the blinds – the motion sensor in the driveway. He takes out the pistol and chambers a round and thumbs the safety catch. He glances through the slats as Tarik draws a key from the lace of his shoe. On impulse Burkett slips into the coat closet. He stills the few hangers and squats in the darkness. Within moments he hears the sounds of the front door, hinges and bolt, followed by heavy respirations just outside the closet. Tarik clears his throat, mumbles to himself in Arabic. A rustling sound: he must be taking off his shoes. Burkett thinks he hears the tick of the laces against the hardwood floor. If he puts the shoes in the closet with the row of others Burkett will have no choice but to carry out his task.

From beyond the door comes only silence. A shift of shadows tells him that Tarik is still in the foyer. He must be sitting in the solitary chair, recovering from his run.

Burkett's hands are shaking, beyond the baseline tremor he's had since returning from Khandaros. He can feel the sweat inside his latex gloves. He passes the gun from one hand to the other. When the ache in his left thigh becomes unbearable, he gingerly settles into a seated position, his back against the deep wall of the closet. He holds the gun in his lap. He can feel it trembling. In either hand it seems to make his tremor worse, so he sets it down on the carpet.

Does he have what it takes? He read somewhere that a man with a horrible duty should convince himself beforehand that it is already done. Before carrying out the deed, he should internalize it, make it an irrevocable part of himself.

Tarik pads toward the back of the house. Burkett hears water flowing in the sink in the kitchen and after a period of silence the mumbling yet again of Tarik's voice. He must be praying.

All Burkett has to do is walk a short distance and aim the pistol and pull the trigger. What is stopping him? Is it cowardice? Is it the idea of Tarik putting aside jihad and devoting the rest of his life to medicine? No, Burkett thinks: the bloodlust runs too deep. Tarik even now could be preparing an attack on innocent civilians. The human race would be better off without him.

Now Burkett too is praying, but it is his brother whose face he sees when he closes his eyes and thinks, *Tell me what you'd have me do.* The darkness of the closet, now complete, allows him to imagine it as a space with room enough for him and Owen to sit facing each other. He remembers that broken bone in Owen's hand, the boxer's fracture. By killing Tarik, would Burkett not fulfill the intention of that final blow?

But he can't bring himself to reach for the gun on the carpet between them. It's not cowardice, he realizes, but something even more prosaic: he simply can't imagine committing murder. That word, *murder*, pierces him like a barb, a twisting pain that he somehow feels in both his mind and his gut. It reminds him of his first days of captivity, his days of withdrawal. And what is this, if not withdrawal of a different sort? Not from drugs or alcohol but from the hatred that seems to be ebbing out of him.

All at once his path is clear: he will slip away unseen, even if he has to leave a murderer unpunished, Owen unavenged. Even if he has to worry for years to come about Tarik – who surely learned the source of the FBI investigation – seeking vengeance of his own. But if Tarik came for him, he would be waiting. The killing then would be easy.

At the sound of the shower Burkett begins to rise. His hand catches the edge of a shoebox, causing the contents to spill. He turns on his flashlight and finds on the carpet a pair of expensive watches and a velvet purse with a drawstring. He sets down the flashlight and dumps out a small pile of jewelry. Spreading out the gold and silver he recognizes the Celtic weave of his brother's ring. He holds it to the light and reads the inscription on the inner surface.

There wrestled a man with him until the break of day.

Now he is crossing the foyer. He passes the prayer rug and stalks toward a frame of light at the end of the dark hallway. He seems to follow himself at a remove, like his own shadow, his body nothing more than an instrument of rage. He pushes into the wisps of vapor and yanks back the shower curtain to find Tarik blinking in a white lather, the watery suds streaming down his body. Tarik shouts, startled, but then his eyes register Burkett, and his face slackens as if Burkett weren't an intruder at all but rather an expected visitor. Tarik shifts his head from the stream, wiping his eyes and pushing back his hair, and for a moment he is looking not at

Burkett but at the fogged mirror, which holds only the dim outline of a man with a gun.

Burkett mops the sweat from his face. When he displays the ring, Tarik gives only the slightest of nods, an acknowledgment of either the ring or the shortened finger, perhaps both. Tarik opens his mouth to speak, but then closes it, making it clear that he intends no argument. Burkett would have preferred some final utterance from Tarik, a word of defiance, anything to compel him to pull the trigger. He pockets the ring so that he can hold the increasingly heavy pistol with both hands.

'Damn you!' he shouts.

At the sound Tarik flinches, stumbling backward with his hands lifted in defense. He slides into a seated position on the floor of the tub.

'Just pull the trigger,' he says, his voice shaking, his twitching eyes unable to hold Burkett's. 'Come on. Shoot.'

Shoot. It is a term from wrestling: to attack the legs. The word brings back the voice of his brother, his brother calling to him, cheering him from the edge of the mat. Burkett has little memory of that particular match, beyond losing it, but now he can see his brother on the periphery of the ring, drenched in sweat and still in his singlet after a match of his own. Owen yelling, 'Shoot! Shoot!', and Burkett failing to do so, Burkett falling short. In that clenched, pained expression he saw what he'd taken for granted as long as he could remember, perhaps since before their mother died, not just that Owen was suffering along with him, but also a corollary of that selflessness: Burkett could hurt his brother by hurting himself, or honor him by striving to become more like him.

29

Burkett sits outside a cafe in Atlanta, near the hotel where he's booked to stay the next four nights. A novel lies face down on the table. He checks his phone, confirming what he already knows – Véronique is fifteen minutes late and she hasn't called.

His colleagues ridiculed his choice of Atlanta rather than some exotic resort, but their gentle childing was preferable to the gossip that no doubt would have ensued had he mentioned his real motive: a woman from his past now in Atlanta for a job with CNN. A woman who might not even be available, who was engaged to be married when he saw her last. But if Véronique were spoken for, he wonders why she would reach out to him after so many years. Why send an email out of the blue?

How did she say it? *I've been thinking about you and meaning to write.*

His reply, even before he was sure he could arrange the time off: *It just so happens I'll be in Atlanta next week.*

But now she's late. Maybe she's standing him up. Perhaps the nurses were right: for his first vacation in years – an advantage of hiring a junior surgeon – he should have done something more tropical, however depressing the notion of a man his age, forty-two, alone at the beach.

But his time in Atlanta hasn't been entirely wasted. This morning he finally emptied his father's storage unit, a problem he'd put off far too long. He spent four hours with a pair of movers processing the dust-covered boxes, clothes, appliances, and furniture. His rummaging yielded at least one interesting discovery: a sheaf of fifty or so letters handwritten by their father but never sent – each with its own painstaking copy, identical but for the name at the top. *Dear Owen* or *Dear Ryan*, written during their first years in medical school. Those he's read so far discuss little beyond the mundane details of a retired surgeon's solitary existence. His tedious account of a grocery store visit and oil change somehow leads to his favorite surgical dictum.

Remember, the perfect is the enemy of the good.

Burkett is momentarily distracted by the driver of a passing car, a woman he briefly dated during his residency. Or someone who looks just like her. There appear to be children in the back seat, which shouldn't surprise him. This has become the salient characteristic of his social circle: a gradual accretion of spouses and offspring. He was recently asked to be the godfather of Rory Bird's daughter, a role for which he feels distinctly unqualified, but it would have been a grave insult to refuse, and Rory knows him well enough not to expect very much in the way of moral or spiritual guidance.

He stands when Véronique arrives. She apologizes for being late and offers a genuine laugh when he says he's glad to see her in something other than Kevlar. It is a joke she's heard before, he's sure.

'What brings you to Atlanta?' she asks as they embrace.

'I did all my training here,' he says, not quite answering her question. He explains the storage unit and the letters from his father, all the while glancing at her left hand as though expecting the former engagement ring to emerge from her very flesh.

When they go inside for drinks, he holds the door and insists that she walk ahead of him, from either decorum or an impulse to conceal his limp. Likely something of both. The pain seems to grow worse by the month, a consequence of joint degeneration on the side of the fracture. Post-traumatic osteoarthritis: it's only a matter of time before he needs a prosthetic hip. But why the embarrassment? Perhaps it's only natural when courting a woman to suppress all evidence of weakness, even if he can't imagine her writing him off for something so superficial as a limp.

After ordering they wait at the counter for a heavily tattooed barista to prepare Véronique's espresso. Burkett sips his black coffee from a twenty-ounce cup, feeling the warmth of it through the corrugated sleeve. Customers nearby whisper and stare at Véronique, no doubt recognizing her from television, and Burkett enjoys watching her pretend not to notice.

'Any word on our friend Tarik?' she asks when they return to their table.

He appreciates the *our*, and also her use of the nom de guerre, the implication that he wasn't delusional after all.

'Tarik seems to be doing well,' he says, rotating the Celtic ring on his finger. 'Last I checked, he'd gone back to his caliphate to practice endocrinology.'

For months after his ill-advised break-in, he feared a visit from the police or, worse, Tarik himself intent on some torturous revenge. He still keeps that pistol in the drawer of his nightstand, and some nights, even while convinced of Tarik's return to South Khandaros, he lies awake anticipating the squeal of the alarm, yearning for a shot of bourbon if only to help him sleep.

He looks at her and asks, 'Weren't you engaged the last time I saw you?'

'That was doomed from the start,' she says.

But she is looking over his shoulder, toward the strip mall across the street.

'Is someone filming a movie?' she asks.

He sees what she does: a barricade holding back a small crowd. Craning, he discerns the standing lights, a microphone on a boom. He catches only a glimpse of the actors, a pair of men in matching suits, whose faces he can't quite distinguish. When he turns back to her she wears a smile half formed, her eyes not on the set but on Burkett himself. They play at guessing the type of movie, eventually settling on a marriage caper, gangsters doubling as groomsmen. Perhaps in the final cut he and Véronique will appear as anonymous figures in the distant background.

'How romantic,' she says.

When they've finished their drinks she offers to show him where she works. A tour of the newsroom holds little appeal, but he takes the invitation as a pretext for spending more time together. They walk out to the parking lot where he finds himself lagging behind. His limp seems worse than ever, but not even halfway to her car she stops and waits.

Acknowledgements

I'm grateful to Rebecca Carter for her invaluable insights and commitment to this novel. It's been a privilege to work with Margaret Stead, James Roxburgh, Tamsin Shelton, and everyone at Atlantic Books. I'm indebted to Geoff Hayden for his incisive reading; Christopher Costanzo for sharing his knowledge of missions; and Jim Wood for help with surgical detail. All mistakes are mine alone. I'm especially grateful to Brooke Smith, without whose patience and support this novel wouldn't exist.